DIRGE OF THE INQUISITOR

D.W. White

This novel is dedicated to my daughter Natalya as is everything I do.

CONTENTS

ACKNOWLEDGMENTS

Special thanks to Darryl White Sr., Tod Goldberg, and Jennifer Lu. Also to Kevin Tom who provided the last push.

1 THE KNOCK

An hour after sundown, I contemplated death. Someone banged on my office door without taking into account my typical response to such gestures. I wanted to eviscerate, mutilate, a couple other things ending in – ate, or yell, *fuck off*. Despite my irritation with… humanity, I couldn't afford to chase away work. I was desperate for a paying client.

Covered by dirt and dry curls of old white and green paint, the sign outside my office read KENSINGTON ASHE, BOUNTY HUNTER. The sign like most of my life was a crafted lie designed to weed out the wrong kind of client and keep the FBI, IRS, and PETA off my back. Anyone wanting bail jumpers caught received an ear-full and a door to the face.

The right clients located me when there was nowhere else to turn, which was typically after a demon devoured the in-laws. The general public denied the existence of monsters even after they've torn off limbs or bitten through throats. The good news? We progressed as a society. Those who believed in monsters got medicated into oblivion rather than burned at the stake.

Knocka-knocka-knocka.

On a second series of knocks, recognition flared and disappointment laced the pit of my stomach. The hollow *ratatata* with a five second pause belonged to my landlord. Whatever his malfunction, it was mundane, normal, and human.

Rising from my seat, I grabbed my Sig pistol loaded with .357 hollow points, crossed the room, and peeked through a bullet hole in wall. I wanted to make sure I was pissed at the right person before I unlatched the

1

two heavy deadbolts.

My normal looking regular office door concealed three inches of solid panic room steel pimped with a spirit trap designed to hold anything corporeal or non-corporeal until deactivation. Though anchored to the door, the soul trap's crafting covered my entire living space, which made forced entry through either a window or a wall ineffective. My thumb brushed the faint sigils etched, near the latch, into the door's wood while I said my security phrase: *glazed and powdered.* The soul trap's crafting slumbered with the soft whisper of air escaping a balloon. I lifted my T-shirt, slid the Sig into my waistband at the small of my back, and opened the door.

The top of my landlord's shiny baldhead came to my nipples. His jaw worked like he chewed bad tasting peanuts. His long arms hung loose in a starched wife beater that hugged the bloated outline of a marble sack gut spilling over the belt line of his crisp Dockers. Despite his million angry ex-con tattoos of Penthouse pinups, battleships, and angels, he considered himself an upstanding businessman rather than a glorified liquor store clerk and slumlord.

He perpetrated his usual runny-eyed look of disdain and I always wondered if he noticed the broad shoulders of my father, a marine from Tierra Santa, New Mexico or the cocoa skin of my mother, a bruja from the Dominican Republic? He probably saw what my driver's license reflected, dark brown eyes, a square unforgiving jaw, two days' worth of stubble, and an aged scar on my left cheek courtesy of a wight girl in Vegas.

"Your rent, Mister Ashe. Three days." He handed me this week's stack of pink and yellow bills threatening a firing squad if I didn't pay. He wiggled three fingers in my face. "Three days late."

My office was a converted storage garage behind Red Cat Liquor, a libation emporium rocking a giant red cat face on a cheap white sign as the crux of its advertising genius. Rent was four hundred bucks a month, dirt-cheap in Tierra Santa. My inconsistent income made paying, even low rent, difficult. I was about ten days overdue and over the past four years my financial tardiness had become legend.

"I'm Mister Nice Guy," he said. "And you try to walk all over it. I won't take it anymore. You want a roof over your head? You pay. I have hundreds lined up for this place. I could make five times as much. No, no, I'm Mister Nice Guy."

He couldn't kick me out, wouldn't, whether I paid him or not. My connections in low places and reputation as a ruthless son of a bitch created a no-fuck-with-zone that kept his liquor store from being robbed, vandalized, or shot up; a near impossibility in this neighborhood.

"Big. Bad. Bounty hunter. Why don't you catch some bad guys and pay me," he said.

His finger shaking was into its third gymnastic rotation. There was no point interrupting until it nailed the landing.

My landlord continued, "You know what your problem is? You need a wife. This is Mister Nice Guy's advice. A wife will kick you in the ass with a broomstick and say, work! So she can have nice hair, and pearls, and then she tells her friends you're worthless if not for her. *Shit*."

I scratched my nose. "Why would I want someone with a hairier set than mine?"

His face reddened. His wedding ring caught the angry light as he shook his fist under my chin. The gelatinous meat under his bicep did the *Electric Slide*. "Only reason I let you stay is because your smell keeps the rats away and saves me in extermination!"

"You'll get your money. Loosen your panties." I tolerated his month to month tantrums because he was the closest thing to normal I dealt with. Sad wasn't it. Paying rent. No angle to it. Nobody's life depended on it. It was a shining anchor in my dark harbor of life.

"Money talks, bullshit sits on the curb next to dog shit, and that's where you be if you don't pay me." He shook his fist one last angry time before turning on his heel and marching back to his store.

Red Cat's parking lot was empty for a Thursday. Tomorrow, cars would be piled atop one another for the weekend beer rush. I had been cooped up for the last couple of days so I loitered in the doorway to enjoy the late June warmth. A dull gray sheen hung about the buildings like pallor on a corpse. The few people walking the sidewalks were too focused on their destinations to note the city's condition. That was life in Tierra Santa, a city where anyone who deviated from the straight and narrow disappeared into shadow.

Headlights from a nondescript cream colored BMW blinded me for a second. It turned into the lot and almost hit a wino in an oversized yellow coat. The guy jumped back and kicked empty air in fury. The BMW parked diagonal to occupy two spots.

The driver was a pale brunette. The passenger, a smaller younger clone of the driver, leaned against the window with adolescent fear on her face. I heard living with a teenager can drive a parent to start drinking though I had no practical experience. My daughter didn't live long enough for me to find out. I staunched her memory before it could make me bleed.

I closed the door, locked it, and scrunched my nose. Fresh air invaded my office and warred with the staleness of half empty cartons of Thai, Mexican, and Italian; the United Nations of take out. Since I already knew the battle's outcome, I turned my attention to more relevant needs, the hunt for my chosen prey... donuts, the patron food of the glucose impaired.

A second door on far side of the room connected my office and my living space. The four drab brown walls of my living space came with a refrigerator, hot plate, and microwave. I dropped the overdue bills on the counter with the heaping pile of other overdue bills.

Hidden in the busted microwave was my emergency stash of donuts. I brought out a square pink box and shook it. The last glazed donut rattled and plopped into my hand. Though the donut was stale with crunch, it tasted a lot better than it looked. I tossed the empty box near the overflowing trashcan where landed on the floor amid the other loose rubbish.

I turned on the water. The kitchen faucet *worgled*. I waited for the brown to settle out before palming my hand like a cup. Water splashed across the blue teardrops tatted on each wrist that covered unwelcome scars courtesy of a near crucifixion.

I drank from my hands, switched off the water, and entered my often mistaken for a closet bathroom to complete my wake up ritual by stripping off my T-shirt and soaping down my armpits. I was in the middle of a good lather when knocks interrupted for the second time tonight. I rinsed, flapped dry, slipped on my T-shirt, and again answered the knock.

I opened the door. "What?"

The teenager I saw earlier stood next to the BMW driver who wore a bad day like a puke floral muumuu. The driver fidgeted and scanned the parking lot as if expecting to be devoured. Dark stains covered the driver's hunter-green blouse and jeans in irregular intervals. Her hair could only be described as askew. Her eyes were red like she had been crying.

"The man from the liquor store said you were open. I'll pay for your time." Her trembling hands gestured to nowhere specific. "Please hear me out. I want to hire you."

Seeing them side by side made it impossible to miss their similarity, probably mother and daughter. The daughter refused to meet my eyes. She sighed and found the floor interesting for no apparent reason.

Maybe it was the mother's stained clothes or her near panic, but my common sense told me to slam the door in their faces and go back to... doing nothing. Before common sense could whisper any more of its wisdom, the driver flipped open her tan purse and pulled out a billowing wad of hundred dollar bills spread like a bouquet of fresh roses.

My fingers twitched as I stared at the cash. This time the knocking was replaced by the *cha-ching* of a cash register.

Rain and floods.

The appearance of sudden money should've sent up red flags. Today, those flags were attached to dessert menus. By the time imaginary cupcakes stopped winking at me, I already invited them in to sit—the potential clients not the pastry.

My office's sparse décor consisted of dust bunnies, a couple of filing cabinets only present to make it look like I kept files, a four year old desktop where I tried to keep up with expenses until the hard drive blew, one of those large square black speaker phones with lots of glowing buttons, and two cheap fold out chairs for clients. Reigning behind the simple desk was a plush, deep, and comfortable black leather recliner, a splurge purchase from more profitable times.

Mother and daughter became Gabriela Rodriguez-Fletcher and Roxana Rodriguez after we exchanged proper introductions painted with pseudo smiles. I concentrated on Gabriela as I melted into the recliner's cushions, tried not to scowl, and waited for her lies.

"Mr. Ashe," Gabriela breathed. A slight Spanish accent crept into her voice. "I don't... know how this works, but I have a problem and I was told that maybe you could h—"

"Before we start let's get one thing straight." I held up five fingers. "My fee is five grand. If I accept the job, I expect half up front in cash and the balance on completion in cash, money order, or cashier's check. If you can't afford it or don't have the money on you, don't tell me your problem. I don't do consultations, free or otherwise. We understand one another?" She nodded. "Good, then the only question is who?"

"I'm sorry?" Gabriela asked.

"As in, who died?" I said, shifting in my seat.

"Oh my god!" Roxana hissed like a cute kitten you wanted to pet, trap in a bag, and toss off the nearest bridge.

Gabriela took it worse. She gripped her purse in a panicked stranglehold, her eyes grew doe wide, and blood rushed to her neck turning it hot pink. As I watched, grief warred against her composure. She churned in her seat like a haggard piece of wash. Roxana saw her mom drowning and leaned against her. Gabriela's reaction was instinctive; arm encircled daughter. The contact anchored Gabriela and dammed the flood.

By their tandem glares, I deduced they regarded me as an insensitive ass. In fact, I was. They didn't understand questions have jobs and mine had earned its pay. I needed to make sure they weren't some mother and daughter con. I attracted a lot of crazies. I needed honest unscripted emotion and I had been pissing people off long enough to recognize it. Someone close to them died, hard and recent.

Gabriela squeezed Roxana's shoulders. "I want you to protect my daughter."

"I ain't daycare." I kept my expression bland. "Take her to the police."

Though her lower lip protruded, Roxana didn't react to the news, which meant this wasn't her first time hearing it. They probably discussed it on the drive over, which explained the kid's fearful expression as she leaned against the passenger window.

"The police can't help. You see my daughter is… special. She's…" She bit her lip and glanced at her daughter, one of those kinds of glances given when the other person wasn't looking back.

"It's okay, Mom," Roxana whispered.

Gabriela pursed her lips before returning her attention to me. "She's half-guajona."

My eyebrows shot up. She mistook my surprise as something else—ignorance.

She tried to explain. "Guajona are…" She said, struggling for the right words. "Do you believe in the supernatural, Mr. Ashe?"

Wow, and with a straight face too.

I had first heard the word guajona during my apprenticeship with the Inquisition. I cleared my throat. "Guajona are blood witches who use ingested blood to power their spells and incantations. They've been known to seduce humans and reproduce through them. Males are known as gargola and are less common. Gargola and guajona traits don't always show in their progeny. Sometimes two normal seeming people with gargola or guajona recessive genes can have a kid with dominant gargola or guajona traits. Those children are called Nescient."

I leaned back and ignored the roach crawling up the wall to my right; hopefully they would ignore it too. "Nescients don't lust for blood, pointy hats, or flying brooms. In fact, they live and die like anyone else unless a certain set of indoctrination criteria are met. In order for a Nescient to transition to gargola or guajona, or in layman's terms from person to monster, they must consume a life to solidify their connection to a source of evil called the Cleave. Tasting blood isn't enough; the Nescient must kill their victim. Guajona equals jar. Blood equals water. Pour one into the other and you get the Cleave, which grants certain…" I glanced at Roxana. "Your mother and father have the genealogy."

"You've dealt with this sort of thing before?" Gabriela was relieved.

Roxana's face was hopeful. "So… there are others like me?"

"Not many." A complete untruth, there were more guajona than I was happy with and most of them were trying to fill the power vacuum left by their mouros masters. It was best to keep Gabriela in the dark, especially the kid. She was at that age where peer acceptance meant more than common sense. If she knew of other guajona, she would seek them out at first opportunity and dance to any happy tune they set even if it meant murder.

Roxana's face crashed and burned. Gabriela stroked her daughter's hair to soothe the flames.

"She hoped—" Gabriela began.

"That there's a big school where a white bearded old guy teaches guajona 101 and practices poor adult supervision so she and her two new BFF's can embark on magical world saving adventures? Look, guajona have two choices, they can live as people or die as monsters. All it takes is one drop of someone else's blood, that's it. One taste, one murder, and they blood binge like an alcoholic; once started, it's impossible to stop. So what I want to know is—" I jabbed a finger at Roxana. "Did she have that one drink?" To emphasize my point I let my gaze rest on Gabriela's stained clothes.

Gabriela shook with fury. "She hasn't done anything like that."

Gabriela could be a guajona, though I wasn't receiving that vibe from her. She was what she appeared to be—a mother scared out of her mind. Her daughter, on the other hand, was familiar.

Brown hair covered her face like shredded curtains and damp brown eyes stared at me through the tangle. She raised her chin and swept hair behind her ears revealing cheap earrings, the kind found at any mall or swap meet. Even the tiniest monsters carried an 'I can eat you' swagger. Roxana didn't have that. What she did have reached into my chest and wrenched out—

Nine years ago, a cold storm howled through the night, water fell in barrels instead of buckets, and thunder roared like a berserker's battle cry. I had gone into my daughter's room because I knew how she felt about rainstorms and found her covers abandoned. There was always a panicked second when her absence tormented me with the irrationality that she left in the night like her mother did, but there were many stormy nights and many abandoned beds.

I knew where to look.

She always felt safe in dark cramped places and like usual she huddled in the closet, a tiny shaking silhouette in a deep corner. When cooed promises of cookies and candy wouldn't budge her, I did the thing a single dad who loved his daughter could do and climbed in with her. My Pequiñita huddled in my lap settling into a deep sleep only a seven-year-old can achieve when she feels protected. At the time, I had no clue she would never grow up. She would've been close to Roxana's age right now.

Gabriela continued, "Will you help us? It'll take me three days to arrange somewhere safe."

She needed a safe place if the monster she was fleeing had eyes and connections everywhere. That meant a monster with a lot of influence. "Who are you running from?"

She shook her head. "For five thousand dollars. Does it matter?"

I kept my expression plain. "If you want my help."

"I was wrong." Her mouth formed a straight uncompromising line. "You can't help me." She grabbed her daughter by the meaty portion of the upper arm and dragged the startled kid out of her seat.

I watched Gabriela grasp the door knob before asking. "Is it her father?"

That did it. Gabriela squeezed the knob so tight her knuckles turned white.

Roxana glared at me red faced. Her voice had gone hollow, "He's gone."

Gabriela nodded to herself, released her manic grip, turned, and raised her chin so our eyes met. "Her biological father... passed away."

There was finality in her gaze, an old wound. She saw him die though I didn't have the impression it was by her hand. Someone killed for her.

I glanced at her purse and the pieces fell into place. Money, where did she get the money? She didn't appear to be a six figure executive type with a lot of disposable income and I doubted she stopped by a bank with her clothes so... messy. She kept a cash stash. She had been prepared to run. People who were ready to bolt were the kind who made deals with unsavory types.

Gabriela probably bargained with a monster who paid her, fed her, clothed her, and let her live a normal life until tonight. Now the monster wanted to collect on the deal and mommy didn't want to pay so she searched for a safe place to stash the kid.

"Without the truth, I can't help and they will find you. Neither of you want that. So do us both a favor and spill."

"Why can't money ever be enough," she murmured. Gabriela squared her shoulders and faced me. "We used to be addicts, Mr. Ashe," she began. "Ro's biological father handled the scoring. He became real sick one evening. I thought maybe because he hadn't used and I'd already used up what he brought. I left to score hoping a pick me up would improve his condition. When I returned, he was... like an animal. He attacked me, he tried..." She shook her head. "He bit me here." She pointed to a scar faded to near non-existence.

She continued, "I didn't understand what he wanted at the time so I fought and... and he would've killed me if she hadn't shown up. I thought her an angel at first, so strong and beautiful. His head came off in her hands." She shuddered. "My savior apologized, said it was necessary and that she would take care of me from now on. I remember feeling numb. I couldn't figure out how she knew about Ro's dad, how she broke into our apartment. I was in so much shock... I was grateful to be alive. I did what she asked. I was afraid she would kill me too."

Gabriela's voice fell into a dull cadence caked with bile. "She got me clean and when I found out I was pregnant, she helped with that too. She even introduced me to Evan, my husband."

Roxana stared at her mother in awe. Apparently, she never heard this story.

"She never asked for anything, for fifteen years," Gabriela continued. "All of a sudden, she starts showing up in the middle of the night asking tons of questions. She made me nervous. I could tell she wanted my daughter. I waited for months. I knew one day she would try to take her away and today when... when we returned from shopping, we found Evan dead." Her voice cracked. "His throat was torn out. I knew she'd done it. I knew we had to run."

The kid's biological father was a Nescient who turned gargola. Another guajona comes along and takes out Roxana's father and offers to take care of Gabriela. I would wager her guajona benefactor knew about the pregnancy and was protecting the embryo. This method of 'adopting' was pretty common among covens.

I put my elbows on my desk, rested my chin on my fists, and leaned forward. "I need a name."

"I-I can't!"

"A name," I growled.

"You don't get it—"

"Dhyana," Roxana whispered. "I heard Mom say it once."

"Roxana Allison Rodríguez!" Gabriela shouted.

First names meant nothing. Everything about a guajona was in their last name—it identified their coven, bloodline, and special abilities. Guajona adopted a last name reflective of their lineage once they became part of the Crimson Consortium, a collective consisting of seven major covens.

I stared at the kid and asked if she knew Dhyana's last name. Roxana refused to look at her mother as her shoulder's shrugged to say, *I don't know.* I rose from my chair and approached them. Gabriela was still angry and unsettled. I pointed at her soiled clothes.

"Evan. M-my husband... Roxana's step dad... he... he..." Resolve broke and tears poured in droves. "Oh damn you!" She slapped her hand against the door. Daughter encircled her mother's waist, arms squeezing hard.

"Did she kill him?" My hand inched closer to my gun. If the kid was already on the monster path, I would end right her before she hurt anyone else.

My tone held mommy's attention. She blinked and replied, "She. Did. Not. Hurt. Evan! Ro loved him."

Roxana stared at her feet; her hair tumbled forward over her eyes. I couldn't read her. "Did he know what she was?"

"Of... of course." Gabriela stammered. "I wouldn't have married him if... if he couldn't love her regardless."

Not many people knew about the existence of guajona and fewer still would accept the offspring of one. That this wonderful man of hers embraced the kid should've been an obvious red flag. Her hubby had been planted to keep tabs and when he outlived his usefulness... There was one way guajona cleaned up after themselves.

"This his blood?" I asked. Without waiting for an answer, I touched the fabric and concentrated on how it felt between my fingers. I knew by their gasps they were horrified by what I did. I didn't smile at their discomfort, though I wanted to. Instead, I took a deep breath, closed my eyes, and let fresh death speak.

The experience of life flashing before your eyes was La Parca speech. I was born with a Lengua-bruja, a tool of communication granting me the ability to understand death rattles—the language spoken by La Parca as they announce the arrival of a new soul into the afterlife. The drawback was fluency so the snippets I caught were confusing.

The feel of Gabriela's shirt disappeared. Time slowed. The world turned into a wasteland of black and white like in those old silent movies. I was stranded on a crop of rock surrounded by a death rattle ocean. Noise rose from the pool and crashed over the rock drowning me with a sound best described as a million rats in tap shoes scampering across hardwood. Evan Fletcher's death rattle filled my brain. La Parca spoke:

He hurt her without enjoying it. Two forces warred. His brain split. Two desires competing. He broke trust, which made it easier for him to be turned. He failed because he died before he could succeed. He wanted her protected. He wanted her dead. He died unaware what was real.

I tottered as the death rattle receded. My head felt like it had been struck by a bag full of hammers. My eyes popped open and two blurry shapes came into focus. It felt like hours passed. It was a few seconds.

Gabriela's expression curdled with disgust while Roxana's was... curious.

"What were you chanting? I couldn't understand the language," Gabriela said as she backed against the door.

Evan Fletcher's death rattle was the cryptic kind. As best as I could tell, he died confused. The worst part about his confusion was that it shrouded his killer making it impossible to confirm Gabriela's story. Evan couldn't face the truth and his death rattle reflected that. I also felt his fear and I couldn't live with the kid having to face anything that could terrify a grown man. I could protect her from that at least.

"I'll take the job," I said. "Though knowing who I'm supposed to be protecting your daughter from would help. I need a physical description at least."

"Y-you want to protect both of us?" Gabriela asked.

I nodded.

She stared as if trying to remember something before reaching into her purse and handing me five thousand dollars in cash. "I... can't. I have to get us safe passage out of the city. Dhyana... has eyes everywhere. Her... Dhyana's last name is Nuberu. She's unbelievably beautiful, maybe five eight, about my build, short dark hair like a pixie cut, strong cheek bones, brown eyes, and she wears a lot of cream clothing and rubies—either a ring, necklace, or earrings."

Gabriela kneeled, held Roxana by the shoulders, and said a few calming words about manners and behaving. Gabriela hugged and kissed her daughter half a dozen times before turning to me. Gabriela's eyes were hard and final.

Being a former parent, I recognized her overprotective stubbornness, she was going try to something extreme to keep her daughter safe. I had the feeling she was destined to fail. Dhyana would make Gabriela hurt before Gabriela died.

That would leave the kid in my care indefinitely. Nuh uh. There wasn't enough cash in the universe to get me to go parental for a pubescent monster. "If you're not back by Monday, I'm turning the kid over to the cops."

"I understand." Gabriela uttered one last sobbing, *I love you* before departing.

Roxana watched her mother run to the BMW. She didn't ask her to come back. Instead, she mouthed, *I'm sorry* over and over. There were a million things a fifteen year old could be sorry for and none of them mattered. Receding taillights would be the last time she saw her mother alive.

2 WAFFLES

Babysitting was my least favorite job. It was dull, involved lots of waiting, and clients whined about everything. The sole consolation in this instance was the pay. My thumb counted the crisp C-notes as I slid five hundred of the five grand into my empty wallet; the rest would go into a hidey-hole under my bed.

Though I had enough to pay Daz, buy some snacks, and even pay utilities, I decided to wait until the job was done. It would be awkward dragging Roxana around while I begged bill collectors to keep my services on.

A second count of the money brought a warm rush of pleasure. It felt good having cash. My loopy grin faltered.

The kid reclaimed her foldout chair and fell into an empty eyed trance. Her stepdad was dead and I knew firsthand what that kind of loss did to a person. My father met his end in a shit-storm of alcohol and demon possession that numbed my emotions for decades until I met my ex-wife.

Part of me was tempted to comfort Roxana. Despite the initial shock, the full brunt of her parent's absence hadn't marinated yet. That moment would hit when she expected to hear his voice, *get dressed, eat your breakfast, go to bed.* That was when the freight train of anguish barreled down the tracks. That was when she shattered.

I couldn't afford to let her succumb to catatonia. She had the answers. I expected she would be more forthcoming about Dhyana Nuberu and her stepdad with her mother gone.

"You eat yet?"

Roxana jumped at the sound of my voice. Color returned to her cheeks and her posture straightened; she picked up the pieces of her wilted little self and reassembled them into something resembling a teenager. She wiped her nose with her index finger before shaking her head.

"If you have a voice," I said. "I suggest you use it otherwise we'll have issues. Have a taste for anything in particular?"

She shrugged another feeble, *No*. The entire decision was apparently up to me. Fine. There was a twenty four hour waffle house called Frankee's a couple businesses over—the kid would like the place. I asked her to sit for a spell while I gathered some things.

I shut the door between my office and living space for privacy. My poor man's safe consisted of a loose piece of tile covering a shallow pit under the bed. I dropped forty-five hundred into the pit and replaced the tile.

Next, I grabbed my duffel and transferred a couple of water bottles filled with gasoline, a shotgun, hand axe, and spare ammo from the footlocker. My lighter, the most versatile of tools, slid into my jean pocket. My custom bulletproof vest lined with chainmail went under a black thick cotton long sleeve and shoulder rig.

Six inches of a military crisp steel blade, reloads, and a penlight were snapped into the rig's various holders. The vest, shirt, and rig were light though a bit hot, especially in summer.

I found my cell phone amid my chipped nightstand's cluttered surface of candy wrappers, wallet, keys, alarm clock, dirty rags, and my shoebox of memories.

Wedding keepsakes and a dizzying cascade of Evelyn's baby photos filled the shoebox. My trembling hand reached for the picture of Evelyn sleeping in the crook of her mother's arm. It was Evelyn's first photo, taken at County Memorial right after she was born. I held the picture to my nose and savored the off-putting gummy residue of the album it once inhabited. Evelyn, my Pequiñita made immortal by film.

I let my daughter slip away, violating the most carnal instinct hardwired into the human nervous system since homo-erectus—parents protected their children. I replaced the photo wishing guilt could be set aside so easily.

The next item was my ex-wife Yanira's gold wedding band, mine had long since found its way to a pawnshop. I lifted it with a thumb and forefinger. The light glinted off the simple oval. No engravings, no jewels, a circle that should've meant forever. I dropped the ring back into the shoebox with a dull *thud* and closed the lid.

14

That was a different time, a different me, before I knew how fucked up the world was. The shoebox went back on the nightstand.

There was one last touch I refused to leave home without. I opened my closet. An avalanche of dirty laundry tumbled out. I cursed while shoving most of the laundry aside with my foot. My hangers were empty except one.

My patchwork brown suede coat boasted a severe steer skull with carnage crimson eyes and a toothy bone snarl stitched on the back. The coat had numerous crisscross patches where new suede had been sewed into the old. Every stitch was a map of my hunting. Each repaired seam was a corpse.

I removed the plastic cover surrounding the coat and placed the empty hanger back on the rack. The suede settled about my shoulders and I took a moment to enjoy its suppleness.

I returned to my office. The kid stared at the huge duffel hanging over my right shoulder. She appeared to be working up the courage to ask what was inside and I forestalled it with a universal head jerk of *let's go*.

Roxana pursed her lips in a petulant way teenagers do before rising to follow.

I reset the spirit trap, locked up my office, and made a quick stop to my car to drop the duffel in the trunk before we continued to our destination.

Tierra Santa's downtown lights sparkled through the darkness like rotten teeth. A dark place in every season as if the grime rose from beneath the concrete to swathe the avenues in gray. This metropolitan dirt-town brimmed with a bustle of folk lounging around the many liquor stores, gun shops, and car dealerships besieging the city. Project apartments littered the deepest recesses of southeast Tierra Santa, flat roofed townhomes frolicked in the suburbs, mansions lamented in the hills while farm communities flourished in outskirts. It was common to see chromed BMW's and beat up Ford pickups overcrowding the same coffee shop.

A few feet ahead loomed Frankee's, the familiar brown, green, and white waffle house shaped like a shoebox wearing a sombrero. Inside, we were confronted by yellow walls covered with framed black and white photographs of late sixties Motown artists. Oblivious to the musical history surrounding her, Roxana left to clean up in the restroom while we waited to be seated.

For a second, it made me nervous that she might bolt. It would serve me right to lose her so soon due to nonchalant care; however, the kid's quick reappearance, her face scrubbed and her hair pulled into a ponytail, revealed my paranoid musings to be what they were—paranoid musings. A couple minutes after her return, a rude hostess showed us to a booth.

We sat across from each other.

Roxana skimmed the menu and set it aside as someone caught her attention. She crinkled her nose, glanced over her shoulder, and then leaned forward. "That lady behind us smokes a lot. I can smell it from here."

I blinked. Perhaps this was some sort of teenage insulting ritual or maybe the kid was looking for some common ground. I leaned to the right for a clear view four tables down at a solitary woman in her early fifties drinking coffee and reading a book; she was one of those Sunday church types. "Then she should die soon."

The kid goggled, pulled a strand of hair from behind her ear, and began twirling it around her finger. "You're mean aren't you?"

I held the menu between us.

She was on some annoying eager beaver trip. I was beginning to regret asking her to speak up only to remind myself that her sullen silence was far more depressing. Lucky for me, the waitress' arrival saved me from any further drama.

A brunette in a white and green striped uniform wore a tired work smile. "I'm Peg. I'll be your server. Tonight's special is a T-bone, comes with cornbread, a baked potato, and an endless mug of coffee."

"Coffee. Black. Pancakes, sausage burnt, and hash browns," I said.

"It'll cost more that way. Why don't you order the number three, it comes with eggs."

"Pancakes. Sausage burnt. Hash browns," I repeated.

"Ohhhkay," Peg said. "And you little lady."

"Waffles please and orange juice." She steepled her fingers on the table while looking across at me. "Is it okay if I have two orders?"

"You can have whatever you can pay for," I said.

Her eyes grew round. Peg's pen tapped her pad like machinegun fire. After the fortieth tap I said, "Two orders of waffles and bring a carafe of OJ."

"Thank you," Roxana replied in a tiny voice.

"How gallant of you," Peg said with as much warmth as a floating iceberg. She finished her scribbles and headed off toward the kitchen. A few minutes later a busboy dropped off our drinks.

I sipped my coffee, the kid downed two quick glasses of OJ and was already pouring a third while the room buzzed with white noise from too many conversations. I added my own thoughts to the static in a feeble attempt to decipher the best way to protect the girl from the trouble that was sure to come. Research took a specific set of skills I lacked. I was a hired gun who preferred to leave information gathering to my clients.

Peg brought the food.

"That's black," Roxana said wrinkling her nose at the three strips of crispy flaky meat on my plate.

"Perfection," I said. Well-cooked meat became something of a necessity after seeing pieces of internal organs splattered hither and yonder.

We dove into our plates; the noises between us were scraping forks and the occasional swallow or *glurp*. She finished before me, polishing off two plates of waffles and leaving enough orange juice for one last glass. She slid the carafe over to me. I ignored it and finished my meal. Peg cleared the dishes and asked about dessert, which I was considering. She departed for the kitchen to give me time to decide.

Instead of studying the dessert menu, I found myself wondering about how Roxana handled growing up feeling different and the impossibility of finding anyone who understood what she was going through. My Lengua-bruja hadn't developed until adulthood and even then I needed mentoring to understand my ability. Embroiled in murder at age fifteen, her childhood was already shot to hell.

"You know about… monsters?" She asked.

The human kind feeding on fear, misery, hate, and violence like they were the four basic food groups, those types I left to the cops—unless paid otherwise. I hunted the people-eating supernatural kind without hesitation.

I wiped my fingertips with a napkin. Her eyes followed the motion. I balled up the tissue and tossed it across the table. She puffed her cheeks and blew it toward me.

"How much do you know about your biological dad?" I asked.

She shrugged and rubbed her thumb along her forearm. "Mom never talked about him much. I know his name, Lucio Miguel Ramirez and that he's from El Salvador. That's where they lived before I was born. My Mom told me they grew up there."

I guessed a file containing her father's background was too much to ask for. I had a name, which was nothing since Ramirez was not a coven surname. Her house might've had additional information hidden somewhere, but it was probably crawling with cops by now.

Police involvement would make my job harder if they posted the kid's face all over the news. If it came to that, I was going to need help.

"Did your mom call the cops… you know, after?" I asked.

The kid shook her head.

I might have time, a dead body could hold for a whole week before the smell disturbed the neighbors. "What can you tell me about Dhyana?"

Roxana's round eyes reflected in the napkin holder's dull polish like a deer seeing its last set of headlights. "I told—"

"Not everything."

She thought before answering, which impressed me. She pushed her hair behind her ears as she spoke. "She doesn't make any noise when she comes or goes, but I can always feel when she's near." The kid's eyes grew distant. A bit of longing threaded her voice as she continued, "She's pretty, so pretty that you can't stop looking at her. She's like a model or an actress only… more like a warrior princess. Sometimes, when she'd visit I'd sneak out of my room. I think she knew I was listening, but she never said anything to Mom."

"What did they talk about?"

She shrugged. "Normal stuff, she'd ask Mom how I was doing in school, if I played sports, had a boyfriend, stuff like that." She met my eyes. "You ever like wish you were someone important so everyone would like you? Dhyana talked like I was important. Her voice it was… cool, creepy, and cool."

"Anything else?"

"What do you think will happen to my Mom?"

It was my turn to shrug. I had no illusions concerning Gabriela's chances. The kid was looking for reassurances I couldn't give. Even as a lie. It wasn't that I didn't have a heart; it was that I didn't bother using it much. "If she's caught, they'll ask her where you are."

Roxana's face darkened. "Wh-what will happen after that?"

A hard edge crept into my voice. "Dhyana will come for you and then that's when I earn my pay."

"But my Mom—" She said.

"Your mom can take care of herself." I sliced the air with my hand to end the subject.

Tears bunched up in her eyes. Her lower lip trembled.

I reached out. She leaned away and wiped her wet cheeks. Her pain brought up a paternal need to ask questions and even worse, to care about the answers. "Tell me about the last time you cried."

More tears fell and then words flooded our table. Slow. Hesitant. They churned and spilled. "We moved a lot. I was like always changing schools mid-semester. We'd stayed the longest in Philadelphia, two and a half years. Then my Mom met Evan. After that I thought we weren't going to move anymore."

Roxana seemed unaware of the loneliness threading her voice. Moving so much probably had made friendships impossible to maintain. If Gabriela or Evan felt the same disconnect, they probably didn't show it in a way Roxana understood.

"This last move was different," Roxana said. "Something changed. Mom and Evan fought a lot. He sat on the couch all day and when Mom got home from work, he'd criticize her until they argued and then he'd get mad and leave. Mom never knew where he went."

"So what happened this afternoon?"

She looked away. "Mom doesn't know, but a few weeks ago he started looking at me weird… like… when I came out of the shower or when I got home from school. He was always staring. It was gross." She shuddered.

"You thought he'd hurt you?"

"I don't know... something. I used to have nightmares about him coming into my room when I was sleeping." She exhaled and wiped away more tears. "And then today, I didn't even do anything. I came home and he totally freaks and shoves me to the floor and starts choking me." She pulled down the sweatshirt's collar to bare the bluish angry bruises in finger length intervals around her neck. "I got mad and my head started hurting and then everything went away." She shook her head and her fists curled in frustration. "Next thing I know, Mom was dragging me upstairs and telling me I needed to shower and change. She didn't tell me what she did until after we left."

Gabriela said they found Evan dead. The kid's version was very different. I studied Roxana's face and neck. Guajona healed fast. Nescient healed like a regular person. Her bruises looked like they would be worse by tomorrow. I was hesitant in asking if he left marks on other parts of her body and even more afraid she would show me. Taken together, her injuries and Evan's death rattle were enough for me. The kid didn't kill Evan. Gabriela did.

"Mom said," Roxana continued. "She saw him hurting me and she broke his neck. She used to… fight or something back in El Salvador. And then she talked about Dhyana being mad and how we needed to find help.

Mom said we couldn't tell you what she did because you might not protect me if you knew. That's when we came to your office."

I didn't understand the reason for the Gabriela's lie unless she was trying to create a sense of urgency. Maybe she was abandoning Roxana and didn't want her daughter to realize it until it was too late. "Did you see Evan before you left, are you sure he's dead?"

Roxana considered my words for a half second before shaking her head in the negative. "Mom covered him with a blanket. He wasn't moving. There was a lot of blood, especially on her clothes."

Broken necks don't cause massive amounts of blood loss or become reasons to change clothes. Knives, bullets, claws or teeth are messy. "Is someone after you?"

"Mom says so. I don't see how. I mean, how would Dhyana know what happened if nobody told her?" She grabbed some napkins, dabbed her eyes, and blew her nose.

I poured another cup of coffee to keep from pounding the table. The kid's story had at least confirmed Gabriela had lied. Evan's programming probably went haywire, human dysfunction or supernatural interference, something or someone made him go off the rails. Gabriela probably walked in while her daughter was being attacked and exercised lethal deterrence. I agreed with the kid on one thing. There's no way for this mysterious Dhyana could know about Evan's death unless someone spilled. "I need the truth if you want my help, understand?"

Roxana nodded.

I held her gaze. "Did you kill Evan?"

Roxana's eyes grew wide. She shook her head and said, *No* though it sounded like maybe she was afraid she had.

"Kid," I pressed, glaring until she began squirming in her seat.

She repeated her *No* without any more conviction than the first time. After a few minutes, I relented. I believed her story. If only belief and trust were the same. I wanted to give her a hug that would take the monsters away. I saw my redemption in her. She might not be my little girl, but she was someone I could save. Her story pretty much crimped my taste for dessert (trust me that was pretty hard to do). I paid. We walked back to my office. At this juncture, all I had to do was wait for this mysterious Dhyana to take the field.

My cell phone shrieked with a haunted house themed ring tone I found hilarious. The face of my cell brightened as a familiar number flashed across the screen.

"Ken," Winnie said in a gravelly voice courtesy of a ruined voice box. "Thank god you picked up!"

About two years ago, I had discovered a Crimoire, a gargola and guajona eatery where the only dish on the menu was people, beneath a freeway overpass. I had followed a couple of guajona to the spot, kicked in the doors, and killed every monster inside. I went searching for human survivors and found Winnie face down in her own puke with her throat like shredded red cabbage. I got her to County in time for emergency surgery. She survived, but the incident left her with scars, a ruined voice box, and growing fear of the night. Her increasing paranoia, insomnia, and self-medicating on company product led to her prompt termination from her pharmaceutical sales job. Now, she tended bar at Jiggy's due to her new preference for the company of shady strangers after sunset. Winnie and I had something of an understanding as a result of me saving her ass.

"I'm on a job," I growled.

"Don't hang up. This is serious. I swear!" When I didn't hang up, she continued. "Marston Lewis, you know him?"

Marston or Mars as he was called struck me as a pit-bull with ambitions larger than his brains and an obsessive-compulsive reflex to bite any hand that fed him.

Winnie continued, "Well, he died four days ago and now he's back. He just walked into Jiggy's like it wasn't nothing. I got so scared out of my mind and got the hell out of there."

Jiggy's better known as the Jungle Gem Gentlemen's Club was one of Mr. P's businesses. Strippers up front. Hookers out the back. G-strings all the time. Mr. P aka Sole Pimberton, named after his father's favorite fish, was the often disputed, ill reputed, crime lord of Tierra Santa. P was a celebrity pimp back when I was a teenager. I heard it said more than once that he licked, at least twice, every lollypop in town worth tasting. Over the years, he dodged incarceration and expanded his interests to drugs, racketeering, murder, and the most heinous—*used. car sales*. P's success came from his willingness to stay educated on every aspect of the city, including its monsters.

Aloud I said, "Anybody killed yet?"

"No. It's strange. Mars is just holed up in his old office," Winnie said.

Money tended to come all at once or not at all in my line of work. Technically, I didn't need another job, especially one that didn't have a paying client. However, if Mars actually turned out to be a monster and I got rid of him, I might be able to trade the favor to P for some cash. "Is P paying?"

"Ken!" Winnie said.

I squeezed the bridge of my nose. I didn't want to do another job. Christ, but I knew the consequences if I left the matter unattended. Someone could die. *Someone innocent like my daughter.* I looked at the Roxana. I would have to do something with her. I couldn't hunt and protect her at the same time.

The problem fixed itself actually. Since Winnie was ruining my paying job, she would have to keep the kid until I was done with the non-paying job.

"Fine. I'll be there soon." I hung up. "This way kid, we're taking a field trip."

My black and silver pinstriped Grand Marquis was as sturdy as a tank and cornered like a boat, I took a used car in lieu of payment about three years ago and never regretted it. In the years that followed, I put my personal stamp on the G-Marq—inches of dirt and dented side panels. It was mine and it ran. That was what mattered.

"We going somewhere?" Roxana asked.

"Hop in." Taped to the visor above the steering wheel was a photo of my ex-wife Yanira grinning from cheek to cheek with her arms wrapped around our little four year old girl, Evelyn. Their mirror imaged faces showed identical eyes the color of rich wood, dark curly brown hair that appeared black until the light touched it, and dimples. A Ferris wheel and cinnamon roll booth from the County Fair was in the background.

I ran my finger across the photo and said a silent prayer. I had won Evelyn a stuffed dragon by shooting out a red star with a BB gun. It was her first carnie experience and she ran herself in circles trying to absorb the lights, smells, toys, and rides.

"Who's that?" Roxana leaned over to look up at the picture.

I flipped the visor shut with a hard snap. The kid took the hint and didn't ask again. The car started on the second twist of the key. We pulled into manageable traffic. It was a short silent drive before the neon hottie sitting in the palm of a hand with the words JUNGLE GEM GENTLEMEN'S CLUB underneath flashed from a few streets over. We arrived a few minutes later. I pulled into the parking lot and cut the Grand Marquis's engine.

Roxana's attention was plastered to Jiggy's flashing lights. Her voice vibrated with that kind of nervous excitement kids have when they're about to go somewhere they shouldn't. "Are we going in?"

She knew what the sign meant and I couldn't help feeling embarrassed about it. I pointed above the club to a set of second story windows. "I know someone who lives up there."

"Oh," she answered, disappointed. She removed her seatbelt and opened the passenger door.

There were two apartments above Jiggy's. Winnie lived in A and a couple of Jiggy's dancers lived in B. I opened the door of the G-Marq and stepped onto the dull black pavement. Something sticky attached to the bottom of my sole. I scrapped my boot across the asphalt and away came the gummy corpse of a used condom. I stole a quick look at the kid; she wasn't looking down. I gestured toward the alley and led the kid up the stairs. I knocked on the door with the crucifix hanging on it.

The patter of footsteps stopped on the other side of the door before the light in the peephole darkened. There was a slight pause of recognition before the triple deadbolts unlocked with three clicks. The door swung inward to reveal a broad bare chest in polka dot boxers.

Covered in tribal tattoos and steel cage scars, Brody was a former MMA fighter who slummed around training camps until he ended up a bouncer at Jiggy's.

"Evening," I said, reshaping my sneer into a nervous twitch to hide the shock of finding him, of all people, answering Winnie's door. I hadn't known Brody and Winnie were an item. Hell, I wasn't even sure Brody could spell item.

"Winnie," Brody called. "It's for you, Hon." He gave me a measured stare.

My surprise visit didn't appear to bother him, which made me curious about what confidences they shared. He was a full head taller than me with shoulders wider than the Grand Canyon, a veritable tough of toughs. I brushed past him without being invited in.

Roxana paused at the door.

Brody noticed the kid, beamed a welcome, and stepped aside.

Roxana blushed, dropped her gaze, and walked in.

"She's not legal," I growled.

Brody speared me with a dirty look, closed the front door, and started toward the bedroom where a dirty blonde in her hard thirties exited. Brody toyed with the frayed ends of Winnie's oversized yellow grandma bathrobe before placing a gentle peck on her cheek. They shared a smile before Brody disappeared behind a closed bedroom door.

Winnie's dark ringed blue eyed gaze criticized before sparking into full-blown glee as she spotted Roxana. In a jagged southern drawl she asked, "What's your name?"

Roxana jumped at the gravelly sound, but managed a sheepish smile and avoided staring at Winnie's neck scars. Good girl. They introduced themselves, Winnie extended her hand and Roxana shook it. They both giggled. I fought the urge to start making gag noises.

"You want something to drink? We have strawberry soda," Winnie said.

"Yes, please." Roxana's smile widened.

Winnie gave me a quick questioning glance as she disappeared into the kitchen. I shrugged.

Attraction to the askew was human nature. We looked for what was out of place when we entered someone's home. We took comfort in other's imperfections because they made us feel like we measured up in some weird way.

Looking around, I noticed the changes since my last visit a little over a year ago. For one thing, she cleaned, organized, and decorated. The artwork was weird enough to be fashionable and bland enough to blend in. The heavy metal CD's, black curtained fringes, monster imagery, and manic newspaper clippings of grisly murders were gone, every last stitch exchanged for a healthy collection of DVD's, mostly romantic comedies, and decorations deep in the earth tone category.

Winnie returned with a large glass sloshing with red soda and ice cubes that clinked and popped in the bubbly liquid. "You hungry?"

"We just ate." Roxana took the offered glass.

Winnie's jaw dropped in shock and her hand flew to her chest. "He fed you?"

"Barely," Roxana added an eye roll.

They both giggled again. The whole camaraderie was so sweet I was going to hurl. I made upchuck noises.

Winnie glanced my direction. "I'm going to speak to Ken for a moment. Help yourself, the remotes over on the coffee table, and there's DVD's. You want anything just ask." She pointed to a laptop. "We have Wi-Fi."

I didn't have Wi-Fi.

Roxana nodded before sitting on the couch and booting up the laptop. I followed Winnie into the kitchen. Once inside, she handed me a shot of tequila.

"I don't have any sweets," she apologized.

I held the glass.

Winnie stared at the un-tasted tequila. "She reminds me of my baby sister, about the same age too. Louise Ann had her sweet sixteen, all barbecue and boys." She lowered her voice. "She wasn't attacked was she?"

"Nothing like that." I set the shot glass down. "I need to stash her here."

Winnie shoved her hands into her robe's pockets. "Who is she?"

"It's good that Brody's here, he can help."

Her voice lowered, which is to say it inflected from pounding boulders to pounding sand. "Leave Brody out of this, he's decent folk and you've made it clear I'm not—"

"You're whatever I need you to be," I interrupted.

After I saved her life, she took me as a shining knight of sorts and made her depth of thanks no mystery. I took advantage, disrobing her mystery and plunging her depths for a wealth of thanks. She tried learning about monsters to become the *Robin* to my *Batman*. I refused. I dissuaded. I finally stopped coming around. She took the hint and moved on.

She flushed crimson. "A whole fucking year since—" Winnie spat. "You wouldn't even let me help before!" The heat reddening her cheeks and throat caused her scars to appear swollen. She closed her eyes, took a deep breath, and released it. "How long?"

I put an edge in my voice to forestall any backtalk. "You hear anything downstairs?"

"You really are an ass you know that?" She turned away from me, switched on the faucet, plugged the sink, grabbed a bottle of dish soap and squeezed it with more force than necessary so the green liquid jettisoned into the mix.

I watched bubbles froth as the water level rose.

She tilted her head and something about her profile told me she made a decision. She reached into the pocket, took out a set of keys embossed with a smaller version of Jiggy's hottie sign, and handed them to me. "These open all the doors and the safe. I've been holding on to them since Mars... He's just sitting in the manager's office."

She turned off the faucet. "I called Mr. P, but his assistant wouldn't put me through. I left a message and waited. When nobody from Mr. P's *security* showed up, I decided to call you. I'm not setting foot downstairs until Mars is gone."

"How does Mars look?"

Winnie wrinkled her nose in disgust. "Pale, rank, nice clothes, otherwise mostly normal. He's not interfering with business though. Some of the girls have walked out. Those that haven't are nervous." She stared as if considering something. "I'm nervous. I wanted to stay at Brody's, but—" She shook her head. "Mostly, I've been keeping low and my eyes open you know?"

"Why didn't you call sooner?"

She covered the scars on her neck with a hand. "Since when do you help anyone for free? I called Mr. P, *my boss*, the person I'm supposed to call."

When we last spoke, I made it clear I never wanted to see her again. All she did was oblige me. Though she deserved her anger, it was still stupid for her to risk so many lives on a grudge. I put a hand on her shoulder. She wasn't someone I called a friend. After today, it was something to consider. "Don't teach the kid any bad habits," I said. "I'll be back."

"If I can undo anything you've done, more is the good." Her thin smile couldn't hide her tension as she shrugged off my hand. She hugged herself as if warding a chill and gave me a look that said I used up every ounce of good will I had coming.

I didn't understand women, most were works of art, polished, primal, abstract, and moody. I was seeing a bit of what Brody must see daily—steel underneath that cotton. Maybe she would've made a good *Robin*. I left her to the dirty dishes.

Roxana rose from her seat as I exited the kitchen. "Are we leaving?"

I glanced at the computer screen. She was watching music videos with bad singing and dancing. "You're staying with Winnie while I go downstairs for a bit."

"No." Her lower lip trembled. She came around the couch and stood in my path, her voice took an ugly tone reminding me she was more than your average teenager. "You're supposed to protect me. My mother paid you. She paid!"

I put both of my hands on her shoulders. "Look Evelyn, do as I say."

Her chin rose. "Who's Evelyn?"

With so many answers, a lifetime wasn't enough to voice them. I squeezed the bridge of my nose to stop the steel drumming behind my eyes.

"Is she important?" Roxana asked.

Important. Very important. The most important. I studied her expectant face. She needed an answer. My breath caught in my throat as if the fate of the world depended on my next response. I had several good lies, but what came out was truth. "She was my daughter. She died when she was still small."

"Oh." Roxana scrunched her nose while studying the middle of my chest, she looked up, and favored me with a wide-eyed smile kids have when they discover ownership, my toy, my bed, my daddy, my hired killer. "I know you'll come back," her voice was a patient echo of her mom. "I'll stay."

I turned to leave and her arms circled my waist tight and brief.

"Thanks for dinner," she said before darting back to the laptop.

"Damn waffles," I muttered, scratching at the warm fuzzy forming in my chest.

3 A LOT OF RED

Guarding the Jungle Gem entrance like Roman Coliseum gladiators were two broad shouldered men speaking in hushed tones. Their eyes kept darting toward the street as if they were primed to make a break for it at any moment. They made no move to frisk me or even make eye contact as I strolled inside.

A dim hallway led to the glass cover charge booth manned by a dancer. I paused for the quick flash of velvet covered cleavage behind the bullet proof glass.

"'Sup Ken," said the cover charge girl with a smile frayed beyond repair.

"Evening," I replied while trying to attach the name to the dual... distractions. "Mars in?"

Her face paled and her pupils shrank to pinpricks. She stole a quick glance in the direction of the manager's office and lowered her voice. "You're going to bust up the place aren't you?"

I smiled, rapped my knuckles on the booth's glass, and left.

Jiggy's interior contained a handful of gloomy regulars present more out of habit than desire. The music hummed, bare midriff women quivered, jounced, and gyrated in one form or another. No one smiled. The molten sea of tension, usually sexual, was some other vintage tonight. Scoping the room revealed zip. I took my usual seat at the empty bar. The bartender drummed a bottle of tequila and shot glass in front of me and glided away to take a waitress' order.

Since drinks didn't pour themselves, I filled my glass though I hadn't planned on drinking on the job. The smell of perfume wafted around the room like heat from a firestorm. Sinuous movement filled with purpose caught my eye. I didn't recognize the breast implants. New blood.

"I give three looks," said a nubile blonde dancer sliding onto the stool next to me.

On closer inspection she wasn't blonde, but a brunette with tons of blonde highlights. Not that it mattered. If you could measure sex appeal in Fahrenheit, she would be dangerous around books and small children. Violet tinted pouting lips added volcanoes of good looks to a flat face, her eyes swirled blue like a gas stove pilot, bountiful breasts were laced into a metal studded black corset, and long pale legs ended in stiletto biker boots with the toe portion removed to show wiggling ruby painted toes.

"The first look is when you walk into the room," she continued. "The second is at the competition." She gave the room a once over. "To know my odds. The third is to see who you're looking at." She smiled. "And it better be me." She reached for the bottle of tequila, raised it to her lips, and swallowed. "All eyes on you the moment you stepped in. The girls say—" She made a vague gesture with the bottle. "—you're some kind of big shot."

The bartender turned and noticed the dancer. They locked eyes like two rampaging rhinos. The bartender looked away first and exiled herself to a dark corner of the bar to mix a noisy drink.

"Didn't notice," I said.

"That girl a friend of yours?" she asked. "I was out back misbehaving and saw you two on the stairs. She looked… young. Not that I'm judging." I glared. She put her hands up. "Look, I'm not saying anything. A lot of girls working here are runaways, addicts, or they have families to support. The one thing we have in common is the willingness to do what we have to."

"What business of it is yours?" I asked.

"That you left her upstairs with Winnie says you're decent." The dancer nodded. "I'm Sera by the way." She smiled giving me a mile of pristine white teeth. "With an e." She tipped the bottle toward my lips. As I grabbed it, she slid her hand away. "I could use decent right about now."

I guess playing hard to get still worked in some states.

"Kensington Ashe," I replied. I set down the bottle. I stole a quick glance in the direction of Mars' office.

"Nice to meet you, Kensington or is it Ken?" She chuckled, tracing a single finger along the bar. "I heard you're friends with Mr. P and well, I have a… work problem. Not with Mr. P of course. But with Mars." She flipped her hair over one shoulder and pouted.

"What makes you think I can help?"

Sera glanced toward the manager's office. "Rumor has it you deal in strange."

Strange? I chuckled. Either people knew what I did or they didn't. There's no in between. Despite her attempts at the mystery, I wagered she was disgruntled talent looking for the toughest idiot to beat down her problems. I dated this type before, sweet promises until it was time to deliver. Still, it had been a while since I encountered the possibility of getting laid *and* I had to kill Mars anyway. "What's in it for me?"

Sera caught her smile before it fell off her face and the way fire touched her eyes told me she expected me to go Lancelot over the booty. She smothered hate with pure Oscar worthy innocence and forced a smile of promise.

"Whatever you want," she said.

"I'll see what I can do." I didn't know why I bothered when I knew she would disappear come collection time. She was gone already, her caboose swishing toward the deejay booth. What she left behind on the stool was a cocktail napkin with her phone number written in eyebrow pencil.

Classy.

The area code was somewhere near the Tierra Santa Galleria mall, with my luck it probably was the mall. I slipped the napkin into my pocket as the bartender returned eying daggers at Sera's back. I addressed the bartender. "Anything I should know?"

The bartender opened her mouth. Before she could expunge a syllable the music pumping through the speakers transitioned into something slow and gothic, the lights dimmed, and a spotlight flared on stage.

Sera shined in a pool of light with delicious limbs mock-chained to a stainless steel pole. She broke loose on the first drumbeat and gyrated slow circles against the rigid steel. A guitar riff shattered the melody hard and raw and she matched its intensity by hooking legs around the pole and spiraling to her knees. As the drums upstaged the guitar, she flashed a wicked smile, and banged fist on the floor with her hair whipping from side to side. Then she leaned back, stroked her breast with one hand, and traced the line from her stomach to between her legs with the other. Cymbals clashed. Her hips thrust outward. As the music resumed its original gothic tone, her fingers tiptoed to the metal studs on her corset.

My heartbeat hammered as each snap came undone and exposed even more pale flesh. She had a way of moving that made the pulse below my waist throb. Her hand continued working the studs until one remained. A grin inched its way along my cheeks. Loud clapping, whistles, and catcalls drew my attention to Sera's corset discarded at the stages edge. Her bare back faced a catcalling crowd of six. The music changed signaling the start of her second set. She bobbed her shoulder to the rhythm.

Enough of the show, I had work to do. I rose from my stool and headed toward the manager's office. My nose noticed the first sign of trouble. The manager's office smelled of rot even with the door closed. I took out the keys and tried the lock. It came open with a click. I pushed inward with a hand close to my gun.

Mars leaned back in a honeyed leather chair with his ankles crossed atop the desk. He wore a starched gold pinstriped auburn suit and gold suede loafers. A duplicate of the Mr. Tickles key ring Winnie had given me, a miniature hand palming a hottie, swayed from his belt. Dirty fingernails capped his long slender fingers, an overbite spilled over thin smiling lips, and pale porcelain skin stood out bright against runny eyes whose iris, pupil, and sclera were as white as a hardboiled egg.

"What's with the new blonde dye job with the nice legs?" I asked.

"So much peroxide in this joint I have new blondes every week," he replied.

"The really nice legs." I rolled my shoulders. "Looking to be a free agent."

"Oh, Sera." An unpleasant thought twisted his unnatural expression into something more human which made it more off-putting. "She's more than you can handle. Worry about your own ass."

"Mars, you're a little shit and you know it." I shut the door, locked it, and approached the desk making it appear like I was at ease because a wight's nose for fear was only surpassed by their nose for flesh.

Wights were invulnerable to most forms of harm except fire and dismemberment. Though the most telling aspect of his new condition was that he was talking instead of trying to eat me. His master had him on a short leash, which meant there was a second monster nearby, probably one of the customers in the club.

A maggot burrowed out of the puckered skin over Mars' left eye and began crawling down his cheek. "They told me about you was supposed to be a bad ass killer."

"If *they* told you. Really told you. You would've run already." I kept my tone civil even as I wondered which *they* he meant. It would be nice to know whose lips my name was on. I made a slow show of opening my coat with two fingers so that my Sig Sauer P239 glittered in full view.

Mars stiffened, dropped loafers to the floor, and stood halfway with his hands gripping the desk's edge. A predatory snarl curled his thin lips.

"Mr. P wants to renegotiate terms." My hand moved Sunday drive casual, showing him I wasn't going for the gun, but instead for my wallet from which I extracted a single dollar bill, change from tonight's dinner. I laid the dollar on the table. "Take it or leave it."

Mars dropped back into his chair looking confused. "A buck? You shitting me right?"

I smiled hoarfrost. There was one useful constant about wights, reanimation didn't make them any smarter. Oh, the fresh one's could speak and put together some good sentences, but any attempt at critical thinking confused their dead minds.

It was almost too easy.

I sucker punched Mars out of his loafers. The maggot flew off of his cheek as he flipped over his chair and toppled to the floor. I freed my combat knife, slid across the desk sending the dollar fluttering like a feather, and dropped atop him. The knife split Mars' coat sleeve and pinned the dead flesh of his right bicep to the floor. I held my breath. Instead of blood, a horrid gagging stench rose from the wound.

Mars goggled in surprise and as expected he took a desperate left fisted swing I caught his wrist with my free hand, twisted it into a reverse joint lock, and jerked it toward his head.

I maintained control of Mars' wrist with my right hand. I took the lighter from my pocket and sparked it with my left hand. I gave Mars my Inquisitor stare, death incarnate, three times cold, and twice as nasty. "Who reanimated you?"

"Dammit!" Mars gaped, "You fuck. I'll kill you for this!"

Mars struggled. I tweaked his wrist until the bones cracked. Mars was stronger and had unlimited endurance of the dead. I had skill and leverage, joints twisted at the wrong angles put him at a disadvantage since wights still registered discomfort.

The fight drained out of him as his attention focused on the dancing flame. "What're you going to do with that?"

Rain and floods, he didn't know about fire. How the hell could a wight be unaware of fire? Wight bodies were dry as kindling so the slightest flame caused an uncontrolled burn. It was the first thing they learned to fear. Whoever reanimated Mars didn't give him a full run down, which meant Mars was expendable. "I'm not asking again."

His eyes darted back and forth with what passed for deep thought and he hesitated as long as it took him to dry lick drier lips. "I'll tell you if you let me go?"

Double dealing? Predictable human thinking. What a shame. I cranked his wrist for the intimidation factor and nodded.

"Ojáncanu," he said eyes darting. I cranked his wrist harder to make sure he was telling the truth. Several bones popped. Mars howled, "Ojáncanu, you fuck pie!"

Ahh, so now the truth oozed out like pus from a chancre.

The Crimson Consortium was a collective of witch covens. Each coven was denoted by its bloodline. There were seven major covens and an unknown number of minor ones. Coven Ojáncanu was one of the major players. They were plague bringers, a bloodline with the unique ability to secrete toxin whose effects differed depending on the potency. A low dose caused euphoria, a moderate dose caused paralysis, and the highest dose was flesh eating acid.

Coven Ojáncanu were also known as the partiers of the Crimson Consortium. They threw grand affairs, shit-faced their victims on toxin, fed deep, and then kicked out any survivors during the seven a.m. cattle call.

"What does Coven Ojáncanu want?"

"I don't know! I don't!" Mars screamed. "They said I can have Mr. P's territory if I help give them inside information. That's all I swear!"

He made no sense. A wight wouldn't care about running P's territory unless his master told him to care. Let's face it, only a complete tool would put a wight in charge of anything. This whole situation bobbed like a custom made lure.

"I know your master is nearby so save yourself some pain and point him out."

"What? I don't know where she is. She told me to keep you talking until she came back."

She? One of the girls in the club... Mars was an expendable pawn. Someone knew I was coming and wanted me to waste time on this idiot. Did this mean his Ojáncanu intel was a lie? Was his master trying to throw me off the trail. Could the real coven be Nuberu? As in Dhyana Nuberu?

"What does she look like?"

Mars took this moment to make a break for it. He drove his knee into my crotch. I pitched forward. The lighter slipped from my fingers and fell into his surprised face. Fire sparked on his skin and *whoosh* he exploded into ghoulish green flame.

I rolled away as thick dark smoke smelling of rotten eggs filled the office.

He screamed, ripped his pinned arm free, and surged to his feet, human customs like stop, drop, and roll were forgotten in his panic. Green flame engulfed his head and torso as he bolted for the door.

I grunted through the pain flaring in my lower region. From my position on the floor, I drew my Sig and squeezed two bullets into his back and one between his ass cheeks. That was for the low blow.

The bullets' impact and his forward momentum sent him crashing through the office door in a hail of splintering wood. Mars stumbled into two surprised dancers, swung both arms in wild arcs, and punted them across the room, one flipped over the bar and the other crashed down on a table hard enough to shatter it.

Fire alarms screamed.

Customers, waitresses, bartenders, and dancers shrieked in panic. They hauled ass away from the monster burning with green flames and made for the exits. They didn't know his unnatural flame wouldn't catch, not that it mattered, pretty soon the scramble of panicked bodies ebbed leaving a mess of spilled drinks, overturned tables, and broken furniture.

Mars swayed like a drunk and collapsed in a puddle of limbs in the middle of the empty club. Green flame danced skyward, belched waves of heat, and brightened the room in white-green light that blitzed my eyes. Mars' body imploded in one burst. The flames extinguished in a burst of smoky air.

I lowered my gun and blinked away the spots blurring my vision. All that remained were black-gray ash, the hissing heat-warped metal of his Mr. Tickles key ring, and the various zippers and studs from Mars' clothing.

I climbed to my feet, holstered my sidearm, and cupped a hand over my mouth and nose to protect against the smoke and stench. The painful throb beneath my waist ebbed to a bad memory.

The club was empty though music still droned, the deejay must've put on a tune before Mars went boom. With the fire alarm smashing against my eardrums, it was only a matter of time before the police and fire department arrived. I had to grab the kid and escape if I wanted to avoid any blame.

The backdoor fire exit led to the alley behind Jiggy's. It was the quickest path to Winnie's apartment. I retrieved my knife and headed through the smoke and found the backdoor ajar.

I pushed open the door. Fresh air punched my lungs. I coughed and spat out gobs of phlegm. Something glistening and wet on the asphalt caught my eye. I wiped my mouth with a sleeve and drew my Sig, gripping it in both hands with its barrel pointed down.

A slick, red, and thick trail of fresh blood pooled around a sockless left foot peeking out from the behind a dumpster. By the looks of the still wet pavement, the bullish corpse hadn't been dead for long—his skull cracked open by collision with the asphalt.

Light from the second floor created harsh shadows. I had to move closer for a better look at his face. I swallowed hard. My stomach knotted as the lump of flesh coalesced into someone recognizable. I dealt with a lot of dead so believe me when I say it was easier when the victims were strangers.

Large chunks of glass protruded from his skin and his boxers were bloodied and ruined. I couldn't find his other sock and I wondered why I tried, sometimes the mind coped by focusing on a simple task. Part of where his scalp was missing had turned strawberry by blood. Impact had forced his eyes from their sockets and they dangled on stems, easy pickings for a hungry rat.

Brody wasn't a stranger. He left life footprints. He was someone P would avenge to keep from looking soft and most importantly someone Winnie would mourn. My gaze left his face and searched his throat, which was shredded into low grade hamburger. The fall hadn't caused those wounds. They were the result of puncture wounds from one long fang.

The highest concentration of oxygenated blood in the human body was in the lungs. Guajona bite the jugular because it was easier than breaking through rows of ribs to extract the creamy filling. I hated when monsters leave behind a lot of red.

Brody was either thrown or he fell, most likely thrown because falling wouldn't explain the glass or the neck wounds.

Roxana's face exploded in my mind. If she killed her stepdad, she would be full guajona with more than enough strength to do this. My stomach lurched. I couldn't be wrong about her. *Please God, don't let me be wrong!* Otherwise, I asked two lambs to watch a hungry lion.

The scene before me, like many others in alleys in cities across the country, was the reason why I qualified guajona as monsters. Carnage was the inevitable conclusion when guajona relinquished their humanity for the power, blood, and hunger. That was the lure of the Cleave, it promised unimaginable power, immaculate beauty, unbreakable confidence, and anything else an individual might be lacking. How could anyone beat near immortality at the low low cost of feeding on the living? It was how corporations made their megabucks.

A crimson gob splashed on my shoulder and neck. I glanced up. The missing chunk of Brody's scalp ripped free on the way down dangled from the slats in the stairwell. That damned hairy serrated lump chose this precise moment I stepped underneath to bleed all over my coat.

My goddamned dry cleaned coat!

Most people believed death was quick and clean. It was not. It took a long time for the soul to leave the body and it could sometimes hang around for weeks. Souls were bound to our flesh like we were bound to this planet. Like Brody had been bound to Winnie.

Brody's blood running down my neck activated my Lengua-bruja. Brody's death rattle dissolved the world's natural colors to Armageddon-gray. I stood in the world of the dead, a tonal wasteland. White coiled reverberations, the size of hula hoops, bounced from Brody's dead body upwards in an arcing path to Winnie's apartment. The reverberations expanded to a more familiar marching of a million scampering rats across hardwood. His death rattle played. My Lengua-bruja tried to decipher what La Parca spoke:

Three laughed. The Unseen came. Unheard was the turn of the door. The Unseen pounced, sank her tooth into his neck. They tumbled, crushing and smashing. So ended the laughter. So began the screams.

He wrestled The Unseen, its strength tore his skin. He felt the burning pain of invasion. Inside his throat. He struggled. The Unseen drank his life. The Unseen discarded him. The carpet pressed against his cheek. Lethargy overtook him. Limbs became leaden. Still. Still. Heart slowed.

He saw The Unseen clearer now, a woman he knew to be Sera though he had been more interested in her legs, longer than sin. Why were her eyes black? Why was her mouth red? Why was a part of him inside her?

Sera knocked his Heart aside with the back of her fist. He watched his Heart crumple and remain still. Sera moved toward the cowering girl. A child. Innocent, sweet child. Sera struck. The child collapsed as still as his Heart.

Searing fury erased lethargy. His feet were strong. His legs and arms responded. He charged Sera. Joyful contact as his shoulder met her ribcage. They thrashed and destroyed the furnishings. Joy was short-lived. Sera clawed his back, lifting. He rose high. Glass sharp, shattered edges sliced him. The wind found him. His Heart's home moved away. He reached and reached.

The promise of ringed gold he had hidden in the pocket of what he mistook as his Heart's favorite jeans would go unfound. He waited for his Heart to find the promise. He was tired. Tired of waiting for his Heart to find gold. His Heart would have gold. He would ask Winnie for her promise. Tomorrow he would—

The world slammed back to normal, color, and shape. Brody's death rattle had been clearer than most. Winnie and Brody were attacked by Sera, the dancer who pretended to need my help.

Sera sat right in front of me, a smile painted on her face, the pearly whites of her teeth glistening deception, and pointed me at Mars' so she could slip upstairs and take the kid. How did she know that I would bring the kid here? Was Gabriela and Mr. P in on this? This whole situation reeked of a set up.

As the last person seen with the kid, I would be the police's primary suspect. Gabriela set me up, as either a murderer or kidnapper, which means she must've been working with Sera. That Dhyana Nuberu crap was bullshit. Dammit! I was going to find Gabriela and when I did…

There was no way to tell how much time elapsed from the events in Brody's death rattle. My Lengua-bruja translated La Parcas' dialect and death spirits like La Parca had no concept of time. It was up to me to figure out whether the victim died minutes or hours ago.

The whole talk I had with Mars and the resulting burning man show took about ten or fifteen minutes—more than enough time for her to kill Brody.

I leapt the first set of stairs, stopped, and glanced back at Brody's corpse; it could be infected by the Cleave, which could reanimate him as a wight under Sera's control. Destroying Brody's body would have to wait. I continued up the stairs with the hope that the dead would stay dead.

The pleasure of motion was its ability to erase doubt. I became more focused as I ascended the stairs. My heart pumped. Each stride brought me closer to knowing if I was too late.

The front door of Winnie's apartment gaped like an open mouth. I pointed the Sig's barrel through the opening and scanned inside. Winnie's living room appeared to be a victim of a smash and grab—hit quick, steal what you can carry, and run—except the valuables were still present.

Her couch was overturned, the coffee table, laptop, and Blu-ray player were smashed. The flat-screen had been knocked off its stand; it was still plugged in and it hissed with the screen of death. Blood covered the cracked plastic DVD cases strewn about the floor.

I followed more of Brody's blood to where the busted window overlooking the alley left glass on the carpet. He had put up as good a fight as any normal man could against a monster. If I had medals to give for dying, I would plant one on his corpse. Instead, I sent a silent prayer of *thanks for trying.*

Not far away, Winnie's disheveled clothes hung limp on the S curve of her prone form. Her matted hair obscured her face so I couldn't tell if she was alive and as much as I wanted to check her injuries, it wasn't quite the time to indulge, for all I knew Sera might still be lurking.

I abandoned Winnie to conduct a quick room by room search. Kitchen. Bedroom. Bathroom. I checked the nooks and by that I mean jean pockets, closets, cabinets, and refrigerators (it was amazing how many bodies you could stuff in those places). I was left scratching my angry brow as I returned to the living room. The other rooms hadn't been touched. Roxana and Sera were gone. I holstered my gun.

Winnie remained unconscious. My decision to leave the kid, my inability to see through Sera's deception, and overall greediness for a paying job caused all this. I went to check her pulse and halted.

If I made contact with her skin and her death rattle came rolling, I wouldn't be able to shut it out. Her final moment would remain carved into my brain, which was the most heinous part about death rattles—you couldn't forget them. My solitary hope was that she made peace with all her inner and outer demons before she died. I could leave her undisturbed, but she might need CPR. I couldn't live with myself if she died because I too chicken shit to touch her. I shook my head. There were no winning choices. I reached out, hesitant, and let my fingers brush her neck before snatching them back.

I waited for the million scampering rats across hardwood sound and a world devoid of color. Nothing happened. With growing confidence, I pressed two fingers to the warmth of her neck and found a steady pulse. I released a tense breath and closed my eyes for a second, sending a silent *thank you* to no one in particular. I turned her so that she laid on her back and brushed the hair from her face to reveal a bright purple bruise coloring her right cheek. I checked her over. No cuts or scratches. Thank heavens, no bites.

I recovered the engagement ring Brody placed in Winnie's jean pocket. The least I could do was see that she received it. I slid the diamond onto her limp ring finger. The ring was a bit undersized and took some work to get it over her knuckle, but once in place the diamond sparkled in its new home. I laid her hand across her chest and stood.

With the ruckus downstairs, Brody's death, and the damage up here, this fiasco had grown beyond my ability to contain. Someone needed to keep me out of jail while I figured this mess out. I took out my cell phone.

Detective Natalie Lacruz's voice hummed over the phone as she answered. There wasn't a single call she ran from and heaven help anyone wasting her time. Lacruz was so scary that solicitors voluntarily banned her from their call lists.

"You busy?" I asked. Lacruz was one of the few friends I trusted, which made her more prized than a pound of French vanilla ice cream. There weren't a lot of people I could share shoptalk with—homicide over burgers and monsters over donuts.

"Damn, Ken. Not tonight," Lacruz answered. Her voice sounded like she had arrested a thousand perps and had a thousand more to book. "Give me a sec." Lacruz barked out orders to a cacophony of excited voices, probably another crime scene. "I'm clear."

"One of mine?"

"No. Strictly native. Domestic dispute," Lacruz answered flat and toneless in her cop's calm—daunting, confident, and incorruptible. "Someone used this homeowner's head as a drumstick and the floor as a drum."

Ouch. "Who made the call?"

"Anonymous," Lacruz said. "There's about an hour delay between time of death and the 911 call. Both mother and daughter are missing."

"Christ," I said feeling red behind my eyes. At times, I couldn't fathom how people could be monsters when the real one's skulked around. Maybe people would be more civilized if they knew about the real horrors. "Kidnap?"

"I'm guessing fled the scene." Lacruz's voice hissed like a spent barbecue pit. "That's not why you called. Spill it, you're wasting my minutes."

Must be a lot a scene fleeing going around. "Major trouble at the Jungle Gem. The monster and dead body variety," I said. "One dead, several injured."

"What kind of monster are we talking about?"

"A wight, which I've already barbecued. You can thank me later. The second is a guajona. She escaped so it's the cleanup," I said.

Lacruz paused. "Your pajama parties are always a laugh," she answered. "Be a couple hours before this wraps up."

"Fire alarms sounded off a couple minutes ago. I'm not hearing sirens yet…"

She swore a string of curses a mile long. "You won't. Pimberton's criminal businesses aren't on the fast response list. It'll be a spell before anyone shows up."

I held my hand up in mock resignation trying to have the common decency to avoid snorting. "To serve and protect."

"Pimberton's a crook as is anyone in his employ! They can wait while we deal with real victims. Please tell me you haven't… God, am I going to find missing hearts or heads or something else odd? I hope not because I am seriously running out of favors with forensics."

"Connelly thinks you're a babe. Boink him and you're good until December."

"Not funny, Ken," she answered, annoyed.

"You boinked him already, didn't you?" I snickered.

"We are not discussing my boink life. I'll meet you as soon as I can."

"Hit the alley."

"You better be there. No Houdini stuff," she sighed and the weariness in her tone returned.

"Don't forget to grab some protein," I chided. Silence answered and I imagined her hand running through her short black hair. A gesture she always did when she was tired. She would be running all night with no time to eat or rest.

"Goodbye," Lacruz said.

"Goodbye," I answered, killing the line. I made a second call to 911 for an ambulance before pocketing the phone. Lacruz could vouch for me when the cops arrived and Winnie would receive the medical help she needed. For now, I had a few minutes of undisturbed silence to comb over the place for a connection between Sera and Roxana. Or maybe not.

There were some sounds that were pleasant no matter how much you heard them. For example, your mother's voice as she called you for dinner, the ice cream truck music on your way home from elementary school, your wife's jingling keys before the front door opened, or your daughter's first and last laughs of the day.

I didn't have many sounds that filled me with pleasure. All my happy sounds were connected to people who were gone. All I had left were the blood curdling sounds that made me want to lock myself in at night. I added another unhappy sound to my lock-myself-in list.

Sirens.

4 COP A FEEL

The Saturday afternoon sun was so bright that I had to shield my eyes to watch Yanira finger comb her dark regal hair away from her face. She stood at the fence marking the separation between our property and the neighbors. We had purchased a two bedroom house on the bad side of town—her choice, not mine. Accompanying her at the fence was our neighbor Tuggy, a bare chest island buck in baggy jeans. Her hand brushed his arm as she laughed.

A little someone tugged at my shorts and I looked down into the caramel apple cheeks of my pouting little girl. "Mommy said I couldn't have ice cream," Evelyn said.

I kneeled, pulled her close, and whispered. "Only Daddy's Pequiñita get ice cream."

Evelyn giggled in my hug. Her soft cheeks rubbed my beard. "I'm Pequiñita!"

I laughed into her hair, which smelled like syrup and baby powder, and glanced over her head. Yanira had moved closer to Tuggy and whispered in his ear. He pushed a plastic baggy into her hand, a quick practiced gesture that would have been invisible unless you looked for it.

Evelyn slapped both my cheeks and squeezed. I felt the stilted pull of my cheeks before I realized I had stopped smiling. I readjusted my expression into something closer to a grin and tickled my daughter. She giggle-kicked in my arms.

"First one to the kitchen licks the spoon," I said as I set her down and jogged for the house.

I fled the sunlight with my Pequiñita chasing after me.

Kensington, a voice pulled me from the past. Terrible music droned, distant and muddled, I tried to identify the haunting noise that crackled like lightning and buzzed like angry bees. Finally, my brain wove the notes into

42

cop radio chatter. The voice calling me was attached to a badge.

Lacruz's fashion was predictable and efficient, a simple blazer, black slacks, and a powder blue button up. Her polished badge hung on her belt next to her Beretta PX4. Her tan skin glowed against black hair cut in a boyish style, short on the sides and back with short bangs. A smooth cute nose and the most perfect slice of lips softened her high cheeks. What captured me were her eyes, a dancing brown that was more Cha-cha than Electric Slide. Underneath it all, she had the kind of body you would take home to daddy because mommy wouldn't approve.

I was handcuffed to a gurney in the back of an ambulance. The rear doors were open so I could see the bustle of cops, firemen, and the curious onlookers held back by the police tape stretching from one telephone pole to the next. Flashing sirens from police cruisers, ambulances, and fire trucks bathed the asphalt in blue and red and for a moment Tierra Santa's haziness lifted exposing the bruised underbelly of a city too familiar with abuse.

The EMT who checked me disappeared after declaring me injury free. A bored moose faced officer in TSPD blues stood guard. We both knew his disinterest was an act. Lacruz nodded and the officer left his post to give us some privacy. That was when I noticed she was holding two bags, one white paper containing what I guessed to be donuts and the other was clear plastic imprisoning my knife and gun. It occurred to me that I would lose any chance of staying out of jail once TSPD ran ballistics on my gun and on the bullets mixed in with Mars' ashes.

With squared shoulders, I reached for the donut bag, which Lacruz released without comment, and fished inside the opening. We were alone, as alone as we could be, but I could see the officers lingering close ready to back up Lacruz at a moment's notice. I pulled out a bear claw donut, nodded at the cuffs on my right wrist, and met Lacruz's steady gaze. She responded with a not-on-your-life look. I put the donut in my mouth to forestall an angry retort. I chewed slowly so the sweet apple filling soothed my aching propriety.

Lacruz waited.

She was the only person I knew who bothered to study silence, from what I understood it was a dead language. She regarded me with a mixture of amusement and anger like a mother whose kid muddied his Sunday best and still looked adorable despite the mess. I knew her well enough to avoid mistaking her expression for forgiveness. I had some explaining to do so I arranged my story in between bites.

Trouble was creeping in the dark. Other than killing Mars, it had all gone so wrong tonight. One bad decision led to the next. How could I leave my office without asking why the kid mattered? Was I so desperate for cash that I ignored all the warning signs?

My carelessness led to Brody's coffin. Almost Winnie's coffin too. And I might need to have one made for Roxana. It didn't matter that I barbecued a wight. My incompetence rendered my accomplishment meaningless. I brought the kid to a hot zone, lost her, and had no clue how to find her.

I lifted my chin and smiled. It never hurts to smile except when it does. "Shitty night we're having."

"I know I asked you to stick around..." Lacruz said, studying the roughness around my edges. "Napping in the back of an ambulance is low, even for you Ashe."

"You asked me to stick so I stuck." I noticed my reflection in some odd metal tool resembling oversized forceps. I set my donut aside, took the tool off the wall, and used its dull flat end like a mirror. I looked like crap microwaved twice over. I set the forceps down, took up my donut and gored it before slurping the filling to keep it from spilling. I made a fist and shook my manacled wrist.

"Try, *Thank you for not hauling my ass in for murder,*" she said. "My boss keeps asking about the weird cases and the exceptions in protocol I've been making lately and 'it's a hunch' is starting to wear thin. My exemplary service record is the only barrier keeping me from being busted down to meter maid." Lacruz's focus wavered for a second. "I can't keep a lid on this kind of thing forever."

"The lids been on it for centuries. Trust me it'll keep." At one time, society believed in ghosts and goblins and told stories about them over campfires. Over the centuries, truth became fantasy and fantasy became Dracula and Dracula became major motion pictures. Humanity made a conscious effort to replace all the bad with as much fiction it could cram down its gullet. I waved my half eaten donut like a lecture stick. "We can send a man into space, put tofu on a pizza, but can't prove the existence of Yeti."

"You told me there wasn't a Bigfoot," Lacruz countered.

"You know what has the biggest feet? Cuélebre. Supposedly he's a mountain-sized Wyrm the color of snow with hundreds of ginormous feet. Some call him the Anti-Adam because he didn't give up a rib and kept procreation all to himself. All of his progeny turned out to be horrible misshapen flesh eating monsters so I guess the moral of the story is a man needs a woman's touch, but you know me and morals."

"In the version I heard, she was named Lilith and she was Adam's first wife," Lacruz said.

"Lilith was Cuélebre's booty call. Terribly toxic situation-ship, God had to flood the earth for forty days and forty nights to clean up the mess."

"You're telling me this why?" Lacruz asked.

"Ahem, rude Padawan. Bigfoot isn't a monster it's a concept. Any hairy monster wearing Shaq-sized shoes is called Bigfoot. Yeti are different. Think offspring of a polar bear and a killer whale with nonexistent IQ. Yeti are bad, but not as dangerous as Eastern Bunnies. Now those are nasty little mongrels."

Lacruz rolled her eyes. "Easter bunnies aren't monsters."

"East-ern Bunnies are flesh-pink long eared carnivores with razor sharp teeth, red glowing eyes, and a nose that can smell prey ten miles off. They're the size of Chihuahuas and hunt in packs of twenty. They live in Germany, on the Eastern side of the Carpathian Mountains. They only hunt at midnight."

Lacruz wanted me to be joking. She rubbed the bridge of her nose and closed her eyes for a second. "Do you try to ruin every pleasant childhood memory I have?"

"Pretty much," I said finishing the donut. I reached into the bag for another—a glazed twist.

"Stalling much?" Lacruz asked. Thanks to me, Lacruz slept with a loaded gun next to the bed and a knife under her pillow. Monsters enter anywhere they choose. Soul traps, hallowed ground, quality locks, or a hefty set of firearms were the only true deterrents. Safety depended on what you could do for yourself.

Lacruz's fingers flexed and I was reminded of her sword training. She was part of a troupe that did medieval fight reenactments during renaissance fairs. She was Sir Tight Ass of Honesty or something I couldn't quite remember.

"You smell girly," she said. The words were light. The glare wasn't.

"I had plenty of singles."

She considered it for all it was worth before snatching the donut out of my hand and dropping it to the ground. Her face was blank and unreadable.

"Let's do this at the station," she said.

I held up my un-cuffed hand in mock surrender. "Is Winnie okay?"

"The blonde concussion? At the hospital. She's still unconscious. The EMTs said she wasn't in any immediate danger. I plan to question her when she wakes up. Who is she to you? More importantly, what will she say?"

"A friend." I was glad for Winnie's safety. "Do me a favor, will you? Keep a cop at her door." Lacruz considered the request and nodded. "Did you find Brody?"

Lacruz paused. "We found a lot of blood, glass, a shoe, and a really huge mess. Right now we're collecting names, numbers, and addresses of any employees or customers who didn't bother sticking around. Hopefully, somebody saw something." She sutured me with a stare that doubled as a lie detector. "We have a couple of eyewitnesses who claim a guy in a brown jacket with a skull on the back set the manager on fire. We asked if they saw him do it, they said no, only that this man goes into the manager's office and then a huge green fireball comes running out. We tried to confirm the story by locating the body, but couldn't find one. Ash and spent shell casings, yes. Body, no. Doesn't help that most of the witnesses are wasted and that goes double for the employees."

I decided to tell Lacruz about Mars being a wight, my run in with Brody's corpse, and Sera orchestrating the whole affair. I left out the part about being hired to protect Roxana and her subsequent kidnap—basically the motive. I didn't want to hear Lacruz's opinion of my stupidity. I needed her to believe I could still hack it and that was the problem. Maybe I couldn't? I left Brody's corpse hoping he wouldn't turn so I told Lacruz to have the body frozen as soon as possible. She listened without interruption until I finished.

Lacruz took a breath and swore. "A guajona and a wight," she snapped. She turned to me, her expression becoming thoughtful. "I'll put out an APB on the dancer."

"Don't. She'll tear any cop a new one. She's mine."

"We've never hunted a guajona," Lacruz said.

We've never hunted anything. She cleared the road and stayed out of my way. That was our arrangement. This we business sounded like she wanted to take our working relationship to the next level. A deep spinal fear of being smothered crept its way up my neck; I had more confidence and control working away from judging eyes. What I did was too dangerous.

"Maybe we can leave and grab a drink?" The words were out of my mouth before I could yank them back.

Lacruz goggled with her thin brows creased in disbelief. "You're serious?"

I shrugged.

"I don't drink when I have dead bodies and suspects."

Lacruz always had dead bodies. I replied, "I'm not a suspect."

She jammed her hand into a pocket and snatched out a key. "Technically, I've had you downgraded to an eye witness. Really, you're a major ass. My boss will probably have my badge for cutting you loose. But there's little choice, is there?" The key entered the lock and with a quick twist the cuff fell away.

She was right. It wasn't much of a choice. Guajona roamed the dark. I was equipped to handle the problem. That was the trust we shared. She depended on me to do my job and was willing to bend the rules even at the cost of her career.

She handed me the plastic bag containing my knife and gun. I tore it open.

"A duplicate of these have been logged in as official evidence so ballistics won't match the bullets we found inside," she explained.

I decided not to ask why she had exact copies of the hardware I used. Some questions you didn't ask in polite company. I put both weapons in their respective holsters. "At least you don't think of me as a friend," I muttered.

Her anger dissipated and she laughed. It was a short bark that ended with several snorts. Lacruz hated her laugh. I liked it. The smile radiating from her eyes held me transfixed for a second and I imagined her lips...

"I try not to think of you at all," she said, averting her gaze as she put the cuffs into a pouch she kept on her belt. She brought out a plastic badge that read, Police Consultant and pinned it to my lapel before I could protest. She gave me a hard look that said she would spear me if I took it off.

I ignored the doodad and I occupied myself with working feeling back into my wrist.

She looked around the parking lot. Her mouth hardened into a firm line. "Come. I need you to tell me what you see."

I nodded and stood.

I left the empty donut bag on the gurney, licked my fingers, climbed out of the ambulance, and followed her through the gauntlet of investigators. The lights were up inside Jiggy's. The odor of burnt flesh clung to its stampeded interior. Most of the tables were twisted. The glass riddled carpet had soaked up its fill of overturned drinks. Stains, whose origins I didn't want to guess at (and never noticed before because of the dim lighting) covered the VIP couches in an odd shadow mosaic. Five gloomy employees were separated and interrogated in quiet corners. The only bright objects in the room were the stripper poles. I hoped P would consider some serious redecorating in the wake of this disaster. This place was tacky as hell.

Lacruz's colleagues greeted her with nods more friendly than professional. Their critical appraisals followed my every move. The officers took in my coat, attitude, and semi battered appearance. Despite my consultant badge they probably pegged me for an all-around bad guy.

They were right.

"Keep your coat closed," Lacruz warned. "I don't want to have to explain your hardware."

A cop approached us wearing gray slacks and a blue police jacket with TCPD imprinted in white over the left breast. The crow's feet surrounding his on-the-job hard eyed stoniness placed him somewhere in his late forties. He had the type of mouth that hadn't forgotten how to laugh and from the undercurrent of bourbon on his breath, he hadn't forgotten how to drink either. The stranger stripped off plastic gloves and put them in a pocket. He greeted Lacruz with a pat on her shoulder and spared a full three seconds, staring down his nose, to etch my face into memory.

"Connelly," Lacruz introduced.

I did a double take. This was my first time meeting him in person. Hell, this was my first invitation to an active crime scene. Lacruz talked about him with varying degrees of profanity, respect, and affection that made me a bit jealous. My mind drifted nine months back to a specific moment at Frankee's when we had coffee and burgers. She was dressed much like she was now, only her hair was longer. She told me about a disagreement with a hardheaded Forensics Tech named Connelly.

"This is Kensington Ashe; he's… going to be helping us." The undercurrent of Lacruz's voice intoned that he not make a fuss.

Connelly heard it. His eyes narrowed into dangerous slits as they touched my badge. It was clear he didn't want me anywhere near his crime scene, but didn't have the authority to override Lacruz. He looked me over, another three-second inquisition, before speaking. "We have two points of interest." He pointed to gray dust on the floor. "Some kind of ash, a lot of it. Don't know from what yet, but it kind of looks like cremains. We also found some metal bits and three bullets. We found signs of a struggle and shell casings in the office. The fight started there. Victim crashed through that door and burned to cinders here. I don't know how that could happen without the whole place burning down. There's not even scorch marks on the carpet." He pointed at a twisted table. "One of the dancers was impaled, either thrown or shoved or fell wrong and well... shish kabob, deliberate or accidental," he shrugged. "Can't really say."

Other guys in jackets like Connelly's were taking snapshots of the blood soaked carpet while another was scrapping metal and blood from the table leg into a plastic baggy. They were all blind to a truth they wouldn't believe even if they were drowning in it.

I was overconfident when I confronted Mars and didn't take any precautions other than locking the door. My carelessness costed a life. I had to do better and now was a good a time to start. I scanned the room for, well, anything that might give me any clue as to how to proceed. I noticed the bartender who tried to help me earlier leaning against the bar with her arms crossed. Her tired and exasperated expression punctuated a woman explaining, repeatedly, why one plus one equals two to a uniformed officer who couldn't add it up. I was too far away to make out her exact words. The officer wrote something down on his notepad and asked another question. She scowled and replied sharply.

I decided to intercede.

I took two steps in their direction when Connelly's girth slid into my path (he moved pretty smooth for a big guy). I stopped two inches from his face and fought every instinct to shove him the hell out of my way.

Lacruz, enjoying our head butting and too professional to show it, regarded us like two bull elephants. She placed her hand on Connelly's forearm, pulled him toward the ashes while dismissing me with a shoulder. She said to Connelly, "Explain it to me again."

I took a deep breath. Let it out. It was going to be that kind of night and I had already lost precious time. Lacruz's authority was keeping me out of the box so it was vital to play nice and snuggly with the lower ranking fuzz. I approached the bartender, smiled polite at the officer, and tried to appear non-hostile, friendly was too much of a stretch. "Can I have a moment?"

The officer scanned my plastic badge and glanced over at Lacruz. She gave him the okay. He nodded, closed his notepad, and walked over to where Lacruz and Connelly pow-wowed.

The bartender let out a quick burst of frustrated breath as soon as the officer was out of earshot. "What happened in there?"

"You have a good view of the mass exodus," I said by way of answer.

"Wasn't much to see," she muttered. "Was that really green fire?"

"What did you tell the Blues?"

She rolled her wrist in circles. "I didn't talk about you if that's what you're asking. They asked what happened and I kept saying, I don't know. Then he kept asking about the fire alarm. I told him, I didn't know about any of that. He kept asking over and over. Fuck him. I'm no snitch. You tell Mr. P. Tell him Kim don't snitch."

The one nasty surety of working in one of P's businesses was seeing or hearing something you would rather not have. How you handled yourself afterward, what you said or didn't was crucial in determining whether you stayed... employed. I asked, "Ever have trouble like this before?"

Kim looked thoughtful. "There's usually all kinds of shit going down. Nothing weird until Mars came back. He was supposed to be dead, not that I went to the funeral. He was an ass," she explained. "Well, anyway, that was a lie because he comes back after like four days and he's all weird. Nobody had the balls to ask him what happened, not even Winnie. She says she called Mr. P."

Wights didn't just come in off the streets on their own. They had to be ordered. "Mars have any other visitors?"

She shook her head. "I pretty much stayed clear and left it all to Winnie. But that bitch bugged out and left. No one went into the manager's office except Sera. Probably fucking or whatever. She was real flirty with him even before his vacation. He bragged about going somewhere in Mexico for two weeks."

Sera probably had been planning this for at least a month. She could've infected Mars as far back as three weeks. What was her endgame? It doesn't take a month to plan such a messy kidnap. I had to discover what or it was my ass taking the blame. "Did anyone use the rear fire exit before or during the fire?"

She chewed a fingernail. "Sera went that way after her set. Some of us smoke in the alley because it's a hassle to smoke out front; sometimes the customers don't let you alone when they see you outside."

"She leave the door open?"

"It locks automatic otherwise you can't reenter in without walking around front," she said. Kim held two fingers to form a V and moved them against her lips in a mock puffing motion. "As far as I've seen, Sera don't smoke. Then again she didn't hang out with the rest of us. She was way into herself."

"Is she...?" I gestured around the room.

Her tone was dismissive. "I haven't seen her since the ruckus. You might want to check for her car, a white Mercedes with the plates CYNFUL." Kim rolled her eyes before tilting her head and studying me as if she was working up the courage to ask a touchy subject. "Was it gas? I mean, did you use gasoline?" I didn't answer. She blushed and said, "I've never seen fire that color. I mean poof he's gone. People don't burn like that without being covered with some kind of special oil or something, right?"

Despite what happened tonight, she wouldn't consider the supernatural. She wanted a rational explanation for what she saw and wanted me to make it make sense. To her, monsters were movies and books. What she saw tonight defied logic and now the thin bubble of delusion protecting her mind was stretched to its limits. Her eyes shone with a bestial fear. Fire isn't supposed to burn like that. With one word of truth I could shred her world.

I lived a delusion once. I thought safety meant living far from the wars overseas so I behaved like everyone else—worked too much, drank too much, and complained too much about not having enough. I made my life's purpose to acquire because accumulating was the best way to go about providing for my daughter. I was working overtime at the office when a guajona tore my delusion to shreds.

I had no idea monsters existed, let alone one would pick my block, my house, my kitchen. Even if I had been there, the end would've been as tragic except I would've died alongside my daughter instead of carrying her death inside me.

In my nightmares, I relived that night over and over. It would be cruel to do that to anyone else. "You ever see green fireworks?" I supplied. Not the best explanation, but it was all I could come up with on the fly. "Certain chemicals change the color."

Kim's relief bubbled from her chest, vibrated her body, and released the tension in her dangling limbs. She studied the bar and began counting the labels. "What now?"

"I clean up the mess," I replied to Kim. That's what I did the night my daughter was murdered.

The night evil showed up on my doorstep, I had pulled into the driveway tired, hungry, and addled by an unfinished report. I had opened the front door and called out to my daughter and the sitter. When no one answered, I walked into the kitchen to find my Pequiñita's still form splayed in cold pink milk. Her babysitter, the neighbor's ebony haired seventeen-year-old into skinny pasty boys and bad vampire fiction, had been left half propped up in a corner with blood dribbling down her punctured throat. Adolescent lipstick was smeared across her bruised face.

I knew my Pequiñita was gone the first moment my eyes touched her. It's a sense I honed from my tour in the Middle East—a body too still, too flat, too rigid when it should be bursting into three dimensions. I opened the window to let in fresh air before I grabbed a dish towel, turned on the faucet, and drowned it under the fall. While the dish towel soaked up moisture, I waited to be consumed by that sense of hope a parent is supposed to feel, a hope that what's in front of them is a horrible prank conceived in bad taste. I felt punished for not loving my daughter enough so death had taken her away.

With rag in hand I turned from the sink and bent to pick up her frail body. Her cheek had stuck to the floor where the milk and blood dried. I tugged and it came away with a sickening *schrippp* leaving bits of her hair plastered to the floor. I dabbed her face, cheeks, and around the open wound in her throat. The rag was red by the time I had finished. The smell of sour milk and human fluids had floated out the open window like a ghost.

Kim smiled, a tired genuine smile, one that let me know she would sleep okay because there were no monsters. I glanced around and spotted the cover charge girl, whose name I could now recall (Viola). She sat alone atop the stage, her legs dangled over the edge while she stared blankly at the floor. I reached out and squeezed Kim's shoulder. She mumbled a goodbye as I left.

Viola looked up as I arrived and made a gesture of arranging her clothes. She became aware of her tear smeared eyeliner and tried to clear the mess using her fingertips. I grabbed a discarded cocktail napkin from a nearby table and handed it to her. "Thanks," she said dabbing her eyes. She composed herself with a deep breath and gave me a sad smile. "What can I do for you, Boo?"

"What's the word?"

Her eyes darted from side to side checking for nearby cops. "Went crazy in here," she said in a low voice with the throaty scratchiness of someone who cried herself raw for the drama of it. "Everybody screaming and breaking for the door and whatnot."

"Anyone leave through the back?"

Viola shook her head. "I can't see that far from my booth. Besides, wasn't like I was looking."

She probably hadn't seen much from her vantage point, but I hoped she at least kept track of a few of the faces streaming past her. "You know Sera?"

"That bourgeois ass broad?" Viola wiggled her shoulders.

"What was her deal?"

"She was double-dipping. She had some other gig and was always trying to pump that cowboy bar, Cattle Branch out on the highway, offering VIP's and whatnot. They into some S&M shit over there and I don't get down with that crowd."

The Cattle Branch was an Ojáncanu Crimoire, which was a fancy way to say fast food restaurant for blood suckers. The silver lining was that I had a place to start looking for Roxana though I shuddered at the kind of torment she would be exposed to. Crimoire were places of pain and misery. The Cattle Branch was a barbecue joint during the day and a nightclub at night. Its very public nature created a shield against Inquisitor retaliation. I hadn't been able to link one disappearance to the Cattle Branch though I suspected they were bleeding people. I had been trying to uncover their angle for some time. It was almost like Coven Ojáncanu had figured out a way to create willing blood donors.

If Sera was hanging out at the Cattle Branch, she was most likely a Ojáncanu guajona.

"You hear anything let me know," I said. I gave Viola my card and I turned to leave when she touched my arm.

"You going to tell Mr. P we didn't say nothing right?"

I frowned. This was the second time someone wanted me to vouch for their dishonesty and I wondered how much pull they thought I had with their boss. I was a hired gun, nothing more, but for some reason they believed he would listen to me. It wasn't worth the fuss so I gave her a vague nod and caught Lacruz's eyes.

Much to my delight, Connelly had disappeared. A group of badges still milled about watching the girls and me. Mostly me. Lacruz waited with crossed arms. I took the time to study her lips, her hair, and the way her tiny ears curled. She grimaced like she had gas. An expression she wasn't aware of, one I found so attractive that I kept it a secret. I was too afraid a shined light would dissipate the shadow of its awkward beauty. I pointed to the blood stains near the twisted table and we met there.

"It'll be okay with the rest of them?" I said eyeing the badges nearby who were pretending to mind their own business.

"Go ahead. Forensics has pictures and samples already." Lacruz raised her voice. "And they aren't in charge." The badges gave us room.

"Connelly?"

"I'm breaking half a dozen regulations by having you here instead of in lockup," she whispered at my shoulder. "What did those two have to say?"

I crouched next to the stain, touched the blood on the carpet, and called on my Lengua-bruja. There was a pause and hitch, the beginning of a putter like the turning of a stalled engine until it quieted. I kept at it for a bit longer before removing my hand and wiped off blood sticking to my fingers. This stranger had made peace before she passed on. I stood up. "I'm going to grab some air."

Lacruz frowned a question.

"Where would I go?" I drew several quick circles in the air. "There's cops all around," I said.

"Three minutes and then I'm coming after you," her voice echoed a clear threat to my health.

"Ye of little faith." I mock saluted, left Lacruz inside, and escaped into the night to make a call. I searched for a semi-quiet spot away from the paramedics, firemen, and badges standing around joking. Watching them was a touch of déjà vu.

I blinked. Memory intruded. The parking lot dissolved and I was standing outside my house watching similar civil servants wheel away my daughter in one of those black coroner bags. Sweet soul shearing pain impaled my brain. I fought off tears.

I stuffed the consultant badge in a pocket and moved toward the darkness in the alley. I couldn't go in too deep, more cops policed where Brody went splat, so I found a niche where I could remain unseen. The safety of the dark reaffirmed my resolve and helped to rebuild the barriers that kept my pain at bay. After a few breaths, I wiped my eyes and put my cell phone to my ear.

The line picked up.

Mick's aged tree bark of a voice was like solid footing on slick treacherous terrain. He patrolled Tierra Santa for decades, smashing monsters with his hammer, before training me as his replacement. He was still in ass kicking shape for a retiree in his sixties. Instead of cashing out for a condo in Florida, he kept tabs on the Inquisitors operating in the States, Canada, and our counterparts in South America and Europe.

We knew each other too long for me to waste time on small talk so I jumped right in describing my meeting with Gabriela, the mention of Dhyana Nuberu, Roxana's kidnapping, the wight presence at Jiggy's, and my current hold up with Lacruz. It took a while to lay it all down. After I finished, I had to admit I sounded like a complete loon. Mick grunted before responding.

"Damn squirrelly mess," Mick said. "It doesn't seem smart to take a job with such a flimsy backstory. I'm sure you had your reasons. If it were me, I would've dug deeper. But that's not why you called was it? You probably want help finding the girl and I wish I could oblige. I'm more worried about this Nuberu your client mentioned. We can't afford to have two covens stirring the pot with all that's cooking right now."

My instincts screamed. "What's going on?"

"Ken, don't be thick," he chided.

"Don't bullshit me." My voice had gone soft with hurt. This was bad. This was very bad.

"I'll let that pass." After a few seconds of silent consideration, he spoke, "I've been discussing our Ojáncanu problem with Jason and he thinks we need a stronger Inquisitor presence in Tierra Santa."

I blinked because I was sure I hadn't heard him correctly.

It was well known among our organization that Jason Arthur and I didn't quite mix. It had to do with me challenging his authority during a Crimoire raid and him shooting me in the leg as a result. It happened when I first started running with the Inquisitors. Maybe I had been green around the collar and maybe a firefight wasn't the time to point out his scorched earth plan was useless on a rainy day. I admit I might've deserved a harsh lecture or maybe a punch to the mouth, but a bullet, even amongst Inquisitors, was a major overreaction.

Jason was a murderous psychopath as bad as the monsters he hunted— he cultivated an inner darkness where kittens died tragically. That was right, kittens. "I don't want that asshole in my city."

Mick cleared his throat. "You've been holed up in your office for so long your ears have clogged. Listen, I've been receiving reports of a brigade of Ojáncanu headed this way. There's also been an increase in Cattle Branch's donor drive like they're expecting to have more mouths to feed.

It's too convenient to be a coincidence. I ran all this by Jason and he agrees with a swift response. We're going to burn the Cattle Branch to the ground and deal with the fallout later."

"And I'm not invited," I spat. Jason's response to any conflict was scorched earth. He ate, digested, and shit scorched earth and Mick knew that!

Mick tried to lecture about how crappy my attitude became around Jason. I didn't want to hear it. Instead I said, I'll keep you posted and pressed the hang up button really really hard. Mick called back. I didn't answer. If Mick wanted to keep the band together, the smart option would've been inviting Inquisitors I didn't want to strangle.

Mick was as wrong to call Jason but right about Cattle Branch. I should've already handled it. That idiot Jason was coming to correct my mistake because I procrastinated a tad. How long were Jason and Mick talking? I was pretty sure the answer would piss me off because it meant Mick planned on keeping me out of it from the start.

It was high school all over again with the cool kids whispering and judging the rest of us. I considered Mick a mentor, a colleague, a friend and he still tossed me to the wolves. Did he think I couldn't cut it anymore? Life turning on you was bad, but that was what life did. When your few friends began to turn...

I shouldn't have let my temper rule me. I could call back, but I wouldn't. I would clean up this mess without help. My best leads were still Sera and Cattle Branch. Even if the phone number she wrote on the cocktail napkin was a fake or a trap, I still had to check it out. Two directions. One me. Decisions. Decisions.

"Who did you call?" Lacruz asked as she came out of the light to join me.

"My priest," I said, scowling.

She snorted and moved closer, her breath tickled my chin while her eyes shone with judicial intensity. "Why are monsters targeting Pimberton?"

"Natalie..." I began.

She shook her head. "Not this time. I'm in. Or you go to jail."

I wanted to keep her off the dark road, not only to save her life, but also to save her sanity. The dark was about negotiating chaos and being able to live with compromised morals. Believing in anything except killing monsters was a handicap.

"Big trouble's coming," I said. "And I have to put a stop to it."

"We," Lacruz smiled sadly. "Have to stop it. Look Ken, I've seen cops try to go at it alone. It always ends in flowers and grief."

I licked my lips. My hands found her waistline and color rose to her cheeks. A faint scent like fresh apples wafted underneath the gun oil. I had never been this close to Lacruz, not one hug or peck on the cheek, and now having experienced it, I didn't want it to end.

She shifted her weight forward and crossed her arms over her chest. "What happened to Brody?"

I blinked, scowled, and firmed my hands on her waist to shove. Her arms shot out and hooked mine. She pressed her pelvis against me for leverage and dropped her center of gravity so that if I tried to push she could reverse the momentum and throw me across her hip.

My arms encircled her waist and my fists locked above her tailbone; I dropped my weight to maintain balance and stilled my body to avoid escalating the situation. I rested my chin on her shoulder, my lips close to her ear. I dipped into my familiar furnace of rage and painted every word with it. "He was already dead when I found him."

I braced for retaliation either physical or conversational.

"Brody was Pimberton's," Lacruz began. "So it stands to reason that whoever killed Brody and set a guajona and a wight loose in Pimberton's club must have a major axe to grind. I'm sure Pimberton wouldn't mind pointing us in his enemy's direction." She pushed against me and forced me a step back. "Why don't you tell me what the bartender and the hostess said?" Her tone was conversational. Her hold hadn't eased.

"Is that why you did it?" I could feel myself grinning. I shoved to see if she would give and felt her twist to send my energy the opposite way. I spun to keep from crashing flat on my back. "You knew they'd tell me more than they'd tell you."

Lacruz's body tightened, letting me know I hit the mark. She pushed forward and when I braced, she reversed the momentum to a pull instead. I lost my footing. I was overbalanced and all it would take was for her to use her hip as a pivot to topple me over. It was stupid to forget how crafty she could be when she put her mind to it. She had me by the shorts, could drop me, and she knew it. But she didn't. She kept me upright long enough for me to regain my balance.

She assumed victory was hers and that she was on board. She gave my hunting habits a wide berth and asked for the only commodity I lacked, honesty. That was life in the dark; blinding friends so they can keep their sanity. She never considered that I fought dirty, which gave me an advantage I could exploit—she didn't know about Roxana, the Cattle Branch, or Sera's phone number. Maybe I could lead her away from the Cattle Branch and most of the serious danger by giving up Sera's number?

"I have a phone number," I said.

Lacruz released her hold and backed out of my grip. Cold air filled the chasm between us. No one had observed our little wrestling match.

I showed her the napkin with Sera's phone number. Lacruz made a call and asked for the address connected to that number. A few minutes later Lacruz received the answer.

"The phone number is registered to a Sera Sarris." She stared at the other badges in the distance for a pensive moment. "Would it be so bad, if they knew? TSPD could at least have a special unit to deal with this kind of stuff."

I gestured at the blinking candy colored sirens with a thumb. "You want to tell them?"

Lacruz ran fingers through her hair. "Let's find Sera."

5 WIGHT HOUSE

We arrived in Delta Terrace, an upscale suburban botoxed minivan haven with housing prices a few happy pills shy of sane. Lacruz navigated her Crown Vic through a twist of suburbia, rows of multicolored mirror image housing, until we found Brook Lane. We parked curbside at the quiet end of the cul-de-sac.

Porch shingles spun despite the lack of a breeze. Even in the dark, Sera's home was a bit of glaze with its white and money-green trim, its dirt garden, cute plaster kitten statuettes, and concrete path leading to the front steps.

The houses in Delta Terrace were built in the fifties. The second stories and modern conveniences were added later when a development company came in and upgraded the neighborhood. Sera's property reminded me of the word *home*, a place fertilized by warmth until smiles grew.

My previous house had good-sized windows, a two car garage, a robust kitchen, and an extra bedroom for the baby. The combination of drugs and monsters destroyed both the place and the word for me. The home and family I worked so hard to keep vanished.

I glanced at Lacruz. Her dark eyes hadn't left the house and I could tell by the way they twinkled she thought it was *cute*. She must've sensed my attention because she met my gaze. The twinkle evaporated. She shrugged and exited the car. I chuckled softly and followed her into the cool night.

"You have a shotgun in the trunk? Let me have it," I said.

Lacruz started toward the house. "Don't let the darkness fool you," she lectured. "Neighborhoods like these are filled with eyes. A shotgun will have half a dozen gray hairs reporting anything from gang warfare to terrorist attacks. We don't need that kind of attention right now." She paused. "Besides, we don't know if this is her house or if she's even here."

"Better reason for the shotgun," I replied. "When hunting a guajona, you bring the heavy guns and don't skimp on the ammunition or you'll be a toe tag and a memory."

If I had my gear, I sure as hell would've whipped out my shotgun and fired a few rounds skyward to make Lacruz's precious gray hairs dirty their Depends. Unfortunately, most of my gear was in my car at the Jungle Gem.

My hand brushed against the soothing weight of my Sig. I grunted assent though I remained uneasy about walking right up to a monster's nest, alleged or otherwise, especially lacking in the artillery department. It made sense to be prepared even when you didn't expect to find trouble.

I glanced at Lacruz. Why was I supporting her bad decision? Because she was my friend and I wanted to have her back. Besides, if there was trouble, I could be her shining knight and prove I was a better man than she believed.

We stepped onto the property. I started toward the backyard. She grabbed my arm and pulled me to the concrete steps leading to the front door.

Her eyes narrowed. "We don't have a warrant so let's at least try and do this proper."

Rain and fucking floods, she was going to get us killed. I jerked free and glared. If by some twist of the knife Sera was stupid enough to be here, it didn't make any sense to behave even more stupidly by knocking, but that was what Lacruz did. She climbed the wooden steps with a gentle *clickity-clack* and put knuckles to door and knocked. I ground my teeth.

Lacruz lived by rules, regulations, and procedures that I thought were a bit old fashioned and anal-retentive. I respected her and by osmosis sort of respected what she believed in… at least, when she was around. Sometimes, her stubborn adherence to the law rubbed me raw. If a guajona or any other monster decided to throw open the front door and tear out her throat, there would be nothing she could do about it. Fortunately, fate was kind and no bloodletting occurred between knocks.

Fuming, I alternated between kicking over the kitten statuettes and trying to look as cop-like as possible by checking the windows for criminal misconduct. Dark olive curtains were drawn shut on the first floor and the second floor except for one window.

Lacruz rang the doorbell a few times before descending the steps in defeat. She motioned for the side gate, the direction I wanted to go earlier. I put on my best smug grin as we walked. She ignored me. I wasn't too happy about her grappling the crap out of me tonight so if anyone should be grudging, it should be me.

Lacruz pushed open the white wood gate and followed the circular stones imbedded in a blue pebble garden to a wide expanse of brown. Beneath the face of the moon, the backyard boasted multicolored flowers—blues, pinks, and yellows blossomed in manicured bushes. The air held their aromatic scent like a mother with an infant needing a diaper change.

"You smell it?" I asked.

Grimacing, she pointed. "That door look open in a suspicious manner to you?"

The backdoor wasn't open or suspicious; in fact, it was outright average flat wood the color of bleached bone with one of the most pathetic locks I had ever seen. In my experience, lame locks always accompanied owners who liked to eat uninvited guests.

"Very suspicious," I agreed.

I approached the door with knife in hand, jammed its point into the lock, and twisted. The lock snapped and busted bits jingled loose. I sheathed my knife and opened the door to a maw of eclipsing darkness. I took out my penlight. Lacruz tapped me on the shoulder. I turned, saw her much larger flashlight, grimaced with light envy, and stepped aside so she could take point.

Her flashlight pierced the darkness and revealed an enclosed patio. There were about nine moving boxes, either Sera planned a quick getaway or she never unpacked.

Lacruz searched one side of the patio while I headed to the boxes. I shined my penlight over their surfaces searching for shipping labels with a previous or forwarding address. The boxes lacked any markings like *fragile* or *dining room* to identify their contents. I was about to pry one open when Lacruz touched my arm and pulled me to follow. She found the door leading to inside the house.

Whatever caused the odor wasn't in the patio so I made a mental note to pilfer some of the boxes contents on my way out. I followed Lacruz to the next room, which was as dark as the patio. She illuminated a white and square object that I recognized as a stove.

I felt along the closest wall for a light switch and when I found it, the kitchen brightened to a space narrower than I expected. The kitchen was rectangular like a corridor with a line of cabinets next to the oven and stove and two stainless steel sinks, dishwasher, and pantry along the opposite wall. In the corner was a large empty space where a refrigerator should've been. Lacruz lowered her flashlight and blinked at me quizzically.

It was my turn to lecture. "Never fight in the dark if you can avoid it. Most beasties have better night vision than you do."

"So you've said a million times," Lacruz muttered. "And conveniently ignore when it suits you."

I made a circular motion in the air. "Room by room."

Our search of the first floor took less time than ordering takeout and revealed a typical suburban home layout: a living room, family room, dining room, a large closet, bathroom, and a set of stairs. The spacious living and family rooms lacked the trappings of permanence like couches, TV's, tables or chairs of any kind. The walls were stark white.

The odor increased in hostility, a mixture of decay and neglect confined in a bubble of stale air. We followed our noses. The rot grew thick and stifling around the stairs. I touched the carved white railing that twisted as it wound spiral-like up to the second floor. Next to it was a second door leading to the basement.

Though Lacruz had respectable self-defense skills, she wasn't a killer. Her first instinct wouldn't be murder. It would be safer for her if we stuck together. "Let's go up first," I said.

She glanced up and down before wrinkling her nose. "Smell seems to be coming from down there." She gave me a look about two degrees shy of hell and cocked the hammer on her Chiefs Special. "You go up. I'll hold the fort in case someone tries to sneak by. We can check the basement together."

As a plan of action, it wasn't too terrible. Safety wouldn't be much an issue with another Inquisitor: one up, one down, and we would meet if all hell broke loose. I could trust Lacruz to keep out of trouble. She wasn't me. "Keep your back to a wall," I said. "And shoot anything that isn't me. Don't ask questions. You hesitate, you die."

"Save the lecture," she said, making shooing motions with her gun.

With a slight shake of my head, I left her to guard duty and climbed the stairs. Darkness pervaded the second floor. I located the lights. I was in a hallway with four open doors. A brief look inside three out of the four bedrooms revealed empty space. I walked down the hall to the master bedroom.

Disorder was too limited a word to describe how Sera kept house. An Italian style plush king-sized with silk sheets sat opposite hand crafted dressers. A large gothic vanity mirror, three mannequin torsos decked out in lingerie, pile of clothes, and hundreds of multi-colored tart smelling candles of varying sizes littered the floor. After my first few steps, I gave up avoiding the candles and just stepped on them.

It would be a bloody miracle to find anything useful in this mess.

I walked to the window, pushed aside the curtains, and looked outside to where I had kicked over the kitten statuettes. This was the window I saw earlier. I closed the curtains, turned, and searched for hiding places. Secrets were at the heart of murder, uncovering them, hoarding them, or silencing them. People died for secrets, theirs or someone else's.

What kind of secrets did Sera keep?

I ransacked her dresser for any hidden nooks or concealed keys. I checked under, over, and even between the mattress. My efforts yielded nothing useful, not even sex toys (not that I looked for sex toys). I gave up and tried sorting through the clothes on the floor, only to decide if anything was under that crap it deserved to stay there. I turned my attention to her closet.

Sera's walk-in closet was large enough to garage a VW Beetle. The clothes, accompanied by a whole rack of complementary colored stilettos, looked like stripper fare. Lingerie, bikinis, and crotch dresses best used for clubbing ranged from skimpy to hedonistic.

A large trunk of black iron and gold like something a pirate would use to bury their booty was hidden under a pile of empty shoe boxes at the back of the closet. I cleared the boxes away. The trunk was locked, but I had my ways, and a few broken lock bits later I lifted its lid.

I would describe the trunk as half full though I tended to be a half empty kind of guy. A silver box about two hands wide sat atop a pile quilts. Inside it were several wooden knitting needles and few different shades of colored yarn. I tossed them aside.

Underneath the box were three hand woven quilts—products of a high level of craft and probably months of work. The first soft-to-the-touch quilt was a deep blue and beige reminded me of the ocean when viewed from an island shore. Its rich perfumed scent made the urge to press it to my cheeks difficult to resist. Setting it aside became more difficult though somehow I managed to do both. I would die happy with a coat that soft.

The second quilt was equal in quality and beauty though of royal gold and dove white with violet stitching in a three diamond pattern. It was so pristine, I found it hard to believe a guajona capable of such exquisite work.

These quilts were probably remnants from Sera's days before she tapped into the Cleave. Some guajona kept mementos from the Nescient period of their lives to remind themselves who they once were. I draped the first two quilts over the shoe rack.

The third quilt was very different, its colors more drab and faded. It was a country scene with a lot of greenery and grazing horses, pigs, and sheep. As I touched the material, a jolt of acidic wrongness ran through my fingers and up my arm. I dropped the quilt and stared for several seconds trying to locate the hidden mouse trap in the material.

I reached down with two fingers; I felt the jolt again. This time I was prepared and held on. I shook the quilt. A burnt edged shred of wizened canvas, the size of a postcard, fell out. And then something strange happened.

The air above the canvas shimmered like heat coming off a kettle of boiling water. The shimmer disappeared as I tried to focus on it. Unease yanked my innards taut as a tightrope. As much as I would have liked to forget what I found, I knew I never would.

Sweat beaded on my forehead. I set the quilt aside, took a deep breath, and picked up the canvas. I was assaulted by bleak despair. My stomach recoiled and I fought to keep my donut dinner down. I wanted to throw the canvas across the room and retch. I held a piece of dark seduction, a temptation of the blood, and it whispered to the rotten cankered places in my soul with voices crying, mocking, and screaming a sinister soprano to infiltrate and sway me.

Anyone else would've been driven insane. The evil in this canvas hadn't banked on my Lengua-bruja's familiarity with disembodied orchestras full of gloom and doom. I ignored the words and focused on volume. It was easy for me to turn the dial to zero and mute the voices one by one.

I turned the canvas over and stared at its image. The best way to describe what I held was as an unearthly headshot torn from a much larger painting. Even yellowed from age, there was no mistaking that the painter had tried to capture a pale entity who's long and narrow face included coal black eyes and blood red lips as thin as worms. His ears rose into points that resembled horns. His hair, the color of the full moon, was long and straight. His carriage had a timelessness that made age and gender impossible to discern.

Without a doubt, I knew what I saw.

It was a mouros, a shapechanging hellbeast far deadlier than most monsters. I had seen a few depictions of them in the Archives at Sanctuary. Guajona and gargola united and killed off mouros centuries ago.

I had the ill notion the painter had suffered for his attempt at transcribing horror and died insane to bring this to art. I couldn't leave the painting here, that much I knew, so I looked around for something to wrap it in. I used my knife to cut a small strip from the third quilt. When I was satisfied with the size, I wound it around the canvas. The sense of bleak despair ebbed and by that I meant it dropped from roaring to simmering. I apologized to my coat as I pocketed the canvas and hoped my coat would forgive me for using it to transport something so vile.

My palms tingled red and hot after vigorously wiping them on my thighs. Scrubbing my fingers with bleach wouldn't be enough to remove this canvas' taint. I felt soiled. I was done with this closet, this room, and this place. But I couldn't leave. Not yet. I had to make one last attempt at finding a clue as to where Sera took Roxana.

The bedroom lacked a CD player, television, or laptop or any other modern conveniences other than a telephone. I checked the call history. There wasn't one outgoing or incoming calls in its memory. I found it hard to believe solicitors didn't know about this number. Those guys annoyed everybody.

Not to stereotype, but the lack of tech usually indicated a guajona born before electricity, which made Sera far older and more powerful than I originally believed. I puttered around some more, found nothing of interest, and returned to the first floor.

Lacruz wasn't where I left her so I called out. She answered from the kitchen. She stood in front of the cabinets. The doors were thrown open and her attention was focused on what she found. She gave me a cursory glance as I entered before returning her attention to the cabinet's contents.

"Lots of cognac." She tapped labels. "Your girlfriend thinks she has class." Lacruz read my expression, pursed her lips, and frowned. "Find anything?"

The canvas churned in my pocket. For a half-second, I considered showing her. "I found the house phone. Her call history was empty."

"I'll order her phone records to be sure. Anything else?"

I shook my head and asked if she was ready for the basement. She crossed her arms, stared, and considered pressing the issue, but in the end, she let it drop. I glanced at the bottles. What did she mean by class? Everyone knows the classy liquor comes in boxes.

We returned to the basement door under the onslaught of a stench ten times as oppressive as stale sewage. Lacruz wore a strained expression. God only knows what mine was. Neither of us was in a hurry to speak because that would mean opening our mouths to foulness.

United in our mutual desire to find out the odor's cause, I grabbed the doorknob and pulled. It didn't budge so I used my knife on the lock. Minutes of puttering, tinkering, and cursing ticked off as the lock rebuked my attempts at entry.

I sheathed my knife in frustration, grabbed the knob again, and shouldered the door. Muscles and veins bulged in my neck. I made unmanly grunting noises as I repeatedly drove my shoulder against the wood. Even with my full exertion the blasted door remained obstinate.

Lacruz touched my arm. I guess she had tired of watching me making a fool out of myself. I turned and gave her a *can you do better?* look. She shrugged so I stepped aside. She didn't try the knob or the lock as I had done. She tapped on the wood with her knuckles, which resulted in a sharp metallic *twang* wood doesn't make. In other words she cheated. Instead of admitting it, she nodded like she had made the most key scientific discovery of the century. She grimaced in anticipation of having to speak.

"The wood's a front," she said as her face contorted in distaste. "Steel underneath. Probably a security door. We're not bypassing it with anything less than a blowtorch."

If the door was anything like mine then she was right. I considered keeping my mouth shut, but if she was manly enough to brave the odor then so was I.

"Too bad we didn't bring the shotgun," I said innocently. The damn air tasted even fouler than it smelled. I clamped my mouth shut. I should've followed my first instinct and kept quiet.

"Uh huh," she answered. Her attention had shifted from the door to the frame. She felt along it and then stepped back. "Whoever installed the door did a half-assed job. They didn't reinforce the frame, look." She pointed at the corners. "Give me room."

Lacruz wasn't going to fool me into speaking again. I grunted. When I had my door installed, the contractor had gone out of his way to tell me about how other substandard contractors skimped on reinforcing the door frame if the customer didn't know any better. The bruja who bound spells into the steel said pretty much the same thing.

Sera's door lacked the carved sigils mine did, which made it both mundane and shoddy. I guess she hadn't known any better. Lacruz had taken up a fighting stance so I moved a couple steps up and out of her way.

"You're going to kick it down?" I grimaced. The damn stench made me want to chop off my tongue. "C'mon, that stuff only works in the movies. Let's shoot the lock."

"I'm going to break the frame, not the door," she said.

She balanced in a cat stance. Her front foot launched forward with a sharp impacting thunderclap striking where the lock met the frame. Wood screamed. The door held, but not as snug as before. Her second quick kick connected. The frame shattered with a snap of flying finger-long splinters, the door swung inward, and smacked hard against the basement wall.

Airborne decay more fetid than a battlefield of corpses baking under a desert sun sucker punched our senses. Lacruz covered her mouth and nose with the back of her forearm and gagged wet and haggard until she was about to retch.

She was the fortunate one.

Lacruz lacked my Lengua-bruja so she only fought the smell. I battled the unrelenting stench plus the press of death rattles. I dropped to one knee as if hit by a physical blow. The rattles screeched through my Lengua-bruja, too many to separate and discern. Dead voices in unison creating white noise.

I cupped my ears even though the sound was in my head. Death steamrolled my insides until they felt liquefied. I was alone in an ocean, a victim of weather and waves. The storm pulled me under until the pressure crushed me flat.

The world turned Armageddon-gray. La Parca screeched as I held my wits stitched together for an eternity of seconds. I found the wall and leaned against it. The odor made catching a decent breath and clearing my head impossible. The fuzziness receded enough for me to stand. I climbed from my knees, peered downstairs into the deep shadows, and wondered what in the hell could leave so much residual rattling?

Thin reedy moans answered.

Lacruz's flashlight sliced the darkness and revealed pale desiccated flesh of several dozen bodies, impossible to separate by sex, with their pallid maggot infested skin stretched tight against bones and atrophied muscles.

Wights, more than I've seen packed into such a tight space, shifted with wide unblinking light devouring eyes. They moved with the explosive suddenness of a dreamer startled out of a nightmare.

We broke their solitude with light and life and now more than a couple dozen heads and twice as many eyes fixed on us. Monstrous nostrils flared taking in our sweat, unease, and flesh raw and ripe for the feasting. Dangerous mouths revealed razor teeth. This two story house became a very tiny place.

The hungriest of them, a thin, dark skinned, high cheeked figure with milky white eyes bolted toward us rasping, "Foooooooooddd."

"Should've brought the shotgun," Lacruz muttered through clenched teeth. With gun and flashlight in hand she took up a shooting stance. "These... are zombies?"

"No," I said, my mouth going dry. "And you had to kick the door into uselessness." I could understand her confusion. These wights were different. They were *rabid*.

Guajona's created wights by infecting them with the Cleave during feeding. If the person died with the Cleave in their system, they would reanimate as a wight. With enough flesh to munch on, wights could retain some semblance of their human appearance, thought, and personality. They became feral enough to eat anything living when starved. Only an order from their Masters could stop a rabid wight from getting its lunch on.

Sera reanimated a small army and must've had trouble keeping them fed. It would've been nice to sit down with Lacruz for a leisure donut discussion about it. Unfortunately, survival warranted our full attention. Waking them had aroused their mindless appetites that, if left unhindered, would devour us, this neighborhood, and maybe this whole city.

I licked my lips. "We can't let them out of the house."

The color drained from her face as she squeezed the trigger three times. The first two bullets caught the approaching wight in the chest. The last bullet split its jaw and sent it tumbling backward heels-over-head into a few of its comrades. The remaining wights, now fully alert, didn't pause as they trampled their fallen to get to us.

They hungered for our flesh as badly as we hungered to keep it. Our only chance was destroying enough of them on the stairs to create a bottleneck of corpses to keep the rest pinned inside. I opened fire. Bullets ripped off arms, legs, and faces. Whoever they were, bankers, teachers, clerks, or doctors, mattered not a stitch in light of the rabid monsters they had become. Chunks splattered, bodies collapsed, and still more came at us in an unrelenting tide.

By the time I slapped in my third clip, they were close enough to play cards. The opening cacophony of our shots dwindled as the wights gained ground. They reached the doorway, their cracked clawing fingernails forcing us backward. Our stand crumbled. They swarmed out of the basement like ants and our last hope of keeping them contained was lost.

As if emphasizing the point, Lacruz's Chiefs Special clicked empty. She holstered it, took out her cute little backup pistol, and fired in four second intervals to ration each bullet like the last drops of water in the desert.

Our ammo would run dry at this rate, we would die horribly, and this neighborhood would be massacred. I couldn't let that happen. We needed to kill the lot of them quickly; a blowtorch would be ideal and a hoot. Mine was in the trunk of my car. We needed fire, a huge one.

"Follow me!" I yelled.

We sprinted to the kitchen with the wights hot on our heels. I made a beeline for the stove. Lacruz, a close second, took position inside the doorway where she continued shooting to slow them down. She was kneecapping the wights in front. They fell and tripped the others. This slowed them down for a few seconds. Right now, seconds were more precious than diamonds and desserts.

At the stove, I twisted the knobs expecting a rush of orange and blue flowered flames. Black oval burners began to glow red. Where was my damn fire? At first, I thought Sera hadn't paid her electric bill and then I remembered the lights. I glared before it came to me…

The goddamn stove was electric!

I heard several dry clicks of Lacruz's empty gun followed by her panicked voice, "Whatever you're planning, do it quick!"

I stole a look her way to see how much time I had before we were swamped. The mass of bodies, about a dozen now, drew closer. She reversed the grip on her cute little backup pistol, gripping the barrel so that the handle protruded like a hammer. The barrel had to be smoking hot after so many shots, yet she held on.

Damn, that was sexy.

A wight reached out, Lacruz pistol-whipped it across the face. She kicked it in the chest and knocked it into the others, which bought us more precious seconds. I yelled *catch* and tossed her my Sig, which had about three fourths of a clip left. She caught it with her free hand and began shooting. Each bullet echo gave me more time to focus on the stove.

Electric fire wasn't like regular fire. Oh, it heated the same; however, most things that came in contact with the burners charred or melted before they caught fire. The ovals by themselves wouldn't be enough. I needed an accelerant or something flammable. Why couldn't Sera have kept a barrel marked *gasoline* handy like any decent suburbanite? Curtains might work, but the closest sets were, in the living room, on the other side of the wall of wights. Clothing was a possibility. Hell, I was almost desperate enough to use my coat as kindling. Well, not really.

"Hey, give me your jacket!"

It didn't appear that Lacruz heard me. I guess she was too busy keeping the wights from overtaking us. She bottlenecked the kitchen entrance forcing the wights to come at her one at time, at least temporarily. Her chest heaved and she bled from numerous scratches. She was slow bringing my Sig around to her next target and the attacking wight reached inside her guard and raked her neck below her cheek leaving long red traces of blood.

Lacruz slithered out of the wight's grasp and countered an open palm sternum strike that sent monster flailing back into its pals. Even though less than a dozen wights remained, there were still too many to make survival a given. Numbers, time, and endurance were on the enemy's side.

"I need a torch." I implored to Lacruz's back. Her shoulders stiffened. She wouldn't give up her damn coat.

Another wight lunged past the one she had struck. She stalled its momentum with a kick to the base of its shin. The wight lost balance, which gave her an extra heartbeat to take aim. The Sig barked. The wight's head split into a shower of dry brains. It collapsed in a twitching heap.

Lacruz picked another target and pulled the trigger to an unsettling click. She lowered the empty gun. Without turning she answered, "The cognac, idiot. Use the cognac!"

I paused. Now why didn't I think of that? I ripped open the cabinets, grabbed a couple bottles like two turkey legs, and shouted, "Get clear!"

She abandoned the doorway and bolted for the patio. The wights stormed the kitchen. I threw the bottles to draw their attention. Glass shattered on impact drenching the wights in liquor and knocking them off their feet. Their momentum sent them sliding into a wall.

I threw more bottles and made it shower glass and alcohol. The wights were drenched and slipping on the messy floor. I snarled and laughed as another wight turned an ankle on a wet spot, lost its footing, and fell like a drunken frat boy. By the looks of it, it might've been a frat boy. The wights adapted by digging their toenails into the floor tiles. They climbed to their feet. Their hunger fixed on me.

The closest wight hissed and lunged. Instead of throwing more cognac, I defended by wielding the two bottles like escrima fighting sticks. I swung the first bottle in a wide arc catching the wight across the temple. It staggered against the cabinets. Another wight attacked after the first; his grubby maggot eaten hands pawed my coat.

Rage filled my next swing. The blow caught the pawing wight in the jaw. The bottle snapped nasty and jagged sheared off the wight's face below its nose. The mouthless wight released my coat, twisted a full three sixty, and collapsed against the sink.

I was covered in as much alcohol as the remaining wights and didn't give a damn that it made my plan more dangerous. Danger was what I did. Fear couldn't stop me from taking a monster down. I elbowed another wight in the chest and sent it sprawling against the hot stove. A dry body covered in cognac was now touching open heat. The wight exploded in a *whoosh* of green flame that shot up from the body and hit the ceiling. Wailing, the burning wight jumped from the stove and crashed into the others creating a cascade of green flaming dominoes. Fire engulfed wight after wight until half the kitchen was a verdant bonfire of burning monsters. Wights flailed arms and thrashed legs as they were consumed.

The fire alarm blared.

Toasting my success, I grabbed the last bottle in the cabinet, yanked the cork, took a swig, and threw the bottle onto the burners. Glass shattered. Flame, the regular wood devouring red-orange variety, snaked up the walls in an inferno. The kitchen filled with dense buffeting smoke.

The last of the wights' dissipating embers left behind extra heat that fed the new furnace causing the fire to sprint from the walls and stove where it nested on the floor and it climbed as high as my chest. In an instant, I was cut off from the patio.

Lacruz shouted something I couldn't make out over the crackle of the blaze, good thing too, because I couldn't imagine it being flattering. Trapped by my own exuberance, I had to escape or be pot roast.

I stared at the firewall through narrowed watering eyes, conscious of my damp coat reeking of cognac. Leaving my coat behind was the rational thing to do. One tiny spark and I would burn. I took off my coat, folded it inside out forming a tight football-like wad, and held it in my breadbasket like Adrian Peterson trying to score from the one yard line. I charged into the flames, eyes shut, and prayed my coat would make it.

At first, I didn't feel anything. A heartbeat passed and then quick agony as my world brightened against my eyelids. My skin stung as if being scrubbed with sandpaper. A suffocating heat roasted the air in my lungs making me feel like a thanksgiving turkey. Another heartbeat, the pain intensified. I kept my legs moving or I would die basting in my own juices.

I was about to scream or wet myself or both when I stumbled into cooler air. I made it through, but the flames had leeched my strength. My legs buckled. I opened my eyes to see the ground rushing up to greet me when Lacruz's arms shot out and caught me before I hit.

Score one for the home team.

As much as I would've liked to body melt against her for the sheer joy of survival, she wasn't having it. With a fire growing around us, she carried me into the safety of the backyard where we collapsed. The fire had taken over. Black smoke belched out of the windows. We gasped for breath. The house, Sera's possessions, and even those quilts were as good as toast. Huddled shoulder to shoulder, we watched the house burn.

Approaching sirens wailed like a betrayed lover.

"Job well done, I'd say," I wheezed. I unfolded my jacket, it reeked of smoke and alcohol otherwise it was in good shape. I shook it out, put it on, and felt safer for it.

"Screw you, Ashe," Lacruz groaned. After several deep breaths, she pulled her knees to her chest and cradled her shins. "You do this every day?"

"Give or take," I said wistfully.

She nodded and buried her face into my shoulder. I put my arm around her shoulders, grateful for the smell of her sweat, the steady rise of her chest, and her warm moist breath. I didn't even care she dribbled snot on my coat.

My limbs ached, the back of my teeth felt hollow, the pounding in my head was a full-blown drum choir, my lungs felt raw, and I could still feel the taint of that evil canvas. Minor inconveniences. I was alive and whole and so was Lacruz.

For once life was good.

6 COMPANY YOU KEEP

The hollering fire trucks pretty much ended any chance of us escaping unseen from the burning misbegotten shell of Sera's home. We saved the suburbs from a wight invasion and made a mess along the way.

Smoke and ash filled the air. Worried neighbors in robes, sweats, and bedclothes paced in front of their properties with cell phones to their ears. Payment would be exacted. Someone had to pick up the check and the badge decided who.

Lacruz agreed to stay behind to explain her involvement in almost burning down the neighborhood. She did this knowing lies would have to be told. Mentioning guajona, wights, or me would be a career death sentence.

Even without mentioning the supernatural, the whole ordeal would require hours of explanation and re-explanation to superiors and their superiors and piles of paperwork filled out in triplicate. It would be a miracle if Lacruz didn't end up writing parking tickets in Canada. Her night was over and I had to do my part by escaping without being identified.

Before I jumped the neighbors' fence, Lacruz tried to make me promise to go straight home and wait for her call. I promised. We both knew I lied.

I boosted a red Mini Cooper parked a couple of blocks over and drove away from Delta Terrace. I was sore, exhausted, angry, and felt used up. We almost lost that fight. The thought of losing Lacruz made me consider how much she meant to me. She was the first woman, since Yanira, I considered in a serious way.

A thrill supercharged my heart every time I saw Lacruz. She was beautiful with eyes that didn't suffer mistakes. I wanted to make her happy. Then again, I wanted a lot of things: home, a shower, salve for my blistered skin, and sleep.

After wiping my prints from the Cooper's interior, I abandoned it a couple of blocks east of Jiggy's and walked the rest of the way. The cops had cleared out. Jiggy's was closed for the night. My car was one of the few remaining in the lot. I got in, started the engine, and pointed my G-Marq toward salvation.

Inquisitor's Sanctuary though officially known as True Holiness Catholics Church was built by Christians and abandoned to the Catholics when the original parish moved to a newer larger upper scale location. Twin towers rose to near sixty feet above street level and became domineering sentries for the arched solid oak double doors. Moonlight lanced through the stained glass windows and casted its reflection off the walls connected to high vaulted Romanesque ceilings of brick and terra cotta. The interior had pews and pulpits and a lot of other things that started with p. High above the dome apse loomed a larger than life crucifix, a testament of having survived arson, drive-bys, riots, and sex scandals.

The side door opened before I was halfway to it. A large man stood in a halo of light spilling into the night. The light was artificial; the welcoming warmth of his grin was natural. Salt and pepper hair and slight wrinkles filled a jovial brown face. Still carrying the muscle from his linebacker days at Florida State, Father Mikel 'Slaphammer' McDowell was one of the best Inquisitors on the west coast until he retired to sift through historical records, rumors, and half-truths concerning people's dealings with monsters.

I met Mick before I knew about monsters. He officiated my wedding and christened my daughter. I climbed behind the wheel of my car after Evelyn was killed. I was going to find whoever murdered my little girl and end them. I blacked out and wrapped my car around a tree. Mick found me in the hospital crotch deep in grief and rage. He opened my eyes to the truth of my daughter's murder. He delivered me from self-loathing and gave my pain a target.

My first guajona hunt was a Coven Ramidreju bloodline with more sadism than good sense. The Ramidreju had kidnapped a pudgy kid for food and play. I was a twisted knot of adrenaline, fury, and exhilaration. We tracked the Ramidreju to the Tierra Santa's warehouse district, put her down for good, and freed the kid.

I remembered Mick's consoling voice absolving me of guilt over the necessity of killing. *In the eyes of God*, he said, *monsters aren't people so there was no sin in their total and utter eradication*. I felt a lot—thrill, satisfaction, and eagerness for the next hunt. Guilt wasn't one of them.

My boots echoed across the church floor. Fatigue made my duffel feel ten times heavier. A warm renewing power most people couldn't consciously detect permeated the church like a tickle of silk across the skin. A lot of it had to do with Sanctuary's defenses.

Sanctuary had wards like my office. Sanctuary's wards were the self-renewing variety that soaked up the positivity generated by Mick's congregation to create an area where monsters couldn't come within miles.

Mick took in my disheveled appearance, fatigue, and the accompanying odor. He had questions and surprised me by leaving them unasked. We walked to his private conference room. He located the trapdoor disguised as part of the carpet, pulled it open, and we descended the concrete stairs into the cellar.

The smell of dank mold permeated the cellars' square footage, which was divided into four areas: the meeting room, the workshop, Mick's Inquisitor office, and the Archive. The lights were on. Somebody was home. That somebody was Deacon. The kid we saved from the Ramidreju turned out to be a talented weapon-smith. He dropped out of vocational college and took up mantle as Sanctuary's resident mad scientist.

Deacon was reading a magazine at a worktable surrounded on three sides by metal fencing. He was dressed like a runaway from a science fiction convention. Gray sweat pants and a black T-shirt that read, MY OTHER SPACESUIT IS IN THE CLEANERS stretched tight across his bulbous form. His long red hair, styled in what could only be described as a deluxe mullet, framed round dough cheeks, a patchy beard, and a lazy right eye that looked left. He inhaled burgers by the pound and quibbled over the calories in a diet soda.

I tapped Mick on the shoulder, letting him know I wanted to talk to Deacon. Mick paused mid-step, exhaled patiently, nodded, and disappeared into his office. Deacon's attention was riveted on the pages of Wildlife Weekly. He didn't notice my shadow fall over his right shoulder. I slammed my palm on his worktable with a hard metal rattling jolt.

Deacon shrieked, jumped as if scalded, and dropped his magazine. He faced me with cheeks flowering red with terror, then redder with recognition, and finally reddest with anger. He started to pick up his magazine, saw my expression, and decided to leave it. He raised his hands in surrender.

"Ammo and a MP5K," I grunted. The rack bolted into the wall held enough weapons to have us arrested as a terrorist cell, K-50M's, Mausers, AR18's, USM79's, countless other things, and that wasn't counting what we kept in storage. I hadn't been a machine gun fan since the military. I preferred low caliber firearms or the intimate destruction of a shotgun. I would need more *umph* to deal with another large number of wights. More *umph* meant machine gun.

Deacon's pudgy fingers reached for a couple of ammo boxes on a low shelf. I noticed his aged dark-pinkish crisscrossed scars near the pit of his pasty white elbow. He had more on the other arm and along his neck, the results of his weeklong captivity. The Ramidreju had repeatedly fed on and tortured Deacon leaving him with far deeper damage than was visible. It was a miracle he avoided being turned into a wight. If it wasn't for Mick and Sanctuary, Deacon would probably stay stoned out of his head to escape the memory of being fed on.

Deacon started to hand me the ammo and paused; his gaze slipped to his magazine. A fiendish glow lit his eyes, his mouth slacked open, saliva pooled on his lips, and a girlish giggle escaped his throat. His hands twitched toward his crotch.

"Deacon," I growled.

Blinking, he recovered, tossed me the rounds, and selected a MP5K, which he checked before deciding it was in working order. My gaze wandered from firearms to claymores, spears, and mauls, some bought and some homemade. A hanging polished steel axe held my attention; it had a wrapped leather pistol-grip handle curved to be wielded with one hand or two and a foot long arching blade opposite a knobby spike. It was a wicked dangerous beauty so sexy it deserved a name.

Deacon saw where I looked and replied, "Custom job for Jason."

Some considered Jason Arthur the best Inquisitor to wear the boots. I wasn't one of them. "Let me see it."

Deacon's eyes darted back and forth in panic looking everywhere except at me, the axe, or the magazine. "Not possible."

I gave him my Inquisitor's stare, death incarnate, three times cold, and twice as nasty.

"Jason'll kill me," he hedged. His jaw set in a way that was more belligerent than stern. "If you want one, I'll make another. It took me a year to refine the metal."

I reached across the table, snatched his pinky, and twisted it to its breaking point. "You want to only be able to count to nine?"

Deacon's tragedy left him without much of a backbone. An inconsequential part of me felt bad about taking advantage and hoped he had grown enough of a spine to hold to his convictions. In the end, I knew he would give in no matter the consequence. And as for Jason… Fuck him.

"A-a-alright. Alright," Deacon whined. I let go of his pinky. He snatched the axe and extended it toward me.

"The rig too," I said.

"O-o-of course," he answered. He rifled through the cabinets and found a leather thong. He tied the thong to the silver ring at the end of the axe handle. The thong was designed to fit snug around the wrist so you couldn't lose it if you lost your grip.

"And…" I said. His face was three shades of purple by now. I hid my amusement and continued to glare. "Incendiaries, the hottest you have."

"All out. I haven't been able to procure them for a while. I've some Molotov's?" He rested hands on his pudgy belly, smug he didn't have to fulfill my request. He looked me up and down and sniffed. "You been tanning?"

I snorted at him and placed the gear in my duffle. "Find some."

"The warp engines can't take no more, Captain," he muttered.

"No one should do that sort of thing with a goat," I replied.

He scowled, snatched the nature magazine off the floor, and tossed it in the wastebasket. An empty gesture. We both knew it wouldn't be there for long.

Dealing with Deacon always left me feeling dirty. I used the five seconds it took me to reach Mick's office to give myself a mental cleansing. I opened the door and walked in. Mick's taste in decoration was still the same love mix of Jesus, football, and medieval maces. The major furnishings were a bookcase, a TV, a square fold out cot leaning against a pint-sized refrigerator, and a work desk occupied by Melody Haley.

Melody sucked a thumbnail while going through a pile of paperwork with a highlighter. She was small boned, five foot something, one hundred and something pounds, and fifty something years old. Her springy hair, dyed green to hide the gray, was pulled back into a nondescript knot. She was one of those touchy feely types, who hugged and kissed everyone hello and no matter how many times I tried to avoid it, she always managed to corral me. I never gave up our duel of personal space without a fight.

The beaded chain on her reading glasses jingled as she looked up and blue-green eyes paused before registering who I was. "Ken!" She smiled, stood, and came around the table so fast she almost toppled Mick, who was standing over her shoulder. "How's my favorite pupil?"

"It was one lesson," I said in a weary voice.

Melody wasn't an Inquisitor. She was a card carrying psychic to most and a bruja to others. She had given me a few tips on how to control my Lengua-bruja and was determined to turn me into a psychic advisor for her internet dating service called Psychic Hook Up where 'real live psychics' (which should be psychic, singular, as she had no employees) located soulmates in the western astral plane for only $19.99 a month. This fee included a monthly tarot reading, dream analysis, and daily horoscope. Besides helping us, she also freelanced for the TCPD.

I stalled her approach by holding my palm face high. She touched her fingertips to mine, a simple gesture. The tilt of her shoulders and hips managed to turn the gesture into something friendly. A sharp prickle of energy traveled along my hand forcing me to yank it away. The damn bruja exploited the opening and hugged me. My consolation was that I managed to avert my head so her sloppy kiss missed its mark and hit somewhere beneath my right eyeball. I pushed her aside.

Melody ran a bony hand through her hair; each finger glittered with silver hoops. Her necklace pouch filled with blessed earth swayed with each movement. Her spaghetti strapped tank top, which would've looked hot on any other woman, showcased the imprints of two nipple piercings, and didn't quite stretch to make it to her belt line, exposing a leathery midsection and emerald stud navel ring. The ten silver hoops in each ear, as well as two in her right eyebrow, one in her lower lip, and another emerald stud in her nose added up to enough metal that made her dangerous to be around during a lightning storm.

Melody sniffed me up and down. Her gaze sharpened. "What's that smell? Have you been barbecuing?"

The smell of fire and liquor still clung to my singed clothing. Mick most likely smelled it too though he hadn't said anything yet. Maybe I should've stopped at home for a quick change and a shower. Mick met my eyes with a brief intensity that promised a hard discussion.

"No, Melody." I always used her full name because I didn't want to perpetuate the idea that I liked her or that we were friends, though she had her own ideas about the nature of our relationship. "Maybe it's your poor hygiene you smell."

"Tut. Tut," Melody said, clicking her tongue. "You reek of lust, smoke, and decay."

I took one of the folding chairs off the wall and set it opposite Mick's' desk. For a second, I considered asking if she picked up anything unusual on her psychic network. It would take her ten hours of sideways explanation to say, *No*. I fixed Mick with my get-her-the-hell-away-from-me look.

Mick dropped his weight into the seat Melody had vacated. The corners of his lips twitched. "Mel, can you pull those Ojáncanu files we marked from the Archive?"

"Yes, but…" Melody stared at us with unfettered exasperation before crossing her arms.

"Thanks, Mel," Mick said.

"Tut." Melody exited, the door closing softly behind her.

Good riddance.

"A fire?" Mick's eyes burrowed into my skull while his chiseled chin moved like he was chewing a piece of rubber.

I returned the fiery glare and readied for a king-sized pissing contest. "Anything to drink?"

Mick grunted and waved at the fridge where he kept his soda collection. I walked over, pulled open the door, and grabbed a can of pineapple soda from a company I swore went out of business a couple years ago. I took a swig. It hit my stomach with sour fire.

"New stuff?" I croaked, looking at the label. I returned to my seat scowling.

"Old stuff," Mick said.

"You need to warn a guy first. I've a delicate palate." I took another drink and held it in my mouth for a couple of seconds before swallowing. It tasted like ass the second time around too.

"Stop stalling." Mick reached over, plucked the can from my hand, and dropped it in the trash.

"You know the first part. A woman named Gabriela Fletcher offered me cash to protect her Nescient daughter Roxana from another guajona named Dhyana Nuberu. I got a call from Winnie about the same time. Mars was reanimated as a wight and he was terrorizing Jiggy's. I headed down there to take care of it. A guajona named Sera Ojáncanu, who was pretending to be a stripper, made off with Roxana while I was murderizing Mars. Me and Lacruz tracked Sera to a house out in Delta Terrace. We found over two dozen wights in the basement. I had to burn the house down to ash them all. Sera and the kid are still missing."

I didn't mention the canvas in my pocket. The only thing I knew for sure was that it was dangerous. I didn't want to expose anyone else to its taint. I could still feel its unearthly warmth.

Mick toyed with his earlobe. "I don't like the idea of any Nescient being kidnapped and corrupted." He softened his voice a bit. "You know her chance at a normal life ended once she was taken. Whatever you may want to believe, she's one of them now. I know it's tragic, but we can't do anything about it. Focus on the human lives you can save." Mick let his words sink in before he continued, "I'll have a chat with Deacon to make sure we're fully stocked."

"Deacon..." I sighed. I put two fingers to my temple and begin to massage in slow steady circles. "The goat was wearing a cocktail dress..."

"Let the goat go. Everyone needs forgiveness for errors in judgment," Mick said in a tired and patient voice. He moved his hand in a chopping motion.

Easy for him to say, it wasn't his retina the image was seared onto.

I did have larger problems than Deacon so I acquiesced and folded my hands in my lap. At first, Sera struck me as beautiful, bold, and none too bright. I had to revise that assessment to add in cunning, ruthless, and talented, at least when it came to quilting. So why would a guajona working to keep her identity a secret suddenly throw it to hell by snatching Roxana in such a violent way? There had to be a number of under the cuff methods she could've used.

And how did she know I would bring the kid to the club? It was a damn convoluted way to kidnap someone. Kids get pinched on their way home from school all the time. Why not do it that way?

Gabriela would've brought Roxana to Sera and not to me if Gabriela and Sera were working together. I believed Gabriela was telling the truth about wanting her daughter protected. Maybe Gabriela was lying about who was pursuing Roxana? Maybe Sera and Dhyana was the same person, one pretending to be the other? Except, Sera looked nothing like the woman Roxana described. I was missing something.

"Is there such a thing as a 'special' guajona, one with more mojo than the others?" I asked.

"One ring to rule them all?" Mick shook his head. He leaned back and stared at the ceiling as if to gather his thoughts. He lowered his chin, clasped his hands on his desk, and looked straight ahead. "A guajona's facility with the Cleave varies. Most of their proficiency is based on their will, practice, and how much blood they've ingested over their lifespan. It's possible for a guajona to temporarily supercharge by gorging on a large volume of blood in a tiny window of time. But to answer your question, I believe so. I'll say more once Mel returns."

The only reason I could see for Sera to grab the kid was to convert her. But why? She was one kid, hardly enough to make any kind of difference.

Mick paused. "Sera Ojáncanu managed to create about twenty wights you said? That translates into a huge ripple in the human population." His eyebrows rose. "I'd bet next Sunday's collection plate it's not isolated. We need to find more ripples."

A whole lot of people missing in a specific area could be a clue as to where Sera had done her hunting. I was still unsure if Sera had left those wights as a trap, army, or both. Locating missing persons is something Lacruz could do for me, but she was probably still tied up at the fire.

Mick studied my expression and wasn't pleased by what he found. "Jason's noted some heavy Coven Ojáncanu movement pushing north: Juarez, Las Cruces, and Alamogordo; they might be on their way here. That's a ripple. We find a third and a fourth and we'll have a good idea of where this is headed."

"Coven Ojáncanu have made plays for the north before," I said. "We bloodied their noses the last time." I stood and located the map of New Mexico Mick kept mounted on the wall. I studied the green stick pins marking Ojáncanu movement. The most northern stick pin was fourteen miles away in Bloomfield.

He shrugged. "Good thing Jason will be here soon."

I groaned, walked to my chair, and sat. Mick's character flaw was that he considered Jason and his crew to be the fucking *Jackson Five* of the Inquisition. With three hundred or so of us active in the states and overseas, you would think he would find a nobler champion. I covered my mouth to hide my scowl. "Do we really need him?"

"Yeah." Mick rubbed his thumb along his robe.

"When will they arrive?" I tried to keep the tightness out of my voice. Jason had a propensity for getting people killed. He was a nuke. I didn't want his brand of fallout in my city.

"They had a few loose ends to bury so I figure his crew will be here early Monday morning. Inaccurate intel is a ticking time bomb ready to explode in your face. That's why open communication is best. It keeps misunderstandings from happening."

I narrowed my eyes. He wanted to say more or maybe he wanted me to say more. I kept many secrets. I assumed others did too. I refused to be baited. I knew better.

Words came slow as if dragged out of him. "You keep the other team from scoring. The rest is up to God and the quarterback." Mick's gaze sharpened as he spoke. "We need the best two minute drive you can muster. Field goal range is all I'm asking. Jason will put it through the uprights."

"Send me in coach," I muttered. Winnie's apartment could qualify as one of those ripples Mick mentioned. I was debating sharing my thoughts when Melody returned.

She handed him a file. Mick scanned the pages until he found the passage he wanted. He turned the file around so I could see and pointed where I should read.

It was a notation circa the seventh century. After the disappearance of the last mouros, two Dueño fought for control over all the covens. Dueño were aristocratic Lords who led a coven. The passage pretty much said Dueño Vega Nuberu fought mano a mano with Dueño Tulin Drac. Dueño Vega won. The phrase, *El Rey del Sangre va al victor* was circled. Underneath it were two translations written in pencil: *The blood king shall pass to the winner* and *The* Sangreino *goes to the victor.*

I covered my mouth and groaned. The Sangreino, always the damn Sangreino, Mick's unholy grail. The Sangreino was a mythical monster throne of power. According to this notation, the Sangreino fell into gargola hands around the time mouros were exterminated.

"Where'd you find this?" I asked.

"Mel's been studying Asturian, Cantabrian, and Catalonian mythology. We've corresponded at length and have uncovered interesting tidbits, pieces mind you, but enough from a variety of sources to piece a tapestry together." Mick leaned forward in his seat. "So to get back to your question about a special guajona or gargola. Tulin Drac was the first to be a recognized power and wielder of the Sangreino though Vega Nuberu still managed to dispatch him," Mick preached. "Vega founded the Crimson Consortium. He became the first king and took the title of Sovereign. He created the blueprint for modern guajona and gargola culture. Vega and his apprentice," he paused and grinned from ear to ear. "Dhyana Nuberu completely obliterated the Drac bloodline. We don't have the slightest clue why."

I had to admit, hearing Dhyana referenced as the apprentice to the strongest guajona in history gave me pause. According to Gabriela, Dhyana had offered protection of sorts while the kid matured. What was the connection here? What was so special about Roxana?

Melody picked up where Mick left off. "References to Vega and Dhyana end sometime in the late eighteen hundreds. The word Sovereign also falls into disuse. We don't think it's a coincidence that Dhyana Nuberu's name reappears when Dueño Lauder Ojáncanu, the current strongest gargola, is headed here. We believe," she made eye contact to make sure I was listening. "Dhyana has hidden the Sangreino in Tierra Santa. This city has always been a hotspot for gargola and guajona activity." Melody and Mick traded smiles. "And now we know why!"

Mick added. "Why else would Lauder go through the trouble of keeping the Cattle Branch poised on our doorstep?"

This was crazy talk. "The Sangreino's probably a fancy loin cloth, even if it exists," I snorted. "And why would I be hired to protect Roxana from Dhyana? Why would Sera snatch her?" My eyebrows shot up in mock surprise. "Unless you guys think the kid is the Sangreino?"

Mick and Melody swayed as if struck.

I started kneading my temples. They were willing to believe anything.

"What do you know about Gabriela Fletcher?" Mick began angrily. "Did you fact check her story or did you just take her money and run off half-cocked? Lying about the child's origins is easy." He held up his hand to forestall my response. "We don't know what the Sangreino is. It could be a person, a place, or a thing. Maybe the child knows where it is or she's destined to become the next Sovereign. Whatever the reason, finding her is a priority. Sera Ojáncanu is a flunky who's most likely holding the child for Dueño Lauder."

Mick and Melody were on the kid finding bandwagon as long as it intersected with their obsession. I had another disturbing realization. Their body language. The way they traded glances. They were fucking. *Eww.*

My belief in the Sangreino's nonexistence would continue. At least we agreed on saving Roxana. I stood to leave. I didn't know how long it would take for Sera to hear about my house warming. I had to locate Sera before she met up with Lauder. If Mick and Melody were right about the Sangreino being here, Sera wouldn't be leaving town until her boss arrived. That gave me some time.

Despite the foolishness of going alone, I was already planning on hitting the Cattle Branch to find a guajona and gargola who knew Sera's whereabouts. Mick would try to stop me if he knew. It was best to make sure he didn't find out.

Melody recognized my change in demeanor. She placed a hand on Mick's shoulder. He looked at her with knitted brows. She kept her tone frank. "We'd ask you to sit and parlay but I've often reminded Mikel that you're a man of action. You're meant to be out doing, not talking. Until Jason arrives, you're our best shot at finding the child and the Sangreino. All we want is a phone call."

"Where are you going?" Mick asked. He rose, placed both hands on his desk, and leaned forward.

I let the silence stretch until Melody's sighed, *Tut tut.* I almost gagged when she patted Mick's hand.

Like usual the only defense against the tidal chaos was the Inquisition— a bunch of murdering degenerates, who in any other century, would've been pirates or worse. This was another opinion of mine Mick didn't agree with and another argument I couldn't win.

My eyes strayed to my wedding photo on his mantle. He married a lot of couples and had a lot of photos. He displayed mine for some reason.

I needed answers. I departed Sanctuary for the Cattle Branch leaving Mick and Melody to whatever the hell was going on between them. *Eww.*

7 CRIMOIRE

At one in the morning, the line of idiots dying to be eaten stretched double file from the Cattle Branch's entrance to the parking lot. Oh, and don't get me started on parking. The cars were wedged together with barely enough space between them to squeeze a cracker through. The spot I found for my Grand Marquis was an exile's walk from the entrance.

I killed the engine and unzipped my duffel bag on the passenger seat. The MP5K Deacon picked out for me was right on top and underneath it was my sawed off twelve gauge, plenty of ammo, a healthy assortment of sharp objects, and my brand new shiny, the new axe I decided to call *Dolor* because it meant both pain and sorrow in Spanish.

My gear felt inadequate for the task ahead; not to mention, I had zero backup. The Cattle Branch was too far out of P's territory for him to give a rat's tit. Mick was the only Inquisitor close enough to provide assistance and he didn't know I was here. The only friend I could depend on was Lacruz, who I left to take the blame for a house fire.

Alone and about to jump into a den of blood drinkers, I took a deep breath, settled into a killing calm, and picked out my weapons. My plan was simple, go into the Cattle Branch, ask some real polite questions, receive some real polite answers, and walk out with Roxana or at least a clue as to where to find Sera. I *wouldn't* have to fire a shot.

I caressed the photo of my wife and daughter for luck, got out of the car, removed my coat, slung the MP5K submachine gun crosswise by its strap so that it pressed against my rib cage, and attached *Dolor* so it dangled from my belt. I put my coat back on and zipped it halfway. My coat was large enough to conceal the submachine gun and long enough to hide the axe's full length without too many unsightly bulges. I looked at the shotgun, as much as I wanted to take it with me I had no place to stick it, and *where the sun don't shine* wasn't an option. I locked the car door and headed toward the entrance.

I strolled past the designer labeled blood donors, masochists, and yellow coat wearing freaks. I ignored their angry shouts, catcalls, laughter, joy, quick kisses, handholding, playful banter, and the fearless faces eager to test their mortality on the latest high. The unlucky or lucky ones, depending on the point of view, were invited to VIP where they would get shit-faced on guajona toxin while being drained of blood. If they survived, they would come back next day and the day after. Eventually, the feeding and the drugging would go too far and they wouldn't come back except as a wight.

At the front of the line, twin pillars of fashion condescension guarded the door. Tight black T-shirts, dark sunglasses, earpiece walkie-talkies, chiseled chins, neat square-cut goatees, and steroid enhanced physiques showed what passed for security. The meatheads were human. The widest, Atlas Wannabe blocked my path.

"Back of the line," Atlas Wannabe said in an I-dare-you-to-piss-me-off-so-I-can-show-off-all-these-pretty-muscles tone.

"Maybe you know a couple of my friends." I smiled reached into my coat as if grabbing cash. Their stances relaxed. I wasn't anything special, some dumb schmuck trying to buy my way in like any other dumb schmuck. I was still smiling when my hand closed over my MP5K.

I whipped the gun in a quick clubbing arc toward Atlas Wannabe's nose. Metal met bone and metal was victorious. Atlas Wannabe's shattered nose spurted blood. He staggered. My follow up kick snapped his knee in several places. He collapsed sideways. I kicked him as he landed, this time in the face. Atlas Wannabe's lights were out before Meathead Number Two could uncross his arms.

So much for the stealthy approach.

I heard several 'oh shit's' and 'damns' as I turned my Inquisitor stare on Meathead Number Two, who froze. I opened my mouth wide. My voice carried into the night. "Somebody has to take him to the hospital or someone else is going to have to take you both."

Meathead Number Two looked at me and then at Atlas Wannabe and then back at me. Understanding came slowly. Putting his hands up in surrender Meathead Number Two said, "No problem, Dawg. No problem."

I stepped back and let him retrieve his fallen friend, who he cradled like a bag of kittens to the passenger seat of a yellow Mustang convertible parked near the entrance. Meathead Number Two speared me with a look of hate before climbing into the car and zooming off for parts unknown.

Those in line cheered, some cowered, the smart ones turned and left. A spiky purple-haired idiot tore the red cord blocking the entry and started for bar. I slid in front of him with my submachine gun pointed at the center of his forehead.

Spiky's arms shot up. "Don't shoot, dude! You're like fucking cool or what?"

Cars peeled out the parking lot in pitches of smoke and squealing tires.

"Only a shot in the ass will get you through those doors," I said. The remnants of the similar dressed idiots, who were probably Spiky's buds, dispersed leaving Spiky to fend for himself. Spiky wasn't shaking in his boots. His dancing dilated pupils and weed breath kept him amused at being held at gunpoint. I reached out a hand. "You have a lighter?"

Spiky reached one hand for his pocket while keeping the other arm straight up and missed the opening several times. "Dude this is like hard, can I use my other hand?" He wiggled his raised fingers while he spoke. I nodded grimly to keep from laughing. "Bitchin'," Spiky answered and with two hands he fumbled for a few seconds before handing me the lighter. "You like a commando or something? Cause if you need some help I like got some bitchin' nunchakus at home."

"Or something. Now get." I slid the lighter into my front pocket. I watched Spiky slink away casting glances over his shoulder while his buddies screamed at him to jump in the damn car.

The Cattle Branch was a middle finger in the Inquisition's face sequestered thirty or so miles outside of Tierra Santa, the Crimoire had been an old slaughterhouse until prohibition hit; then it was converted to a moonshine distillery. It had garnered a passion among the criminal elite, changing hands as each new crime boss claimed the spoils of the old, each adding more black market commodities. Coven Ojáncanu bought it in 2001 and refurbished it into a happening bar and night club while still keeping the secret underground tunnels intact. Tunnels that once funneled booze and bang across state lines transport gargola, guajona, and blood donors in and out.

I pushed open the swinging double doors. My boots kicked up the sawdust covering the floor. The vibe inside was wild with a pinch of nasty. The DJ was spinning loud and thumping bastardized techno-hip hop. Men and women crowded in claustrophobic groups, umbrella drinks in hand, talking, giggling, and encouraging the danger around them.

I scanned the room for a familiar face or someone to take me to their leader. Every make-up caked brunette and bleach blonde looked like Sera until the dim lighting shifted, they danced, or snorted coke off their BFF's breasts.

To be honest, I expected more monsters waiting to kill me. Despite hiding behind too human pretty faces, two gargola and guajona radiated the unmistakable predatory hunger (some people mistook for desire) of big bad monsters about to pounce. They weren't even aware of my arrival. A gargola and guajona were on poaching duty to pick out the healthiest and freshest stock for VIP. Another gargola guarded the stairs leading down to VIP. The guajona bartender poured drinks and chatted up the crowd.

Before I could make a second sweep of the room, the gargola poacher looked up from a crowd of eager young coeds he was schmoozing to where I blocked the doorway. He saw the gun, the grimace, the Inquisitor stare and mouthed, *Oh shit* before he took off toward VIP. He slithered between bobbing bodies like a snake.

I would be swarmed if I waited for this to play out. I had to take the fight to them before they realized I was alone. I chose my first target carefully. It was a shame how much they charged for drinks in this joint.

I aimed the submachine gun and obliterated the guajona bartender's head. The second burst knocked her body into the liquor bottles with a crash of glass. The remaining shocked bartenders stared in at their fallen comrade. The crowd froze unsure if it was part of a show, then the music swerved, the room erupted in screams, and patrons dove for any dark spot of cover they could find.

"Get down!" I shouted. Though I doubted anyone heard me.

The human bartenders ran screaming from their post. I squeezed the trigger again, this time aiming at the alcohol. My spray of bullets tore through eighty proof delights whose liquid entrails soaked the cabinets.

I grabbed a guy crouching low and yanked him toward the door. Those nearest took the hint and followed him out. I ignored the press of people running for safety to inch closer to the bar. I sparked Spiky's lighter, tossed it into the spilled liquor, and made this the second time tonight I started a fire. It was beginning to become a theme. Smoke billowed as the bar caught flame. There was more screaming and fleeing toward already clogged exits.

With any hope, the fire and commotion would sow confusion among any Ojáncanu responding to the trouble. I crouched near the flames and waited for the warriors to come out and play. I didn't wait long.

The second poacher, a guajona with violent red hair, charged at me through the smoke. By the time I realized she was there, she was too close for the submachine gun. I slid my knife from its sheath, sidestepped her rush, and slashed her eyes as she passed. The blinded guajona crashed face first into the bar with a loud crunch of a broken neck. I put a few slugs into the back of her head to make sure she stayed down. I sheathed my knife and returned my attention to my surroundings.

Through the thickening curls of smoke, I spotted the gargola VIP guard holding his position like he expected backup. He backed against the wall so I couldn't get a clear shot, glanced down the stairwell, and back at me. I could see his confusion. I anticipated more Ojáncanu fighters pouring in by now. None appeared. The VIP guard's unease grew. He was probably thinking I was the cause of his buddies' absence. I took full advantage of his apprehension and flipped him the bird.

He snarled. His body began to shake and ripple. His clothes stretched tight against his chest and ripped. He gained muscle mass, which transformed him from a pencil-neck geek to a champion weightlifter. His fingernails elongated into sharp black claws, a long yellow fang extended from blood-red gums on the right side of his albino alligator face, and his eyes turned inky black. It took seconds for him to shed his illusion of humanity. This was the real face of gargola when they dispensed with masks. This was the beast.

My balls tightened against my abdomen.

The VIP guard zigzagged from the stairwell using the cowering patrons who weren't smart enough to escape when the trouble started as cover. He raked claws dripping with acidic toxin across their torsos as he passed them. The acid ate holes through their clothes, skin, and flesh. His victims screamed and writhed until the acid reached a vital organ and then the patrons would go still as a grave.

I gripped my gun tight and tried to get a bead on the VIP guard without killing any bystanders. I used my rage to keep from being overwhelmed by his victim's death rattles. He moved from one group to another, clawed their flesh, and more died from his acid. His black-ink eyes boiled with the threat of a linebacker unabated to the quarterback. With claws dripping, saliva slavering, and mayhem, well, hemming, the guard coiled his legs and dove.

Gargola and guajona can't fly by broom or any other means. They do, however, have powerful legs capable of smashing long jump records. The VIP guard was of the Olympiad variety and swiftly cleared the distance between us. He dropped on me.

I fell backwards and raised my submachine gun to compensate for his skyward descent, but my burst went awry and missed. As he collapsed atop me with claws darting for my face, I tucked my knees against my torso, and shoved both heels into his chest and used his momentum to flip him toward the fire. The jarring impact of his weight sent shocks into my knees.

The gargola flipped over my head. He hit the smoldering bar top, rolled through the flames, and came up a screaming fireball. I rolled to my stomach, aimed upward at an angle, and shot. The burst of gunfire popped his lung and heart. I pulled the trigger a second time shearing off a section of his skull. Flame grilled brain matter leaked out of the serrated bone edges. He slid dead to the floor. I climbed to my knees and scanned for more targets.

The white noise in my head dimmed. The sounds of moaning, coughing, and crackling filtered in. Those that could still walk, hobble, or drag themselves or their friends decided to use the break in the action to make for the nearest exit. There were dozens either too hurt to move or unconscious. I couldn't drag them to safety even if I was inclined to.

They would die because they were in the wrong place at the wrong time. I couldn't protect them and I cared more about killing monsters than saving lives. Accounting for innocents was Mick's most challenging obstacle. I wasn't so altruistic. I came for information not sainthood. I pushed aside any thought of casualties and pushed ahead for answers.

I made my way through bodies and overturned tables to the VIP area. The lack of a stronger monster response to my gunshots worried me because it created the strong possibility of an ambush. I descended the stairs anyway. The air at the bottom was more breathable since smoke rose upward.

With any hope, the door wouldn't be bolted because I didn't have any explosives to blow it open. The door was solid steel with a handle and a peephole. It lacked a locking mechanism on the outside. The door frame was solid concrete. No shoddy workmanship here. I put my ear to the metal and heard nothing.

Their lack of Ojáncanu response boiled down to an enemy arranging an ambush or escaping through the smuggling tunnels. Either way, their advantage increased the longer I waited. A third gentler possibility tickled my brain. Maybe they wanted to talk? Yeah, fucking right.

Overall, I didn't like my odds so I took a deep breath, did the good mannered thing, and knocked. To my surprise the door swung inward. I paused at the spill of light and the sour astringent odor wafting from the VIP interior. My heart hammered. I poked the MP5Ks' nozzle through the crease. I made a quick sweep of the room, frowned, and pushed the door completely open.

Rain and floods.

An electric thermostat whirred. The VIP room was a modest-sized velvet lounge of soft colors and plush couches. Three large empty bowls like enormous bongs filled the center of the space. Each one was surrounded by four feed-chairs, which resembled dentist chairs with mouth gags, restraining straps, and syringes connected to plastic tubing designed to extract blood and deposit it into the bongs for gargola and guajona to drink at their leisure.

Something or someone had damaged the feed-chairs leaving deformed frozen hunks with pitted crumbling cushions. The glass bongs were empty and frozen. The icicle remains of blood donors, humans who voluntarily loaned their flesh to monsters, were frosted into the seats. The corpses lucky enough to still have faces possessed deathly expressions contorted in pleasure as if they were too high to feel the cold that killed them. The most eerie thing about the carnage was the lack of death rattles. The blood donors welcomed oblivion.

More than a dozen beasted gargola and guajona corpses were scattered across the floor. Most had fist-sized holes where their hearts should be. Others were missing their heads. I recognized what remained of the gaudy clothes of the poacher who spotted me.

His death differed from the others. He had been bisected at the waist by something cold, jagged, and sharp. The parting left no blood. Both sides of the sundered wound were frozen. His death was recent and yet his killer was nowhere to be found. Dread filled me as my eyes jumped from cold death to cold death.

A shadow coalesced into a black leather mid-thigh waistcoat, skirt, and sheer stockings covered creamy legs. Sera stepped out of hiding near the rear of the room and smoothed her outfit with black-lacquered fingernails.

She paused, hands on hips, and regarded me from head to toe the way someone appraises a buffet before paying.

"We need to discuss our future," she said with a ghostly smile.

Why did the future always come up with women? You started dating; they wanted to know your future together. You got married; they wanted to know about your future kids. You got caught cheating; they wanted to guarantee your future was hell. I rarely thought beyond my next meal so when a woman wanted to talk about the future, I knew within the next few minutes I was going to be that much closer to the grave.

I held my submachine gun tight and gestured at the bloodshed around me. "Did you go through all this trouble so we could have a date? You dirty little vixen. You shouldn't have." My voice fell into a growl. "You. Really. Should. Not. Have. You've rattled the people who set prices on heads and I'm the collector."

Sera lorded over her handiwork with the pride of artisan. She tapped her cheek in mock thought. "No inquiry into Xana's wellbeing. She'd be so disappointed by your lack of concern." Laughter bubbled from her lips. "You *were* hired to protect her."

Who the hell is Xana? I thought about it. Ro-*Xana*. Is that what she had taken to calling Roxana Rodriguez? It was odd to nickname someone you kidnapped. "The only motherfucking way you will see dawn is to hand over the kid."

Sera spread her hands as if displaying a game show prize. "You weren't supposed to be involved yet. Imagine my surprise when I saw you take Xana to Winnie." She held up a single finger and moved in back and forth in a no, no, no, gesture. "You were supposed to save me from Mars. I was going to reward you... Enthusiastically. Then we'd become such good friends. The kind of friends who do things for each other. Together, we were supposed to claim Xana. And then, you were supposed to kill Dhyana."

All the madness with Mars had been a lure to get me to the Jungle Gem so she could seduce me. She hadn't expected Roxana. Sera changed her plans once she knew the kid was at Winnie's. Not only that. She was pretty much confirming Dhyana did exist.

I didn't like being a pawn in anyone's game and I sure as hell wasn't going to stand for it. I wrecked games. I was going to wreck hers too... as soon as I figured out the rules. I had to keep her talking in the hopes she would let Roxana's location slip. "Why kidnap Roxana when you knew there'd be witnesses?"

She moved closer. "I killed Brody because he didn't have the good sense to stay down. I could have killed Winnie, but I knew she mattered to you. I didn't want you angry. I still have plans for us."

She was talking in riddles. The only factoid I could pluck from the crazy jumble was Roxana still lived. As much as I wanted to start shooting, I needed information more than a corpse. I was willing to listen until I could piece together the kid's whereabouts. "Was P part of your master plan?"

"All good plans have scapegoats and Pimberton is the right bitch to be a goat. No matter," she waved it away. "You're already involved so I'll reveal your part." She smiled proudly. "You're going to help me rule the Crimson Consortium."

Sera wasn't the first guajona with designs for rule. Coups seemed to be common among the covens. It took power, major stones, and a bit of insanity to want to be boss of bosses. Underneath her beautiful exterior she was bananas topped with an unhealthy dose of nuts.

"Dhyana Nuberu has been mentioned a lot in the last few hours. She doesn't mean squat to me. Why don't you explain it?"

"Dhyana," Sera sneered. "You've never met her, then. Good." Sera's laughter cut like swallowed glass. "She is a smart, cunning, powerful, and manipulative insignificant pest past her prime. She probably sent Xana to you for protection. She didn't expect me to account for you."

That raised my eyebrows. Dhyana was making a lot of ripples for someone who hadn't shown her face. I had no clue about Dhyana's motives, but Sera had pretty much confirmed they were working against one another. Maybe I could kill Sera and use Dhyana as a means to find the kid? I smiled. I repositioned my MP5K so I could shoot from the hip.

Sera continued, "The fact that you've come this far demonstrates your tenacity. You are perfect for what needs doing. My proposition is quite simple. Kill Dhyana and I return the girl."

Yeah, right. So now Roxana was leverage to force me to do Sera's dirty work. If Sera had been keeping tabs on me, she should've known I always finish the job once I take the cash. "Where is Roxana? I won't ask again."

"Or you'll kill me? Then who will keep her warm, clothed, and make sure she eats her vegetables," Sera mocked.

Sera's ghostly smile displayed human teeth though something about the twist of her mouth forced me to realize that I was probably too late. Mick was right. The kid was already corrupted. I felt my heart skip. I feared the answer more than I wanted to. "Is she still human?"

"Who decides what's human? Humans and guajona share the same number of chromosomes. We have souls too." Sera raised her hand to stop my response. "You have my word Xana is the same as when I took her."

Her ghostly smile taunted me and for the moment we traded stares. My rage expanded like a balloon with helium shoved up its backside. I couldn't let her sit smug in her belief that she had me. I had to pop her confidence. What could I use as a pin? When leads were at a minimum, issuing a threat, no matter how illogical, was a good tactic to see which way someone would jump. I had one crazy word, a word that would go a long way to clear up a dispute with Mick.

"I can guarantee you'll never get the Sangreino," I snorted.

I waited for the word to take effect and wasn't disappointed. I expected confusion or cold mockery. Instead, Sera's contemptuous humor melted. Her eyes widened and inky blackness flowered and faded across her cornea like fireworks. Recognition, fear, and, doubt cascaded for a breathless instant. She knew the Sangreino. She recognized it as a real object with history and meaning. Her reaction couldn't tell me what it did or what it was, but it did reveal that the Sera believed the Sangreino was real.

"You know nothing," Sera growled as she began pacing. "I've been aware of you for quite some time. You are the type of man who would've spurned the direct approach. But this," Sera gestured at her grisly handiwork. "Death is something we both understand." Her voice became soft, pitying. "You had a daughter. I heard what was done to her. I've seen others do worse to countless like her. The world is filled with dying children. You kill guajona because our hunger drives us to atrocities. Don't you see? By ruling the Consortium, I can prevent tragedies and keep children safe." Sera spread her hands. "We aren't enemies. That we interbreed makes us the same species. Guajona and humans can share a purpose. We both want what these pretty lips can do."

"One thing about pretty lips," I said. "They lie."

My daughter Evelyn was dead, gone, and buried. And yet Sera had the arrogance to bring my Pequiñita into it. She didn't know me like she thought because if she did... Fuck it. I would find Roxana the hard way.

I aimed my MP5K. Sera stood motionless, in fact, her gaze didn't register her impending death. Then I understood why. Voice carried faster than a trigger pull.

"Feel your blood, Hijo de Dirige," she chanted. "Feel it call to the dark.

Imagine how we can be together."

Her eyes burned with darkness. Power hit me like a bullet to the brain. I staggered as if struck. The machinegun burst missed. Hijo de Dirige, those words churned my blood like a secret whispered in my ear while I slept. Sera's power invaded my mind, hijacked my senses, and its death-chilled fingers clutched my brain and squeezed. Sera's ghostly smile warped along with the VIP room. I lost all sensation in my limbs and hurtled into a chasm of endless night.

I smelled barbecue sauce spiced with cayenne, lemon, and brown sugar. The sun shined overhead and the ocean breeze pushed cool air and cookfire smoke across the green grass and tall trees. My KISS THE COOK apron caught the wind. I grilled ribs and enjoyed the scent and sizzle of meat. Sera hummed while setting her glass tray of killer macaroni salad on the concrete picnic table. A few feet away, Evelyn played in the grass with Dhyana, the family cat, while her newborn brother sucked blood from the right ear of his favorite stuffed teddy bear.

A scream tore at the back of my throat. I stumbled sideways into a feed chair. My hip reverberated off the steel and lances of pain shot through my back. Were the horrors attracted to me? Was it my fault Evelyn died? I didn't believe it. Couldn't believe it. Hijo de Dirige. What the hell kind of monster was that? I spent most of my life fighting darkness. Could I be the real monster? Something gouged my cheek as I slid to the floor. I turned and noticed a glint of metal, a single gold band on the corpses' finger dripping with my blood. I concentrated on the ring, remembered the one like it I wore and everything that came with it. This dead stranger was someone's husband who wouldn't be coming home.

Anger anchored me. It filled my head with red fog. I stood, squared my shoulders, and faced Sera with resolve stamped in steel. My Inquisitor stare, death incarnate, three times cold, and twice as nasty, bore down. "You come into my fucking city!" I roared. "You lie, kidnap, kill, and you have the nerve to call me a monster?"

Her devil's dream wasn't the life I wanted. She wasn't the woman I wanted. "I don't know what you did, but I do know what I have in my hand. So why don't you wrap your lips around this."

I devoured the satisfaction of seeing Sera's jaw drop. She didn't understand how I broke her power's hold on me. Hell, neither did I.

My gun barked. I felt the pleasing recoil of .223 caliber hollow points being jettisoned at eleven hundred and forty-eight feet per murderous second. Sera dodged. The bullets cracked the masonry behind her. Her closed fist snapped open. Power pooled in the center of her palm.

Guajona abilities vary and a few called Dueños had the ability to manipulate their bloodline to its highest degree. Sera chilled the moisture in the air in the center of her palm. That wasn't an Ojáncanu bloodline ability. It was Nuberu! What the hell kind of twisted game Sera was playing?

As the temperature in the room dropped, I heard the thermostat whir into action to compensate. It took a team of Inquisitors to take down a Dueño. I faced a force I could never hope to defeat alone. I continued firing in short steady bursts while fighting my rising internal panic. Sera dodged my line of fire easily, smiled menace, pulled back her arm, and snapped her hand forward.

An ice spike came at me like a homing missile far faster than I was ready for. I lunged and tucked my arms tight against my body hoping to become a smaller target. The ice spike sailed into that space where certainty and luck engaged in a brutal street fight. Luck was brawling dirty because after a few well-placed elbows to certainty's throat, it prevailed. The ice spike missed and shattered against the wall.

It was too late to stop my lunge. My shoulder smashed into the floor. Needles of agony danced along my collar bone. I scuttled for the protective cover of one of the feed chairs. It wasn't the best choice of cover though it was better than being caught in the middle of a storm of ice spikes. My breath puffed into the chilled air. The tips of my ears started aching. Ice formed on my shoulders. It was getting co—

The VIP door blew off its hinges, sailed the length of the room, and crashed to the floor. A winter crosswind, the kind that freezes your insides at night so that a trip to the toilet has you pissing ice cubes and shitting igloos, flurried around the VIP room from the open doorway. I looked toward the stairway where the second wind originated and nearly shit myself.

She descended the stairs. Sin, saint, and sex wrapped up in a nice red candy package. A cream sash bisected Lacruz's blood-red leather cat suit tucked into knee high boots. *Damn.* She flowed into VIP and the electric thermostat wheezed and went dead. A mini gale whipped snowflakes around her shoulders and teased her short cropped hair into spikes. To be honest I was frightened, not because of her entrance, but because Lacruz's dancing brown eyes were displeased.

Lacruz raised one arm with her palm facing Sera. Lacruz's eyes flared black for a brief moment. A compressed airburst took Sera in the chest, launched her into the ceiling. Her impact splintered the rafters. Plaster, broken wood, and Sera crashed down.

Sera landed with her right arm curled protectively against her torso. Her scalp had been sliced open. Blood streamed down her face and neck where it stained her collar.

Lacruz smiled cold, took a step forward, and put her hands on her hips. "Give me Roxana," she commanded. "Or I promise torment."

Sera snarled, "I'm disappointed, Ken. I hadn't realized you were already her dog. I should've realized she was backing you up. Only an idiot would think he could assault a Crimoire alone and fight his way to success."

I poked my head up from cover and glared at Sera. Lacruz was dressed like an S&M model and used air as a battering ram. And I was supposed to be a dog for working for her?

Sera must've recognized my complete and utter confusion because her scowl transformed into pure malice. She rose slowly from her crouch. "Oh, he doesn't know." She met Lacruz's glare with mock astonishment. "Oh, that is so rich!"

"Lacruz, what the hell is going on?" I asked.

Her manner of speaking, posture, and pleasing hot new look was different. Her voice and attitude was the same. She was Lacruz. My Lacruz...

Sera addressed me. Her eyes held the twinkle of a winning poker hand. "Don't you know who this is? The guajona standing before you is none other than Sovereign Dhyana Nuberu."

I rose from cover and aimed my submachine gun at Lacruz's chest. Her expression hadn't changed. Her full attention was on Sera. There was a subtle shift of her shoulders. She was less bold than before. I had an unsettling feeling in my gut.

"Is it true?" I asked.

Lacruz's reply was soft. "She seeks to divide us, Kensington."

Kensington. My full name? Oh, hell no! "Bitch, you better talk."

Lacruz tilted her head my way and I saw the planes of her face harden.

Sera's coy laughter echoed throughout the room. "She won't tell you anything, but I'm more than willing."

Lacruz's pointed at Sera. "Seravina Nuberu you tread closer to death."

"Stop," I said. I took aim. "Let her talk." Lacruz and Sera belonged to the same Nuberu bloodline. They had some kind of shared history I was oblivious to. They sure as hell weren't on the same side. I could practically smell their mutual hate for one another.

An emotion too alien for me to decipher crossed Lacruz's face. She lowered her arm and spoke with conviction, "You will dislike her answers."

Sera grinned coldly. "Xana's Drac bloodline is feared throughout the Consortium. Dhyana's job is to eradicate it. Fifteen years ago, she stumbled upon a child conceived of that lineage. Instead of destroying Xana as is Consortium law, Dhyana chose to hide Xana with a guardian, Evan Fletcher. Dhyana has a *preference* for humans because she feels they draw less attention to secrets."

I couldn't believe Lacruz was a guajona and that she managed to fool me over the last two years. She showed none of the usual giveaways, predation, arrogance, or sociopathy. She kept me out of scrapes, tampered with evidence, and generally kept me off the radar of the authorities. We had laughed together, talked, and even shared desserts. She never tried to eat me. None of it made any sense. She was a cop. She upheld the law. She couldn't... Not the woman I...

Sera grinned in triumph. "Xana is a power unseen since mouros walked the earth. Dhyana tried to keep Xana pathetic, average, and invisible. Do you know the hell I saved Xana from? Xana didn't know who she was, the power she possessed, or that she was descended, not from kings and queens, but from a God. That poor teenager felt stirrings for blood and no one was willing to tell her those stirrings were perfectly natural."

Sera pointed at Lacruz. "She let Xana feel shame, confusion, and isolation over the changes going on inside her body. Dhyana let the child believe she was a freak. I planned on guiding Xana gently into her birthright, but she had already awakened." Sera's mouth curled in contempt. "The stress of Evan's attack triggered it. Xana opened up his throat, embraced the Cleave, and fed on him like he deserved. The first kill for a guajona is always darkness." Sera's eyes grew distant and her voice shrank. "We only remember what's after." Sera's expression held cold menace. "Don't you see, Ken? I liberated her."

I was moved to cry buckets of kitten tears for such a tragic tale filled with betrayal and sadness. I was almost, nearly, practically quivering. Really? Sera must've thought I was a total tool to swallow the dung she was shoveling.

If the Fletchers were on Lacruz's... I mean... *Dhyana's* payroll, then I doubted she would choose people capable of harming the merchandise. I recalled the duality in Evan's death rattle, he battled divided loyalties and died conflicted. I remembered the power Sera used in her attempt to control my mind. She couldn't have known what happened unless she initiated it.

I met Sera's eyes. "You made Evan to attack the kid."

She recognized cold hatred in my stare, her impending demise in Lacruz's. Sera's smile lost its conceit the way an extinguished light bulb goes dark.

That was all the confirmation I needed. Sera had mindfucked Evan into attacking the kid.

Inky blackness swallowed Sera's tsunami eyes, frost coursed through her pores, she threw both hands forward sending two ice spikes, three times larger than the one she threw before. I ducked. The ice spike shattered against the feed chair and sprayed ice. Lacruz didn't bother dodging. She backhanded the spike out the air with her fist.

Snarling, Lacruz lowered her head. A black halo surrounded her like a coffin. Her skin took on a pale reptilian texture while her muscles rippled sleek and deadly. She didn't grow any taller. She became lither, more compact. When she lifted her chin, a single long white fang emerged over the right side of her mouth. Her jaw narrowed. Inky-black eyes pierced Sera with tumultuous contempt I had only seen on the face of my ex-wife.

Seeing Lacruz in truth, a creature of merciless killing beauty designed for the sole purpose of devouring life gave me chills and erased all my doubts. I wasn't given much time to admire her new form. On the back wall, a secret door connected to the smuggling tunnels opened up and out rushed decay, scuffling feet, and long *oooish* moans echoing out of the shadows.

The first signs of dead flesh, a gaggle of pale masculine arms attached to clawed curled hands stretched into the light. Rabid wights in business suits, jogging suits, a variety of service uniforms, shirtless, or nude to the toenails poured out of the tunnel with mouths howling for flesh. Sera had plucked men from all walks of life and reanimated them into her personal strike force.

The first ones formed a wight wall in front of Sera. The rest, like a hungry pack of buzzing locusts, lurched toward us. My stomach knotted even as my finger squeezed off rounds. The submachine gun's recoil shook my arm as the smoky insistence of the spent shell casings filled the air.

Ice and bullets, murderous enemies passing in the open, turned the VIP lounge from a guajona eatery to a killing field. I scanned the room to locate Sera through the many dry rotted hostiles of varying nationalities, an African American chef, a Chinese businessman, a Caucasian clerk with a name tag that read, Skip.

I moved closer to Lacruz so we could face the wights together. A *boom* lurched the ground causing me to stumble. A few wights lost their footing and ended up on their butts. Lacruz kept her balance. Explosions were a familiar noise from my tour. Enemy territory often held the danger of IED's, improvised explosive devices. I remembered patrolling and feeling the terror of the anticipatory *boom* of my last step. Hearing an explosion in the present filled me with a sense of survival.

I hit the deck.

More explosions reverberated, about four in a row, louder and closer. I shielded my head as best I could while the floor bucked violently. The explosions turned stones into projectiles. Pieces of wood, plaster, and metal fell from the ceiling. I stole a panicked glance upward through the gray haze to see if the roof was collapsing. Support beams snapped. Huge chunks of debris hurtled toward the floor.

The wights ignored the falling sky. They pushed forward and were either crushed under falling debris, knocked aside, or stunned. The lights exploded. Dirt and filth vomited into the VIP lounge from the mouth of the smuggling tunnel.

The explosions clogged the smuggling tunnel with wood, stone, and metal piping. Water dribbled through the cracks and formed brackish puddles that smelled of sewage. The stairway was an impassible carcass of burning wood. A section of the ceiling near the stairs had collapsed; the ceiling's asymmetrical chasm showcased the upstairs' bonfire, which provided enough light to see in the new darkness. Shards of brick, bloodied human remains, latrines, tables, and chairs had fallen into VIP from upstairs. The remaining feed chairs were covered in dust and ash. The VIP walls sagged with finger width zigzagging cracks. Long beams of wood leaned at odd angles.

Finally, the groaning of stressed wood ceased. I exhaled among the loose rubble. The surviving wights, blinded by the dust fog, searched for someone to tear into.

I was belly down on the floor. My bruised body ached. Dumb luck and body armor managed to keep me from getting seriously hurt. I kept still so my movement wouldn't attract the wights' attention. I scanned for Lacruz. I found her unmistakable rigid silhouette. She stood in halo of the floor lacking any debris. She probably used wind to deflect most of it. Her attention was on the gaping ceiling. There was a second hole in the Cattle Branch's ceiling that revealed open sky with stars covered by dark clouds tinged by moonlight. Thunder cracked.

The wights located Lacruz through the settling dust and had begun to gather for what appeared to be a final assault. My MP5K, busted by a piece of debris, was effectively useless. I dropped it, drew my Sig, rose to my full height, and whooped like a madman. The wights turned to the sound of my voice. I opened up with cover fire.

Despite the roar of my gun, Lacruz's attention stayed fixed on the damn ceiling, which had begun to teeter or maybe the last part was my imagination. Perspiration dotted her forehead as her eyes flared darker than the darkest night. Smudged circles stained the neck and armpits of her leather.

Seconds ticked off. The bark of my Sig dwindled into empty clicks. Enough wights remained to be trouble. Lacruz had moved at last. She reached skyward like it was a stick up. She shouted something to me, but I was too busy listening to a support beam snap.

This is it. This is the end.

I didn't even bother looking up. The room grew warm with the electric tang of a tongue touching a nine volt battery. A bright pure white flash followed by a sickening rending crash flattened me. My cheek smacked against the floor and killed the girlish scream bubbling in my throat.

Right on time, otherwise, dying would've really been embarrassing.

8 COVEN NUBERU

I woke up in Hell.

Heavy darkness choked off the light while warm-blooded snakes wrapped me tight. The swell of panic burned my lungs as I struggled. Muscles flexed. Arms burst free. My eyes shot open as I took in a lungful of air. As my sight adjusted to the dark, I realized I was surrounded by billowy pillows and satin sheets instead of serpents. I took a deep calming breath to let my dream panic fade. I had gentle warm curves of flesh pressed against my pelvis and backside. What I thought were pillows were bodies, two to be exact, pressed fore and aft in some major spoonage.

I reached out and caressed the flesh of the woman snuggled against my chest. Her skin was warm, rough, and scarred. She smelled of mud and exhaustion, a dry bed waiting to bloom again. She snored in an unobtrusive not-to-be-disturbed deep sleep. I pulled the covers off her shoulders to see the slope of her neck marred by a fresh bite puncture and recognized the familiar brown hair of Gabriela Rodriguez-Fletcher. Panic rose. I scooted back and into the swell of breast and flat stomach behind me. The body pressed against my rear shifted, softening without yielding.

Her hand moved up my bare thigh, to my hip where it plunged forward, taking me in hand. I stiffened. In both meanings of the word.

"Let Gabriela rest, Cariño," Lacruz whispered. "I was forced to take too much from her last night. She needs sleep to fully recover. Let me be your desire."

The sound of her voice made me pause. Okay, so I might've jumped, but if anyone asks, I would say I paused. I closed my eyes, took a couple of breaths, and locked my discomfort into a dark corner of my mind. I pressed against her, this time more cautiously.

Lacruz smelled of nostalgia. The crisp memory of a favorite moment like my first ballgame: packed flesh, alcoholic triumph, rooting for the home team, mustard and meat, volcanic noise always erupting, swearing by the gallons, an organ soliloquy, and blue-capped security escorting that drunken idiot in general admission, body painted in his favorite team's colors, out of the stands. She didn't smell like any of those specifically, but rather the moment itself, exciting, exhausting, special, and unforgettable. My sudden awakening carried me back to earlier this evening.

Gabriela had made a surprise reappearance rocking a coal-black sporty BMW that should've had the words *bat* and *mobile* decaled on it. We had climbed in and motored away leaving a smoking crater in place of the Cattle Branch Crimoire. We were completely exhausted by the time finger-thin tendrils of sunshine broke the horizon. Bleary eyed, grouchy, and rudderless we arrived at Lacruz's Estate (think mansion with its own butler surrounded by walls as tall as any you would find at a state prison).

Hold up, I was getting ahead of myself.

Before any of that happened, there was my limb throbbing self on the VIP floor realizing I hadn't been crushed. I didn't know guajona could shove clouds together to generate lightning and that was what Lacruz did. The bolt crashed down with sniper's precision as it hit the VIP lounge and fried the wights.

Standing too close to ground zero during the impact knocked me ten feet backwards where I landed on my side. My cheek smacked against the floor and killed the girlish scream bubbling in my throat. I lost consciousness.

I didn't know how long I was out. Seconds? Minutes? I regained consciousness to blurred swatches of color and deep ringing in my ears. The muscles in my body felt pierced by needles. My skin felt like I had been dry roasted. I tried to rise, but couldn't find my feet. I looked down past my stomach to make sure I still had feet. Two blurry appendages I assumed to be my legs were attached to two blurry boots. I breathed deep, too tired to be afraid of permanent paralysis.

Hell, I was too tired for anything except mourning the loss of submachine gun. I wiggled my toes and my boots rocked back and forth. My feet worked despite the lack of sensation.

Strong hands lifted me off the floor. Lacruz hefted me easily by the waist. I groaned from the pain lancing through my seared nerves. She muttered something soothing I was too dizzy to understand. Her hold tightened. There was a sudden dip before the shudder of rising acceleration. We rocketed out of the VIP lounge and up through the hole in the ceiling. The sudden wind made my eyes water.

We smacked into sheets of rain. Wetness like tears ricocheted off my face waking me against my will.

Hostile oyster gray clouds occasional lit by brief flashes of electric gold drowned the Cattle Branch carcass belching black like a chain smoker. I don't remember our landing. Apparently, she stuck it because sometime after she dumped me onto the sodden earth. Lacruz wandered away.

I spent some time recovering in a muddied fetal position. Minutes? Seconds? The ringing in my ears grew distant. Feeling and motor control returned. The cold pelting rain soothed like an ice pack. I felt dry inside like dusty paper brittle from age. I rolled to my back and opened my mouth. The cold rain falling from the sky slid down my throat and soothed the raw places. I took two last quickened gulps. When I sat up to figure out my surroundings, I noticed Lacruz's silhouette.

She kneeled in the mud, her scorched red leather soaked to the bone. The beast was reabsorbed leaving the illusion of a beautiful vulnerable cop. Rain plastered her hair against her face, sodden shoulders rose and fell as she gasped for breath, and blank brown eyes carried listlessness. To say she looked weak was to say an out of fuel M1 Abrams tank looked weak. She looked *impending*—looming, scary, and so fucking daunting.

Her eyes sparked with black living hunger so palpable it ran the space between us and punched my survival instincts in the kidneys. Her mouth unveiled a glistening wet fang three inches in length. She stood with devilish grace despite the clumps of mud dripping from her soiled leather and took several steps.

Running was an excellent idea. I was so tired, I couldn't climb to my knees. I watched helplessly as the woman I trusted disappeared behind the monster hungering for my death. Each step Lacruz took burned with bitter betrayal. Each foot was a dagger to the heart. Hadn't I bled enough?

For an answer, she took a step, another, then another step, and stopped. She stared down at the mud sucking at her boots. Pause. Seconds passed and she began shaking, either from exhaustion, hunger, or cold. Color returned to her cheeks. She turned, dropped to her knees, and bowed as if praying… or crying.

I trembled. My death had been written in her steps. My life restored in her kneeling acquiescence. Any thanks I could have given was forever swallowed by rumbling. Lacruz looked up, eyes alert, her body expectant. I tensed. The earth groaned and shifted. I stood on wobbly legs. I misjudged the proximity of the disturbance. The ground wasn't opening beneath me. It opened beneath the parking lot. My head snapped around.

My car!

More than two dozen potholes sprang up around my G-Marq followed by an explosive echo of rupturing gas pipes. The shockwave splintered the pavement. All the secret tunnels beneath the Cattle Branch caved in. Thick ragged gashes trailed from pothole to pothole until the section under my car crumbled. The G-Marq's rear dipped; its weight slid backward into its grave with the funeral procession of honking, twisted metal, and shattered glass.

I stared while feeling as if a bullet punched through my chest as the gloriously hypocritical earth swallowed my car one bite at a time until only the chrome grill remained. And gone with my car was my photo of Evelyn and Yanira.

I slumped. Another explosion. Another tremor. I hardly felt any of it.

The Cattle Branch received what it deserved as it collapsed in a cacophonous roar of rending wood, concrete, and ashes before it sank out of sight leaving a puffing black muddy crater smelling of smoke, decay, and ruin. Tomorrow, there would be police cars, fire engines, ambulances, and construction crews digging through the rubble for corpses. Their efforts wouldn't change anything. This time the Coven Ojáncanu Crimoire would stay buried.

"Let us go," Lacruz said wearily.

She stood; her control issues had apparently passed. I probably would've pulled it together a lot faster if I were a monster. But I was human. I needed a second. Hell, I needed a lot of them followed by a dozen donuts.

"That was lightning." My voice rang hollow. I faced her. "You *made* lightning and jumped a mile."

What I really wanted to say, *you're a monster. I trusted you and you're a fucking monster!* How much bad luck could a guy have in a night? Lacruz was a guajona, a blood witch. The Sangreino was real and Sera wanted it. I wasn't any closer to recovering Roxana. The words Hijo de Dirige made my head hurt. I lost my fucking ride and the photo of my daughter and ex-wife.

At least I still had my coat—my foul smelling, soiled, ripped, punctured, frostbitten and too far gone to be repaired coat. I sighed. I read the tally, but no matter how interesting I made the math, I still computed a losing equation.

Lacruz avoided my gaze. "Hardly a mile. The lightning was necessary."

Another female silhouette approached through the darkened rain. Dhyana wasn't alarmed so I decided not to spare the energy to be either.

Her face was still shadowed, but I could make out red leather so dark it was almost black and a tactical vest lined with explosives and ammunition. She carried an assault rifle crosswise against her chest like she knew how to use it. Her boots were military issue shit stompers.

I met soldiers during my time in the service, career skirmishers who preferred the uncertainty of the bush to the predictability of the concrete city and a firefight to a vacation in the Alps. She reminded me of them.

The woman ducked under Lacruz's shoulder, wrapped one arm around Lacruz's waist, and helped her walk. Now that the new arrival was closer, recognition gave me another shock of the night. The new arrival was Gabriela Fletcher-Rodriguez!

Gabriela brushed against me and interrupted my reverie. I shuddered and let the memory slip back into the dark. I was in a different place now, a different sort of danger. Gabriela had been wearing so much then. Now she was stripped bare. More like the woman who walked into my office.

Her proximity magnified the intensity of Lacruz's insistent touch. My body tensed before gentle convulsions rocked the neurons in my head and brought on a serene fatigue. Finished, Lacruz's hand drifted away. I turned to her. She met my eyes with a slight lip curve of enjoyment, the kind of smile women have when they hold sleeping babies or maybe when guajona are about to feed on sleeping babies.

She caressed my cheek with the back of her hand. "You take no pleasure in what I offer."

"Is your new odd way of talking a guajona thing?"

Our faces were close, kissing close, but even after her courtesy I couldn't bring myself to willingly place my flesh into her jaws. I would've kissed Natalie Lacruz without hesitation. Dhyana Nuberu was a monster and a complete stranger. That they were the same person made it confusing. It also made it hurt.

Lacruz sensed my hesitancy, smiled sadly, slid out of bed, and sauntered over to a trio of robes hanging on a decorative rack.

Sunlight leaked through the heavy curtains. I used the dim lighting to study the room. Plush surrounded me, not the kind listed as four bed and three bath, the decadent kind that screamed money to burn. The room held a scent of fresh cut wood. The fabrics were cream and crimson. The wooden furniture probably had fancy French names.

There were a lot of knick-knacks, doodads, and high quality classy stuff I didn't have the pedigree to comment on. The decor accentuated the fireplace, which was so clean I was sure it had never been used. Golden Spanish rapiers hung crisscross over the fireplace and above the rapiers was a portrait. Lacruz's or should I say Dhyana's canvassed eyes glared malice straight ahead while her head lay on the shoulder of a guy wearing a crown of roses that accented his pale, sterile features. His hand stroked her long dark flowing hair as if he had been petting a porcupine.

"Come," Lacruz said. She pulled her cream robe over her shoulders and cinched it at the waist. She held out a crimson one for me. I climbed out of bed leaving Gabriela to discover the wet spot.

"Where the hell am I?" I slid into the robe.

"The Mason Estate," Dhyana said. "My real home."

Natalie Lacruz had an apartment in the city filled with a few simple treasures. Awards for exemplar police work, mock blades and armor for her medieval fantasy stuff, and a collection of Molly Ringwald movies. Dhyana Nuberu rolled differently.

I was familiar with the Mason Estate. You could find it pictured on postcards at the Tierra Santa Airport. The Estate was old pale stone like bleached whalebones surrounded by dense trees and ivy covered walls. It was built in the nineteen hundreds in La Joya Hills by Laverne Mason, railroad tycoon. Mason died without heirs sometime in the late thirties.

The Estate exchanged hands until the seventies when the city took ownership, declared it a landmark, and upgraded the interior to hold weddings, graduation parties, and Bar Mitzvahs. The city stopped renting it out in the early nineties though it remained under the stewardship of the Tierra Santa Historical Society. Now, it belonged to a monster.

Lacruz quietly opened the door and I followed her into a hallway filled with expensive vases, thick rugs, and shiny baubles. The decorations were simple, perfect, and elegant, but lacked the personal touch of someone who filled their home with memories instead of museum pieces.

We entered a lounging area with lots of antique couches. Lacruz chose the largest one and stretched serenely like a feline on its favorite pillow. I lounged at the other end because the couch was too damn comfortable for plain old sitting. She shook her head in amusement, slid closer, and placed a hand on my shoulder. My skin warmed beneath her hand.

"Please excuse my ill manners," Lacruz said. "Your belongings are being cleaned and repaired. They will be returned once we have finished our conversation."

"And my car?" I tried to sound angry, threatening, or even menacing. Instead, my tone came out sullen, petulant, and pouty.

She searched my face. "I cannot rewind time though I can replace what has been lost. I suspect you would consider any recompense to be of lesser value to your precious Grand Marquis, yet I shall endeavor to make amends. For now, be assured you are not dinner."

Her new mannerisms and speech patterns were going to take some getting used to. I let the matter of the G-Marq slide. Not because she offered some kind of vague promise of replacement, but because fixating on it was going to make me cranky and when I was cranky, I behaved stupidly. Doing something stupid in a guajona's home was sure suicide.

"Then what am I?"

She smiled more fully, showing a row of perfectly human teeth. "A mint."

"Mints are eaten." Her uppity attitude was really starting to grate.

"Mints are not eaten, Cariño. They are savored."

I grimaced. My options weren't great. I was unarmed. We both knew she had the upper hand if this conversation devolved into a brawl. As long I was still breathing, an exploitable, table turning, advantage might come along.

"Any reason you've decided to start talking like a robot?"

She gave me a wry smile. "This is how I normally speak. This is who I am. Natalie Lacruz is the mask. Her performance requires a complete change in speech, body language, and carriage. Otherwise, Inquisitors like yourself would recognize my true face and cause me difficulties. I experienced constant discomfort at the possibility you would unravel my secret. It is quite a relief to dispense with the illusion. Be truthful, we would have not become friends if you had suspected my true identity."

Hell, I wasn't even close to suspecting anything. "So back at Delta Terrace, you could've beasted out and saved us without the house burning down?"

"You should have told me Gabriela hired you and that you allowed Roxana to be kidnapped."

I flinched. "You, uh, knew about that?"

"I trusted that you would not deceive me when it came to something as significant as a child's abduction."

"Why all this? Why pretend to be a cop? Why help me?" I should've realized something was up at Delta Terrace when she gave up shadowing me so easily.

"I'm not pretending. I'm a cop. I graduated the academy at the top of my class." She brushed invisible lint from the couch cushion between us. "My deception was not intended to hurt you. It was the best way to keep Roxana safe."

"And that worked out so great. What happened with Gabriela and Evan anyway?" The part of about Gabriela needing to arrange safe passage made sense. She knew Lacruz was a cop and could put out an APB. Gabriela could only escape if she evaded Lacruz's radar.

"I was surveying the crime scene at the Fletcher's home when you called about the Jungle Gem. When I saw Evan's remains, I knew Roxana was no longer a Nescient." Lacruz absently caressed the couch's fabric like it was the last time she would enjoy its feel. "We planned for this eventuality. Gabriela was supposed to bring Roxana to the Estate immediately. Only in the event of my death was she supposed to approach you."

Anger threaded Lacruz's voice. "Gabriela called, told me what happened, and assured me both she and Roxana were waiting at the Estate. I believed Roxana was safe, which is why I chose to aid you instead of checking on them." Lacruz scowled. "After Delta Terrace, I came to the Estate to confront Gabriela." Lacruz held my eyes. "She tried to kill me. After I subdued her, she told me she left Roxana in your care. before she tried to kill me. It was then I truly understood why Winnie and Brody were attacked, why you were searching for Sera, and why you were being secretive." She turned her hard gaze on me. "You lost Roxana."

I found it difficult to refute her accusation, mostly because she was right. I didn't take the kid's protection serious enough. I thought I learned that lesson with my daughter. Apparently not. "Sera turned Evan, I don't know how—wait, Gabriela tried what?!"

"She feared I was grooming Roxana for an illicit purpose and believed eliminating me was the best way to protect her daughter. I was able to... convince her otherwise. As to Evan, Seravina must've infected him."

I gave her a confused look.

"Crimson have two types of bites. One to feed and another to infect," Lacruz said. "Our infection spreads a portion of the Cleave into our victims. Over time, the Cleave acts as a mutagenic poison capable of killing the host while readying their bodies for reanimation. Repeated bites keep the infection at bay. The victim remains healthy unless they die of other means. An infected bite is the best method to enslave. I never infected Evan. He was paid handsomely to serve as Roxana's guardian."

It was interesting that Lacruz used Crimson, a term referencing membership in the Crimson Consortium, to describe both gargola and guajona. So *Crimson* bites aren't hit or miss when it comes to reanimation. They can control them. What was more interesting was Lacruz's naiveté. A paycheck meant zip when living under a death sentence. Sera probably bit Evan and threatened to let him die if he didn't do what she wanted and she wanted him to provoke Roxana. I shifted my weight. Evan was a victim; it would be a shame if he returned from the dead as a pawn.

"Did you?"

She nodded. "Neither Brody nor Evan will return as wights."

That was a tiny victory at least. "How did you find me?"

"I'm, as you say, a cop. I tracked the GPS on your phone. When I realized you were headed to the Cattle Branch, I deduced you must have located Roxana, otherwise why do something so suicidal. I assumed you would need back up."

"So you didn't lose your badge because of the fire?"

"I talked my way around it. My suspension starts Monday and will last until an internal investigation clears me. It's a real pain in the ass."

Lacruz didn't realize she changed the way she spoke. She was sounding more like the Lacruz I knew. This happened, once before, when she spoke about graduating the academy. Maybe there was more Lacruz in her than she realized. The danger of wearing a mask was that it became too real.

"They're canning you," I chuckled, feeling sad at the thought.

"I won't be canned. I have the best arrest record in my unit and a lot of friends who'll go to bat for me. This is my first major screw up. I—" She paused, her eyes growing round. She put a hand to her temple and shook her head a bit as if to clear the cobwebs. When she spoke, she was back to sounding like a robot. "Probation accompanied by months of desk duty is the most likely punishment."

Nice to know she wouldn't lose her fake job and would have to slum it back to this wealth. I tried to make my voice casual as I gestured about the room. "Who'd you rob for this?"

"I founded the Board of Trustees for the Tierra Santa Historical Society that acts as caretaker for this property. Since the Board's inception I have, through one proxy or another, managed Tierra Santa University and the Tierra Santa Public Libraries."

That was *blah blah blah* for I was filthy rich. If I had known, I would've asked for a loan. So Lacruz's alter ego was a philanthropist type with a hard-on for dusty books.

"Never seen your picture in the paper," I said.

"Nor have I seen yours." Her lips curled into a half smile. "Yet, we both do important work."

"You don't know me, lady. And I certainly don't know you."

"Would you feel more at ease if I resumed the mask?" She studied my face, looking for an honest answer. I looked away. She continued, "I make it my business to know citizens with lives outside of public domain, especially those who cause the Crimson Consortium considerable difficulty. As a native of Tierra Santa, your insights are especially useful."

We tried to kill Sera, ended up putting a bunch of wights out of their misery, and lowered the San Juan County's property values. Everything we had been through and 'As a native' was her grand fucking pick up line. I mean, damn, talk about halfhearted effort. I deserved better than that.

I rolled my eyes. "What, no blood sucker mission statement?"

"I find that term... unpleasant. Please refrain from its usage." Her tone remained even.

I snorted. I thought back to the painting in her bedroom and remembered the canvas I had in my coat pocket. They say there's truth in art if you study it. "Who was the guy in the painting above the fireplace?"

She stiffened. Her face remained a mask of serenity. None of it could hide the hate in her eyes. She craned her neck to study a vase in a corner of the room. She combed fingers through her short locks. "I have changed much since then, it hardly portrays me." A devilish spark ignited in her gaze. She closed the distance between us, pinned me against the backrest, and straddled me. "I have use of you."

Except for the longer hair in the portrait she looked identical. The differences she felt were internal. I grabbed her collar and pulled her close. "You want my immortal soul?"

"Oh nothing so seventeen hundreds," she laughed as our eyes met. "I am happy with your companionship." She slid a hand inside my robe and caressed my chest. "Our interests coincide. I want Roxana found and retrieved. Quickly. I want Sera eliminated. Discreetly."

She must've notice my skepticism because she paused and her voice softened.

"I am not threatening you, Cariño. Threats would make you... difficult."

I enjoyed the feel of her weight atop me. I slid my hands around her neck, my thumbs pressed under the hollows of her jaw. If I exerted full pressure, I might be able to snap her neck before she knew what happened. "What happened between you and Sera?"

Her lips became a thin line as her other hand found my arm and pulled back the sleeve revealing the tear drop tattoo on my wrist. She fingered the scar the tattoo tried to hide. Her response was careful and patient. "Her story is for later. That I promise. Let us remain focused on Roxana."

I saw resolve in her eyes, Lacruz's resolve—daunting, confident, and incorruptible. Her touch sent chills frolicking along my skin. I inhaled feverish air through clenched teeth. "Fine. What can I expect from her Drac bloodline?"

Lacruz regarded me thoughtfully. "Roxana's lineage is rare. Those of the Drac lineage were masterful shapeshifters who could assume the forms of all manner of beasts. The most powerful could turn flesh to stone like the Medusa of legend. After the Heritage War, the Drac lineage converged upon the single destiny." She held up a hand to forestall my question. "Do not ask. It is a long story I do not wish to tell. This much I will share—our Heritage War was like your American Civil War, Cariño, with a far sinister outcome."

Heritage War? It wasn't war I knew, read, or even heard of (there's public school education for you). Then I thought about the context and remembered a conflict between gargola, guajona, and mouros that fit the description. The details were fuzzy, the alcoholic kind of fuzzy. Eleventh or twelfth century, give or take, gargola and guajona turned on their mouros masters and exterminated them down to the last.

Mick would know more, but the main gist was that gargola and guajona were responsible for the genocidal extermination of mouros. The war was about power. The Crimson Consortium supplanted the old mouros regime.

Lacruz's sigh was followed by a slight headshake. "I had planned for Roxana to live out her life as a Nescient; in that form she posed no danger. Once she taps into the Cleave—" Lacruz made a decapitating gesture with the flat of her hand. "No mas, Cariño. There is as much folly in too much knowledge as there is in too little. Do what you will do anyway. Save the child. Kill her abductor. Your city and world is dependent. We are running out of time." Lacruz pouted seductively while caressing my cheek. "Make no mistake, I would see Roxana destroyed to ensure she is not misused. Perhaps, with the proper guidance, she can be kept in enough ignorance of her abilities to avoid breaking the world."

I searched her face for that nervous tick or tell that would let me know she was full of shit. It was obvious she was keeping her coven and Dueño out of the loop. Lacruz, like Sera, appeared to be operating independently. "Why me when you have a whole coven at your disposal?"

"Discretion, Cariño. It guarantees victory and is the most essential weapon one has at her disposal. When used properly, it defeats enemies quickly, quietly, and leaves no trace. You have a level of discretion I do not." She looked thoughtful. "I exist outside of my coven and the Consortium. I go through great lengths to keep my whereabouts and actions unknown. That is why Natalie Lacruz exists; she affords me a measure of freedom." She grinned suddenly. "I am a bit like you, something of a rogue."

She tightened her thighs around my waist. "Roxana is a matter I do not wish entrusted to anyone but you. If the Consortium were to learn of her, they would destroy her. None save you and I understand the value of protection. You can help me discreetly. I offer my companionship and answers to some questions. Others must remain buried until their proper resurrection. I have looked after Roxana since birth. I have watched her grow into the young girl she is today. I give my word that I intend you and the child no harm. Let that be enough."

I paused as if considering her argument despite already knowing how much I was willing to compromise. I grabbed both her wrists and pushed to create space. "No deal," I said, raising my voice. "I kill monsters. And now I'm supposed to stop because you want me to be your boyfriend?"

Her muscles tightened. I was keenly aware how much stronger she was and how vulnerable she made me feel. Dhyana Nuberu's proximity stripped me bare in the same way Natalie Lacruz's proximity did.

"I am not asking you to discontinue hunting Crimson," Lacruz whispered. "I ask that you save one girl." Her tone was frank in its disappointment. "If you have no desire for what I offer, then tell me what you would have."

I blinked. Could she make my Pequiñita breath again, run, laugh, and play in the sun? Could she save me from the dark? I wanted to stop reliving my daughter's death and go back to being a regular husband and father. I knew the impossibility, but I would settle for the illusion. Behind Lacruz's lips hid a fang, behind her complexion roamed the beast, and inside her heart hungered the Cleave. Lacruz was justice. Dhyana was death.

I could trace a line from the bridge of her nose to her athletic stomach. She licked her lips. Shivers of sweltering heat frolicked up and down my skin. My desire returned. I shoved finality into my tone, "You don't have anything I want."

Her face remained impassive as she eased off me. She uncoiled her legs with spider-like grace and crawled to the opposite end of the couch where she sat cross-legged and avoided my gaze.

I scooted up to a sitting position and tightened my robe's belt into a stranglehold. I already missed the warmth of her skin. Our waists had been so close that I was almost inside her.

"Knowledge?" She whispered, facing me again. "Only a fool refuses knowledge."

The electrified air between us hinted of passionate possibilities. Her robe had come open a little at the waist. I had the sudden urge to lick her exposed navel.

So tempting.

I clenched and unclenched my fists, closed my eyes, and pictured a half-ton geriatric in a bikini. When I was once again in control of my loins, I answered, "Call me, Jester."

"You have limited knowledge of the Crimson." She touched her neck right over the pulse point. "It is foolish to hunt what you do not understand. Eventually it will… bite you." She gave me a flash of fang. "Knowledge keeps you alive. I can teach you to see through our facades. No Crimson would be able to hide from you."

The more Lacruz used Crimson to describe gargola and guajona the more I hated it. It sanitized the monsters they were. It made them sound cute and harmless. "You'd sell out your own?"

"I ally with the strong, Cariño. The strong continue. If not…" She shrugged.

Having to drink blood as a morning pick-me-up rather than waiting in a long coffee line made me realize Lacruz saw one side of things. She was one of those survival of the fittest types. I sneered, "You're a Darwinist."

"Lamarckist." She corrected. "I believe in the inheritance of acquired characteristics. The strongest are predetermined by the fact they inherit the most profitable traits."

Lamarck? Okay, don't know that guy. "No matter how fit you are there's always someone stronger," I said. Her predatory nature prevented her from protecting the weak. She was a parasite who got fat off others. A guajona ascended or died at the cost of someone else's life. Her desire to protect Roxana had nothing to do with the child. Lacruz wanted power.

"*Sí?* I have yet to meet… that special someone."

Friendship meant nothing. I was a tool, a means to an end. No use feeling angry over it when she was ready to hand me a way to even things up. If I played this right and got Roxana on my side, Lacruz would have to deal with me as an equal and I would have something special for her ass. "What's Sera want with the Sangreino?"

Lacruz gave me an exasperated look.

"Me and Sera are of different minds where Roxana is concerned," she said.

"That doesn't answer why two guajona from the same coven are fighting over a kid. I want to know everything." I spread my hands. "Sorry lady, that's my price."

She stood and said nothing until her face darkened. She nodded gravely, the tiniest of yeses. "Diablo," she cursed. "My companionship stands, whether you reciprocate or not. Before I grant your request, you will need a shower, clothing, and food. I will see to your needs." She stood briskly and took several determined strides as if she was trying to walk herself into a bad decision.

I stood, rubbing circulation into my tense limbs. Victory felt like an empty box of donuts. Softly, I asked, "Were we really friends?"

She left the room without responding, but that didn't mean she never answered. In a few hours, I learned truths I wished I hadn't.

9 TAINTED OFFERINGS

The second guestroom was the type of space you would choose for a favorite uncle. The guestroom possessed a masculine coziness, sharp angled furniture, hard flat surfaces, and sparse decoration. A light breeze came from a pair of glass balcony doors thrown open. Cream curtains billowed in and out in smooth fluidity; the sun cast its glow through the fabric.

My focus was the bed. Draped across it were thick black cotton slacks, a long sleeved black and cream shirt, and a custom tactical vest with a built in holster. The prize of the litter was a sturdy black coat with cross-stitched elbows and shoulders, a blue inner lining, and Velcro vertical slits up to the waist to make side draws easier. I stumbled forward as if in a dream, sat on the edge of the bed, and smiled as I rubbed a hand over the coat's bullet proof Kevlar inner lining.

Lacruz leaned against the door frame, her face unreadable. I held up the coat, watched its darkness play in the light, and admired its sleek lines. The cracked steer skull emblem had been removed from my old coat and stitched onto this new one. I had a strong urge to try it on, to feel it settle across my shoulders. But with her scrutinizing eyes, I had to pass. Styling a new coat was too intimate an experience to share. I forced neutrality into my expression and returned the coat to the pile. Out of the corner of my eye, her shoulders drooped a bit.

"I suppose it's for me," I muttered, wondering when she had time to do this. "This looks custom."

"I like to be prepared, Cariño. Take a bath, get dressed, and I will send breakfast," she said coldly. "We depart within the hour." Stiff backed, she

116

turned to go.

"You promised the whole story."

She gave a slight nod. *And you shall have it*, she murmured before closing the door softly. I considered mulling over our conversation, but I was tired of words.

My rig, weapons, body armor, and tattered long coat were neatly placed on the floor next to a pair of sturdy steel toes. My Sig was cleaned, oiled, and loaded. Lacruz must've retrieved it while I was reeling from the lightning. The pistol-gripped axe leaned against the bed frame, shiny and sharp. Whoever serviced my weapons knew their trade.

This was all I had left; I lost my other gear and my photo of Yanira and Evelyn when my car was crushed. I stared at the tattered remains of my coat and wondered what else might be missing. I searched the coat; the fabric was shredded, frozen, singed, smelled of smoke, gasoline, blood, and rot. My wallet, the wrapped canvas filled with menace, and my cell phone blinking with urgent messages were still in its pockets.

With a sigh of relief, I set the phone on the bed and decided to check the voicemails later. I had a pretty good idea that it was Mick asking about the Cattle Branch. That was a conversation I didn't want to have right now. I began transferring weapons and ammo from the old rig to the new. Someone knocked. I drew the Sig, padded across the carpet, and opened the door.

Waiting patiently outside the threshold, Gabriela wore a simple red shirt with a black leather vest, jeans, and flat-soled boots. She carried a linen covered serving tray. The corners of her mouth tightened when her exhausted raccoon eyes touched my gun.

"If you need anything, use the intercom." She gestured to a brown call box on the wall. Gabriela removed the linen with a terse snap of the fabric and revealed a tray of fresh strudels, Danishes, fardelejos, and muffins. "The Mistress says you should eat."

I mentally ticked off points for the lack of glazed donuts, took the tray, and asked, "Aren't you supposed to be sleeping?"

Gabriela looked to where the clothes were laid out on the bed and pursed her lips in an unfriendly manner. Her attitude made me want to shoot her in the foot and watch as she hopped around in pain. I chuckled at the mental image.

She snorted in disgust and turned to leave.

Like I could leave it at that. "Is she really your kid?"

Gabriela's hair was pulled back into a disheveled ponytail and on her neck was a freshly scabbed over pinprick of Lacruz's bite. Gabriela twisted sharply, her body rigid and eyes flashing rage. She started to say something, thought better of it, and turned away again. "Please do use the bath."

"So, you're full of shit," I spat, crossing my arms over my chest. "That little song and dance in my office with the crocodile tears and the *you're-my-only-hope* routine... Seems you're a better liar than a mother."

She spun, fists clenched, livid with animal fury. She took a step. I activated the Sig's safety, shoved it into my waistband, and raised my fists.

Guajona might kick my ass. Her, I would knock into next week.

She raised her hands offensively and took a step. Sweat broke out on her forehead. Another step. She swayed and stared down at her shaking fists. In fact, her whole body had begun to tremble.

Looks like, this time, her betrayal came from within. I smirked. I bet she didn't like how it felt. I remembered Lacruz's description of the two types of bites and wondered which kind Gabriela received. An infected bite could be the reason for her lethargy or it could be a trick to catch me off guard. I sighed, lowered my fists, and stepped away from the bed.

Gabriela, breathing deeply, stared at me. She nodded acquiescence, stumbled to the bed, and slumped down with her face hidden behind her hands. Too much blood taken and not enough rest left her with too little gas to fire up the engines for the defense of her pride. Her slack skin was sickly pale. She looked used up. She sat as upright and used her knuckles to wipe away the tears in the corners of her eyes.

"I tried to betray her," she sniffed. "Back at your office, I tried to betray Mistress Dhyana. When I saw what Roxana had done to Evan, I knew. I knew what Mistress Dhyana would do if I told...." Gabriela used the sleeve of her shirt to wipe away snot dripping from her nose. "Roxana *is* my daughter. Whatever you may think. She is mine. And I failed." Her voice cracked and she began sobbing the dry kind of distress.

I used vinegar and now it was time for honey. I stepped closer, kneeled in front of her, put my hand on her knee, and stared into her tears. "I had a daughter, too. There's no worst crime for a parent. No heavier guilt than failure." She winced. I continued, "It doesn't matter if you do everything you can. It doesn't matter if you couldn't anticipate the danger. All that matters is there's a hole in your heart. Always a hole. They like to say time heals wounds, but it never does. Never." I would always be empty without my Evelyn. I stopped, took a deep breath, and continued, "Roxana is still alive." I twisted the knife. "You still have a chance. Maybe I can do something. Maybe. But I need the full story."

Gabriela stared as if I was some alien creature fresh from Saturn who must've body-snatched Kensington Ashe. Whoever this new guy was, she must've liked him a whole lot better because she began speaking in a thickened accent.

"What I told you before about Dhyana saving my life was true. I grew up in El Salvador during the tail end of our civil war. Being a guerrilla for the FMLN taught me everything I learned about fighting." She paused. "It was there I met Lucio Miguel Ramirez, Ro's father." She smiled tired and genuine. "He was twenty-two, handsome in a shaggy way, troubled eyes, and a fellow guerilla in my unit. He had a long scar here." She traced a line from her chin to her shoulder. "He loved talking social reform. He wanted to be a political science professor so he could teach the next generation how to make changes in policy without bloodshed. He had, at best, a fourth grade education." Her mouth twisted at the irony.

"Neither of us could handle the fighting," she continued. "It was too much chaos, too much fear, too much uncertainty, and we were too young. We fled the fighting to the north. We travelled on foot, in trucks, and sometimes under them. We settled in Mexico City. We found work. Not high paying, but enough for a place of our own. We'd escaped the war. Or so we thought... Some things you can't run from. For two years, we tried our hand at normal living, but the things we saw and did during the fighting... Drugs helped, for a while. We didn't know anything about gargola, guajona, mouros, or bloodlines. I didn't know Miguel was a Nescient gargola. I don't think he knew either. I wasn't there when it happened. All I know is that Miguel returned home one evening a changed man. A gargola." She shrugged. "The rest I've already told you."

"So how did you end up here?" I asked.

She shuddered and smiled bitterly. "I failed to see the changes in Evan. Sure, Evan seemed emotionally distant and less interested in sex, but marriages have rough patches." She spread her hands as if to say, *It's not my fault.* "Imagine my shock when I got home on Friday to see him splayed on the floor with my daughter leaning over him." Gabriella swallowed hard. "Feeding." Her expression twisted in pain and grief. Her voice dropped to a dim echo. "There was a contingency."

She took a deep breath and plowed ahead. "In the eventuality that Ro drank human blood, I was supposed to bring her straight to Dhyana. But I couldn't." Gabriela dug fingernails into her scalp and her hair piled up like a freeway accident. "It wasn't fair. During the war too many children died from hunger, sickness, for being too small, too dark, for playing in the wrong spot when the bombs exploded or from the firefights with the government." She met my eyes. "I wanted Ro's life to be different."

I nodded because I understood. I would've happily pissed in the devil's ear to wake him if it meant protecting my daughter. "I was plan B."

"My Mistress told us to leave Roxana in your care if she were killed," Gabriela said.

"You tried to take her out."

"Yeah," she breathed. "It was a quick and pathetically one-sided fight. I figured she'd kill me for turning against her. She said we should work together to save Ro." Gabriela touched the bite on her neck. "When I told her I left Ro with you, she got very angry. I thought she was going to eviscerate me. It turned out she knew you had lost my daughter."

"Did you know she was a cop?"

Gabriela's eyes widened. "It's why I couldn't go to the police."

"Sera worked at the Jungle Gem. I think that's where she sunk her hooks into Evan," I mused.

"Do you think I would've let Evan go anywhere near that place?" Gabriela snapped.

It was the rare wife who didn't mind her husband going to strip clubs. My knees creaked as I rose to my full height. I began pacing to let the scenario marinate a bit. Despite Gabriela's protest, I was pretty sure that was where Evan and Sera met. Sera either seduced or infected him and threatened to cut him off, in both senses, if he didn't follow orders. I remembered the confusion in Evan's death rattle. The contradiction between Sera and Lacruz's orders drove a wedge down his center. He was torn between trying to hurt Roxana and trying to protect her.

Sera probably ordered Evan to attack Roxana knowing it would unleash the kid's inner beast. Gabriela walked in on the tail end of a lost fight and rushed Roxana to my office before Sera or Lacruz could grab her. I frowned. Why would Sera wait if she knew where the kid lived and who her guardians were? Why not kill the guardians and take the kid? It was far less risky. Then I remembered, Sera said something about wanting to seduce me first. That was her plan. Seduce me and then nab the kid. She never got to the first part because I hadn't left my office in over a month. Sera's plan turned to shit when I showed up at the Jungle Gem with the kid. Sera panicked and was forced to improvise.

"It wasn't supposed to go down at the house," I realized. I stopped pacing and faced Gabriela. "I don't think Evan was supposed to attack Roxana at all. Sera already knew where to find her. The only reason she wouldn't immediately grab the kid was if she had something else to accomplish first."

Gabriela frowned at me.

I slapped my forehead with the palm of my hand. This whole time I believed Sera was one step ahead. But she wasn't. She had been trying to hold together a busted scheme. It wasn't easy to create a wight. A guajona has to be at peak power to make one, which meant a lot of feedings. On average, guajona could create a wight every two to three days. Sera must've been reanimating for months to amass the amount of wights she had in her basement and those she threw at us in the Cattle Branch.

A monster wouldn't invest that much time and power without an endgame in mind. Sera created an army as if preparing for war... Sera definitely hadn't banked on losing a good chunk of her army due to yours truly. A cold death's head grin etched its way across my face.

I loved ruining someone's day.

Another thought occurred. Maybe tracking the kid was a waste of time. Maybe the best play was to make Sera come to me. To do that, I would need something she desperately wanted. I fixed my eyes on Gabriela and gripped her tight by the shoulders. "Do you know where the Sangreino is?" Her head flopped side to side in more or less a no. I squeezed tighter until she winced. "But Lacruz does?"

Gabriela's eyes dropped to her lap. Her silence was all the answer I needed. I shoved Gabriela. She slipped off the bed, arms flailing, and thumped onto the floor.

I grabbed the clothes, the tray, and headed to the bathroom to take myself a quick shower. I left Gabriela in a confused mess on the floor. Why bother? I knew she would be gone by the time I finished.

The bathroom was pretty much more cream and crimson. A large mirror, plenty of toilet paper, thick cream rugs, matching towels, and a stadium-sized marble tub with rows and rows of shampoos, conditioners, oils, and soaps filled the ample space. I balanced the tray on the sink and piled the clothes, coat, and boots atop the toilet.

I picked up the shower gel. My nose wrinkled.

Lavender and Jasmine Twilight.

I set it down.

No way in hell.

I grabbed the edge of the sink feeling the walls close in. I was trapped in potpourri reminders of another life, another me. For eight years, I had a family. For eight years, I had a wife who made sure the bathroom smelled like a damn garden. That was gone. *Gone but the hurting.* I swallowed the past, pulled myself together, turned on the faucet, and dipped my head so the warmth ran down my face.

As the droplets dribbled under my chin, I forgot guajona, dead children, and ex-wives. There was me, the sink and the water. I cherished the sound of each drop reverberating against the marble, together yet different, like people. It was a simple procession, no fear, no lust, no regret, only the gentle singular purpose of gravity.

I shut off the faucet, dried my face, and started the shower. It took a minute to scrape the soot, grime, and dried blood off my skin. When that was done, I exited the shower feeling refreshed. I toweled dry, held my breath against the earthy scent of perfumed soap wafting off of me, and eyed the pastry tray. Though the pastries were moist from the steam, I devoured them between pulling on each piece of clothing. The underwear, shirt, pants, and boots fit perfectly; it was remarkable how exact Lacruz guessed my size. After lacing up my boots, I brushed crumbs from my fingers.

One thing was missing.

I held my new coat up to the light. The black had iridescent blue undertones the same hue as the teardrop tattoos on each of my wrist. The looped weave gave the coat a chainmail appearance. Its Kevlar and Nomex blend made the thick fabric bulletproof, fire resistant, and water repellent. The coat had two large zip hand pockets, inside cargo pockets, full length zip front, removable cross-stitched padding for the shoulders, elbows, and back; adjustable cuffs, two chest pockets, a drop tail rear hem, and Velcro vertical slits for easy draws from a waist holster.

The blue inner lining had strange sigils that would've appeared to be a stylish design to anyone unfamiliar with brujeria. The jacket had wards for extra durability—a coat like this wasn't sweatshop made though it probably cost a few souls. I slipped into the left sleeve and a shudder of bliss ran up my arm. This coat felt like home. I slid my right arm into the other sleeve and let the fabric settle about my shoulders. It was feather light despite the density of the material.

I spun around while enjoying how freely the coat moved; it was like wearing air and wouldn't hamper me in a fight. I cleared the mirror of mist, pointed my index finger like a gun, and cocked my thumb. I looked damn good. Dangerously stylish. *Gangsta.* The pastries were gone leaving fruity glop on the tray, which I scraped up with a finger and sucked clean. I rinsed the sticky residue off my hands and left the bathroom.

The guest room was empty. I was happy to see Gabriela gone. I tried to find sympathy for what she was going through as a mother with a missing daughter presumed to be a monster, but all I had was anger and blame. This could've all gone so differently if Gabriela had trusted me with the truth. I shook my head. I mean, I would've understood... after I tried to kill her daughter... Maybe.

I drifted over to the bed and finished switching over my gear. I made doubly sure to put the wrapped canvas in the pocket of my new coat and noticed a different effect; it appeared the coat's warding shielded the evil spewing from the canvas. Impressive. Done with the mundane tasks, I started looking for trouble when she reappeared. Lacruz pushed open the door and stepped into full view.

I stared.

Brown suede hip huggers covered her legs like she had been dipped in milk chocolate. The cream low cut blouse fringed with ruffles was like whipped cream, and the sparkling ruby signet on her finger, the adorning cherry on top. I did my best to slow my pulse because my heart was over the speed limit and I didn't want a ticket or a heart attack.

A broad grin split her cheeks. She gave me a couple minutes to pull myself together before motioning for me to follow her down the hall. "You appear ready for answers. Come." As we walked, she said, "As a Nescient, what I desired most was family, a hard working husband, four strong sons, and two daughters. Simple it must sound to you, I know. I come from different sensibilities."

I considered her words. Lacruz was so devilishly sexy; I couldn't picture her as a soccer mom doing minivans and lattes. "Never had any rugrats?"

"I discovered sexual pleasure after I had taken my first life," she shrugged. "Vega Nuberu, a rogue, a drifter, and scoundrel singled me out from my family and introduced me to my heritage rather abruptly. The trauma left me barren." Her expression soured. "He devoured my dreams for a normal life. He set a future for me I did not request." Lacruz stared blankly. "As a male, you cannot understand the loss. Women are the bearers of life and when such a choice is removed from our lives without consent we become intractable. Many years of terror followed; I preyed upon village girls and their families. I forced mothers to watch while I destroyed their children. I did so out of malice and jealousy. It took several centuries for me to rise above such pettiness."

Why the hell was she telling me this? I felt myself growing angry. I pictured her standing in my kitchen, over the corpse of my daughter, smiling that breathtaking smile. Was she the monster who invaded my home? My hand moved closer to my Sig. At this range, I couldn't miss. At this range, I would take her fool head off.

"I tell you this," she said. "So you have complete understanding of my past sins." She looked sideways at my hand inching closer to my gun. Her gaze remained fixed until I relaxed and moved it away. She continued talking as if nothing occurred.

"Next came self-deception. I thought perhaps my body was okay." She touched her stomach. "So I had sex, century's worth of sex." She spread her hands to show the emptiness between them. "When no children conceived from those unions, I began adopting. But human lives passed too quickly. I tired of funerals and making excuses for why 'mother' did not age. I distanced myself from my adopted family, my coven, and the Consortium. I came to accept my fate." Her lips parted. "Never let anyone decide your path, Kensington. Not even me."

"What happened to Vega?"

She glanced at me, shrugged, and remained silent. I could've pressed, but I sensed it was one of those corpses she would keep buried despite my digging. She touched my arm. "The Fletchers were not my Servants. They were free of infection. I believed I had earned their loyalty. No sabía!" Lacruz said. "After I questioned Gabriela, I discovered what that mierda Evan had tried. I could not even sate my rage with his slow death. Fue mi fracaso, the mistake is mine. Had I—"

What more could she say? She fucked up.

We exited the Estate's front door and onto a cobblestone driveway wide enough to host the Indy 500. A BMW waited, Gabriela sat in the front seat looking better groomed though still crappy.

Dhyana turned to me. "Gabriela is my Servant now. She will die before she disobeys."

She was pretty much admitting she infected Gabriela. It took all my composure to keep my expression blank, but I wasn't going to jump because Gabriela let herself get played.

As if to change the subject, Lacruz touched the pocket holding the canvas. "You found this in Sera's home."

"Yeah," I said warily. A shiver ran down my spine. Why wasn't I surprised she had gone through my pockets? It was probably because she was a cop and cops were nosy.

Lacruz's features hardened as she stared off into the distance. She nodded. "That scrap is one of the few remaining mouros portraits in existence. Only a dozen or so were commissioned to begin with and most of those were lost or destroyed making it difficult to sift truth from myth. Man may have forgotten; those who you label as monsters have not."

She stared at the manicured trees populating her estate. "There is a truth we all believe," Lacruz continued. "Every millennium, Cuélebre, El Padre de los Monstruos—the father of all monsters..." She gave me a sideways smirk. "It is good you know of him," she added. "Cuélebre awakens and challenges his children's right to exist through combat. If his children are victorious, then Cuélebre slumbers for another millennium and if Cuélebre is victorious, he razes the planet, human, and monster alike, clearing the landscape for a new generation of his progeny. Mouros, the monsters man feared, hunted, and scorned, were the guardians who defeated Cuélebre every time he awakened. Man owes their prosperity to mouros."

"Why would the mouros protect us?"

"Mouros were protecting themselves. Cuélebre would've considered them too weak to deserve life and destroyed everything—mouros and human alike. Cuélebre would cleanse the earth and father even deadlier monsters. Mouros fought to preserve their existence. Preserving humanity was a byproduct." Lacruz pointed at hidden canvas. "Our history says, the mouros who struck the victory blow was Vasco and he commissioned that painting at the mouth of Cuélebre's cave, a location in the hills of Spain lost to time. The entire image was Vasco standing over the defeated Cuélebre. The hunger seeping from the canvas is tied directly to Cuélebre and there are those who would use it to locate him. Have care Kensington. Keep it safe."

Apparently, I had a ticking time bomb in my possession. I agreed the canvas was dangerous, but I wasn't quite sure about it being a compass leading to Armageddon. It was another mystery to figure out after Roxana was safe.

"Why would Sera have it? Does she want to wake up the big boss?" I could tell by the harsh line of Lacruz's mouth she didn't like that idea.

"Possibly," she said. She climbed into the passenger seat, leaving me to ride in the back.

I stared at the Mason Estate's unforgiving gray stone. Lacruz offered me a place where I didn't belong—at her side. My next visit to the Estate would include a few Inquisitors, some blowtorches, and lots and lots of explosives.

We drove into the sunny afternoon a little past two o' clock. I expected to be taken to some super-secret guajona lab, a defunct haunted castle, a secluded warehouse district or anyplace else except where we ended up.

The Southside Galleria, the largest and most profitable mall in Tierra Santa, loomed like a giant glass state prison with more advertising and fewer fences. The mall had everything else, why not the deep dark secrets of the gargola and guajona? The most evil location in the city was a consumer's wet dream stocked with goods you would have to hawk a kidney to afford and a triple-decked social hub where desperate housewives caught movies or maybe clapped to the seedy jazz players who hadn't the luck or talent to make it big.

The twenty-plex movie theatre on the first floor, near the main entrance, remained accessible after the stores closed. The food court took up a two-fifths of the second floor and the remaining three-fifths were designer-imposter boutiques stacked like books at a library. The third floor contained mostly electronics, toys for kids and adults, and the other pricey garbage. The mall was bookended by two consumerism wardens masquerading as major department stores.

We pulled into a cordoned employee lot and parked in an executive space near the front entrance. A packed mall on a Sunday was hardly surprising when spending never sleeps.

Lacruz stared at the crowd of people. She whispered in Gabriela's ear. Gabriela nodded, put on a pair of sunglasses, and leaned back in the driver's seat as if to take a nap. Lacruz and I exited the BMW and joined the mindless thralls jumping and skipping their way to happy happy fun time of shopping.

Cool air hit me in the face as we passed through the mall's electric doors. A boy and a girl about Roxana's age hugged goodbye outside the twenty-plex. I watched them part, faces and cheeks flushed with youthful enthusiasm. She gave a wave that was all fingers. He nodded but couldn't hold in his metal-braces smile.

I envied them.

That was what teens should be doing, handholding and first kisses while responsible parent should be scaring off parasitic, oversexed, pimple-faced suitors... with firearms if necessary.

That would be the life.

Lacruz took my arm as we passed the directory, some benches, and Giovanna's Lingerie. I kept pace in silence as she pulled me along like we were a couple. She spared a fraction of a second to look at the expensive merchandise in the display windows as we walked. I didn't understand the reason for the pretense. At best, I was a glorified wallet when it came to shopping.

My heart had practically given out on my first trip to the little girls section with Evelyn. I had brought her to the mall while Yanira stayed home sick. As soon as we entered the kid's clothing store, my Pequiñita ran in, grabbed this and that, and asked, *is it pretty, Daddy?* (I said yes to everything.) We marched a pile of brightly colored shirts, pants, and dresses totaling more than I had to spend to the checkout counter. My daughter's puffy flushed cheeked grin had made the debt worth it.

Despite the faux-shopping, I leaned closer to Lacruz. I inhaled her roses and vanilla perfume and found myself missing the apples and gun oil. The last time I felt relaxed next to a woman was during my blissful, won't-be-able-to-pay-next-month's-mortgage, expensive, honeymoon dinner. Yanira had a salad, which she assured me was worth the flight to Miami. Later that evening, after she excused herself to powder her nose, we snuck down to the beach where the blue waves lapped feverishly to lay in each other's arms.

Lacruz came to a complete stop.

"Something wrong?" I scanned the faces around us and saw regular people going about regular business.

Lacruz gave me a quick squeeze before pulling me toward a silver door marked for employees. I noted the subtle tension in her stride. Her hesitancy made me feel protective. With all the confusing emotions Lacruz/Dhyana generated, protective was an emotion I could understand. Lacruz removed a plastic badge from her pocket and clipped it to her shirt. She handed me another stamped with some semblance of official mall credentials. I put it on while she slid a key into the door and twisted the knob. How many plastic badges did this woman carry?

We entered some sort of service tunnel large enough to drive a car through. The ceiling lights were spaced apart by ten feet. The smooth walls were devoid of any decoration or personality. Numbered silver doors matched the echoing brown tile. The tunnel appeared clean though it smelled of grease, urine, and stagnate heat.

I began to sweat.

She turned left and kept a steady pace with me following close behind. I was content following the hypnotic sway of her butt until I heard a distant squeak-scrape. A few minutes later, a couple of uniformed deliverymen pushing a squeaky loading cart stacked neck high with boxes came toward us. I tensed. They could be more dangerous than they appeared.

Lacruz flashed a wide grin, said good afternoon, and moved to the side to give them ample room to pass. The workers replied joyously with eyes riveted to her plunging neckline. They kept looking back over their shoulders, whistling and nudging each other in the ribs until we were out of sight.

It was entertaining, to say the least, to see how other guys reacted to Lacruz especially since nobody reacted like that when she was in 'Detective Lacruz' mode. It made me more aware of my impulses, how juvenile they were, and how it was best to keep them bottled. There wasn't any cool way to drool.

"These service tunnels are used infrequently," she said as she traced her fingers along the wall. "They connect the entirety of the mall. The major outlets prefer their private delivery entrances."

"You own this mall, don't you?"

The shadows hid her expression. "If you remember correctly, this lot had boasted the city's largest library, a park, and an open stage for concerts and farmers' markets. I always intended this location to be a place where people gathered. They did not. Study and the arts proved less of a draw so I paved it flat, built a mall, and this location has been heavily frequented ever since."

The Galleria was at least five years old, which meant she had been operating in the city for at least that long. A crafty enough guajona had no trouble keeping off the Inquisition's radar. It was troubling to think how many monsters were on the down low. Until today, I considered myself an expert at picking them out of a crowd. Yesterday, I faced two women who successfully fooled me; one of which I considered a close friend. Maybe Lacruz was right about my ignorance.

We stopped at a door etched with the number fourteen and Lacruz produced a second key. As the door swung inward, the light from the tunnel spilled onto a narrow corridor connected to a slash of stairs leading down. We stepped inside the corridor. Light disappeared as the door *thumped* shut, leaving us stranded in black. I blinked, waiting for my eyes to adjust. I waved my hand in front of my face. I couldn't see it or make out Lacruz's silhouette. Her perfume was the only indicator of her proximity.

She took my hand. "The decline is steep."

Was a handrail really too much to ask for? Heaven forbid an accidental death when there were enough purposeful ones to go around.

Guajona had night vision and impeccable balance so navigating a darkened stairway meant nothing to them. Those of us humans with poor balance and aversions to broken necks considered the lack of lighting on the ruthless side. Still, I refused to be led like a child. I shook off her hand, took out my penlight, and flashed its narrow beam down past her shoulder to see where the stairs ended. Shadow swallowed my light.

She began her descent. I sighed and followed, resigned to the insanity of the whole situation. This was the second time I was walking into danger under-armed and ill-informed. Why did beautiful women make me so stupid that I was willing to dive into the most horrible situations despite my instincts screaming otherwise?

I did this in my marriage when I followed Yanira into the abyss of her addiction. Maybe it was the thrill of the unknown, or because bad girls had so much more fun that I wanted to be at the party.

We descended single file to the droning *clack* of our footsteps. The temperature dropped. Goosebumps rose on my arms. It felt like I entered a second ice age. The cold didn't bother me nearly as much as the dark. My eyes still couldn't make out anything beyond my penlight's halo. The door, the only way out, had disappeared some time ago. The smart part of me, the part I rarely listened to, wanted to turn around, climb back up, and make a break for it.

My calves were starting to cramp. I was sweating profusely despite the lower temperature. I wanted to stop and rest. Lacruz easily kept the pace. I decided to suck it up and deal. I didn't mind if she thought I was soft in the head. Soft in the body? Never. After about forever and a day, to my groaning relief, we reached the bottom, a low ceiling dead end perfect for a tomb. This was the right spot to leave me bleeding where no one would come searching.

Up ahead was a stone wall that didn't look natural. She found a curved stone and twisted it upward. Underneath was an electric keypad. She punched in digits. There was a silent *whisking* sound. Rock slid inward and sideways.

We entered a square blank room full of light, a lobby of sorts spacious enough to garage a tank. I put away my pen light. A vault door was imbedded into what appeared to grayish stone. The vault door itself was five foot high and three feet across, perfect for a pygmy. In its center were a large ring and an unmarked circular disk that appeared to be a combination lock.

Lacruz put her ear to the metal, her face a picture of painted concentration while her fingers danced deliberate along the tumbling disk. Metal *clicked* and *whirred* until the final twist. She stepped back, grabbed the ring handle, and pulled.

The steel door, thick as my forearm from wrist to elbow, slid open painfully slow on the silence of well-oiled hinges. Pale sickly yellow light spilled through the opening. A stench flooded the lobby like an ill wind through a diseased sphincter. I gagged at the taste of thrice cursed decomposed flesh and sweaty ham. I cupped my mouth and nose.

My tongue had gone dry. Those pastries from breakfast rose up in revolt. They rocketed out of my stomach and burned their way up to my throat where they fought to be the first partially digested mush out of my mouth. I clamped my jaw shut and forced my throat closed. Nothing was going in or out. Not even air. Vomit splashed against my will. In the end, my breakfast turned back the way it came and slopped back into my stomach where it plotted its revenge exit from the opposite orifice. I clenched my buttocks until cramping and discomfort subsided. When I was positive my undies would stay white, I relaxed the gluteus.

Lacruz ducked and shimmied sideways into the vault. I hesitated, checked my stomach first to make sure it was still somewhat settled, and then clicked off the safety on my Sig. A deep breath would've spelled disaster. Instead, I let air pass shallowly through my nose before ducking and shimmying behind her.

The odor was even worse on the other side of the door. My stomach gurgled. My will wavered. A sharp clinging stench of a field of the dead gouged my nostrils. My eyes ached from the brightness. I blinked rapidly until they adjusted.

The overhead lights left an eerie yellow glow on the dull chiseled stone.

Not the most romantic spot for a first date and to be honest I expected classier digs from a rich guajona. Lacruz dragged me to what appeared to be a medieval prison, one of those nice ones without the screams, rats, or sadism. A damn unimpressive patchy crimson rug on the floor like a dime store toupee faced a stone chair.

My hands ached. A tingling numbness crawled up my limbs where it needled its way into my chest with its poisonous cold. My lungs rattled raspy and thick. I coughed. Pale puffs of warm air billowed and disappeared. At least, I was getting used to the smell so I no longer felt the urge to vomit

"I can dispel your chill," she offered.

"Where's the light coming from?" My skin had cooled from the walk down. I shivered. I pulled my long coat tight against my body, crossed my arms over my chest, and buried my fists under my armpits to conserve warmth. The cold wasn't the worse thing in the room. There was something far more sinister and frightful. I hardened my soul to be as unyielding as a black diamond.

A seven foot tall garish monstrosity of a chair, so twisted no human hand could've carved it, loomed. The hair on my arms stood at attention. The chair's appearance had a scaly quality that revealed deeper shades of bruised reds and wounded purples. Its reptilian overlapping plates lacked symmetry and artistry. It was a mockery of a throne, a corrupted gypsum of sharp jutting spines radiating cold like a winter storm.

Rain and floods.

Two bipolar voices gibbered in my head. The first urged me to run while the second cackled that it was already too late. I was frozen in place as if the chair had reached out a huge fist and gripped my soul.

"Welcome, Kensington. The Sangreino awaits," Lacruz's voice boomed awe and lust.

I shook my head to break the chair's hold on me. I jutted my chin at the chair, more angry than scared. The Sangreino? I wanted to laugh and cry. A chair? A fucking evil chair?

Mick would've pissed himself to know how fucking wrong he had it. All of his guajona and gargola interrogations as he pressed heated crucifixes to their eyes, smashed their bones into paste, and fed them poisoned blood until they puked up organs yielded nothing. Not one of his victims revealed the Sangreino was a chair. All those goddamn years I thought he spouted crazy.

Talk about your ironies.

"You are the first human to see this." She nodded gravely. "Try and run Cariño and its image will be seared into your mind. It will even follow you into the deepest depths of madness. You must face it like any beast. Respect it. Conquer it. Find the *belleza,* the beauty, in the blackest shadow."

She climbed the dais and eased into the seat; her back pressed the spines. She crossed her legs and regarded me with a hunger that caused my testicles to rise up tight against my groin. Unbothered by the spines, she languidly stroked the armrests reminiscent of how she touched me this morning, which caused heat to rush to my cheeks.

A slow smile crested her lips. She touched her nose against the right armrest. Her gaze held me. Her tongue darted, fast and pink, licking the armrest until she found the spot she wanted. Her fang lengthened, white against the purple, and scored the surface of the stone. The powerful muscles in her jaw tensed.

My eyebrows shot up. For the life of me, I couldn't figure out why she would want to bite a chair. I was ready to laugh, point, and unload a smart assed remark. A soft crunch, stone gave, her fang sank in as if the seat were made of chocolate.

A burst boil *pop* echoed and black liquid as thick as crude oil oozed from the puncture. The liquid was thick with a reflective sheen like polished metal. The odor hit in one solid wave. It wasn't the kind of odor that made you gag or turn away. It was the kind of awful that was interesting enough to make you inhale and try to decipher what it was. It was seductive, that proverbial bad girl you couldn't turn away from. The closest odor that came to mind was that of bushels of partially rotted cherries.

My agitated throat caused me to swallow heavily. I licked my lips.

Lacruz buried her face in the ooze with a ravening joy that would paint the walls red and sucked in the rush without losing a drop. I admit curiosity. Like at a restaurant when you see a guy eating a juicy steak you can't afford and you wonder what the steak must taste like. That longing enveloped me. I hated every moment of the temptation.

I trembled. Sheer shock, false bravado, and the belief she might rip me bloody and staple the chunks to the wall kept me from making any sudden moves. Her expression altered to one I hoped to never see again. The same expression my wife had when I found her, half-lidded eyes staring off into the distance, slumped on the living room carpet in a curve of a loose C as if she had fallen off the couch. Her arm was noosed with rubber. A bent burnt spoon blackened with remnants of something foul smelling caked in its bow lay with a lighter where both must've tumbled from her fingers. A needle had quivered in her arm.

It was hard to see someone you love crawling into their personal hell, the slurred words, the lethargy, the guilt—yours, not theirs, because they were too damn high to feel anything and that was the point. Yanira had been trying to erase herself for years, first by running away from home at fifteen, then with marriage by assuming the role of wife to someone she never cared to know, and later by being the mother to a child she couldn't nourish.

In the end, she completed the ultimate erasure and disappeared from our lives. Her death would've been easy to handle because I could've ordered a death certificate as evidence of her departure. She went *poof* with all the question marks it entailed. If I was honest, I had difficulty dealing.

Lacruz asked me to face the chair. She was wrong. I needed to accept that I couldn't save my wife because she couldn't save herself. As a man and as a husband, there was only so much you could do with a partner who decided to rush headlong into destruction. In the end, you were given two options: you could be dragged into oblivion with them or you could enable them to an early grave.

Stopping an addict was impossible unless you reached them. Reaching an addict was impossible while their personal needle drip dissolved their souls. Seeing Lacruz taking a hit from an evil stone chair reminded me of my marriage, my failure, my guilt, my hurt, and ultimately my deniability.

Lacruz pulled away from the armrest. The puncture wounds sealed into a smooth stone callus that cut off the flow of the black liquid. The remaining droplets on the armrest's surface were immediately reabsorbed. She relaxed against the Sangreino's hard planes. Her eyelids fluttered over inky black irises while her tongue cleared the residue from her trembling lips. Her chin drooped to her chest, nodding for about fifteen seconds, before her head snapped up alert. She sat up straight, smoothed her shirt until she was once more composed, and reached out.

I licked dry lips with a drier tongue. "I'm flattered that you want to exchange crack pipes. But this... this is insane."

Her hand dropped. She took the patient tone of a kindergarten teacher. "You must understand what you hunt. This is your opportunity. An opportunity no human has had." A lone finger traced slow circles along her thigh. "You will be unable to protect Roxana unless you submit."

I wondered if life as a monster solved needs like food, hygiene, finance, and love. There was always a point in an Inquisitor's career where some beasty offered you power, riches, or a fifty percent off coupon for underwear and socks in exchange for their life. After so many bribery attempts, the offers just seemed silly.

I met her gaze with all the force of my denial.

She smirked. "My invitation is mere courtesy. I choose to placate your ego even though your prior encounter with Sera has aptly demonstrated you are ill equipped to handle what comes. You must understand; the next time she will throw her full strength against us. You must be prepared."

"Make your point," I said. I kept my face blank. My reluctance had nothing to do with what happened at The Cattle Branch and everything to do with what dangled between us. Trust.

Her expression hardened. She shook her head, tapped the armrest impatiently, and studied me as if deciding which lie to tell. "Kensington, your ignorance is—" She clicked her teeth, leaned forward, and answered like a dare. "Stubbornness is your least desirable trait. I am sure you know that. To 'make my point' as you say, Sera will attempt to free the last mouros."

There were a lot of replies I could've given, but what shot out of my mouth was, "Mouros are extinct. They have been for centuries."

Something about the way she held her body, poised, straight, rigid as if her muscles were holding a collective breath. My unease grew as I tried to wrap my head around the possibility of the return of an old evil. I had to confirm the truth and warn the Inquisition. I swallowed the knot in my throat and stepped toward the chair to seize understanding. Lacruz beckoned gravely. I would know why soon enough.

10 REVELATIONS

The Sangreino stared at me. I swallowed the growing knot in my throat and stepped toward it.

Dhyana eased to the edge of the seat. "Come see what you must," she said. She rose reluctantly as if it pained her to be physically separated from the chair. She circled behind it always keeping one hand in contact with the stone. "Sit, Cariño."

My saliva fled for a place of safety leaving my mouth deserted and dry. My stomach was into its fifth gymnastic rotation, and my balls lodged themselves into my belly. "You're trying to shake coconuts from an orange tree."

She stared. Her anger gathered like a storm. "Flee. Forget about covens, the Crimson and Cuélebre," she spat. "Be happy. Enjoy a life free of your own pain. This I would give you if I were able."

Sincerity played hopscotch with the fury. There was more than lust between us. From the first pair of handcuffs, she was so wrong in the right ways. My choices brought us closer. I was an Inquisitor. I thought she was a cop, but she turned out to be a guajona. We were natural enemies.

Blink.

History repeated.

I had met Yanira at a rest stop bar an hour outside of Tierra Santa. She had been on the run from creditors, an angry dope fiend boyfriend, and a drug itch she had been trying to shake since she was fifteen. I was fresh out the military, horny as hell, and filled with uncertainty about my future. The only skill I mastered during my tour was recognizing a sure lay.

135

I studied Yanira from across the bar. Her limp shoulder length black hair, low riding jeans jostling from an undernourished waist, and the cubic zirconium nose stud emphasized the lonely around her eyes. I called the waitress over, ordered up a Long Island for my future ex-wife, and introduced myself as it was delivered. The smile Yanira had given, part annoyed, part flattered, part relieved let me know we were players in the same game. And the rest, as they said in the funny books, was history.

"Why me?" I asked Lacruz.

Her eyes widened and somewhere between the seconds she found the words. "To be long lived is to be adrift." Her gaze drifted. "So much time passes we lose bits of who we were. With you I can remember, la mujer, the woman I was. It is how I—" Her eyes asked me to not make her finish. "I care, Kensington. And I will use you despite that, even if it means your death. To care more would break you. I am striving to care less."

I'm already broken, I thought. Aloud I asked, "Do I have to bite it?"

She shook her head. "I will protect you from its taint. You have my word."

Lacruz never broke her word. Except my trusted friend Detective Natalie Lacruz was an illusion. I knew Dhyana Nuberu for a total of twenty-four hours. Hardly enough time to build anything resembling trust.

"Before I do this I want to know the truth between you and Sera, the real truth."

Lacruz stared into a dark corner and a bit of forlorn crept into her voice. "Sera was my apprentice. I am Sovereign. You must wonder what that truly means. A Sovereign is the chosen overseer and guardian whose duty is to hunt Drac bloodlines and protect the Sangreino from those who seek to use it unwisely. As you know, Crimson are not immortal. Dueños appoint apprentices in order to preserve succession. The apprentice becomes the new Dueño contingent upon the Dueño's death or retirement." She smirked. "We do retire, Cariño, but not often." She crossed her arms. "I am the third to hold the title of Sovereign." Her voice softened. "I found Seravina close to three hundred years ago thieving in Greece. She was a guajona newly indoctrinated. Her previous Sire had run into… local trouble resulting in his death."

"Can you explain the whole Sire thing to me?" I had a good idea of what the relationship meant, but I thought it would be interesting to hear it from a guajona perspective.

"A Sire is a mentor. Sires indoctrinate a Nescient into the Cleave by coaxing or forcing the Nescient to commit their first kill. Within covens, Sires are assigned to Nescients. Outside of covens, Sires search for gargola or guajona in the wild and take them under their wing. In both cases, the gargola or guajona are taught what they need to survive. These teachings range from how and where to hunt as to not reveal our existence, the use of our bloodline abilities, our history, laws, and formally inducts the Nescient into the Crimson Consortium."

Lacruz uncrossed her arms, leaned forward, and cleared her throat to let me know the subject was closed. "I became Seravina's second Sire, honed who she was and what she could do."

I tried to picture Sera and Lacruz all buddy buddy, but the image didn't fit. I saw the way they fought. I heard the underlying venom when they exchanged words.

Lacruz continued, "Seravina was to be my successor as Sovereign. As her Sire, I should've recognized her hunger for power and taken steps to dissuade it. Instead, I gloried in her quick mind and growing facility with the Cleave." Lacruz clasped her hands in her lap and her eyes lost focus for a moment. She licked her lips and spoke softly. "From Gabriela's salvation, I had unknowingly carved the blade that would sever our three century bond. I wanted Roxana to live her life as a Nescient and to never become a guajona. Seravina wanted Roxana indoctrinated in order to co-opt her power."

Lacruz's voice vibrated with suppressed anger. "Soon philosophical disagreements became physical and our 'custody battle' ended violently. I almost killed Seravina for her transgression. She managed to escape or perhaps I lacked the conviction to end her life," she added wistfully. "Either way, I knew her intent. I had Roxana moved from city to city to keep Seravina from uncovering her whereabouts. Seravina's dogged pursuit ended five years after the dissolution of our partnership. I thought she had recanted her foolishness. Yo fue una idiota. She simply withdrew to steal Roxana from my grasp."

I pointed an accusing finger at the chair. "Does she know that thing is underneath the mall?"

Lacruz shook her head. "She knows the Sangreino is in Tierra Santa though its precise location eludes her. I had planned on disclosing that information when she assumed the mantle of Sovereign." Lacruz spread her hands and shrugged as if to say that time has passed. "This room is designed so the Sangreino cannot be removed. She will need to come here to claim it."

"That's why you're calm; Sera has to go through you no matter what." Ah, so now I knew the real reason for Sera's hesitation. Despite knowing where Roxana lived, Sera wasn't prepared to move forward until she found the Sangreino. My early involvement forced Sera to kidnap Roxana before Sera was ready. What did she say? *You weren't supposed to be involved yet.* "How is she planning on using Roxana? I want specific details not cryptic double-talk."

"You will have to sit." Lacruz patted the armrest.

I could tell by her tone she was through talking. Did Lacruz refuse to use Roxana or was it that she refused to share? There was more to their rift. The Lacruz I knew was practical, tenacious, and deadly. Lacruz wouldn't let Sera escape once she had her in the crosshairs. "Sera's stronger, isn't she?" I nodded at the chair. "That's why you're feeding. That thing gives you a boost."

Lacruz blinked. Her mouth quirked upwards. "I can match her in a sprint though she easily outdistances me in a marathon. Her ability to create so many wights is one facet of her talents. She could easily replace the current Dueño of Coven Nuberu."

But Sera wanted much more. She wanted the whole damn Consortium. Lacruz had called lightning to end the fight because she knew a prolonged battle put her at disadvantage. As interesting a tidbit as it was, it wasn't important.

Both guajona were going to great lengths to involve me, Lacruz by pretending to be my friend and Sera through seduction. I was vital to them for reasons still unknown. Had tragedy missed my doorstep my Lengua-bruja would've remained dormant. I wouldn't be an Inquisitor. A cold chill frolicked up and down my spine. How far would she go? I fixed my Inquisitor's stare, death incarnate, three times cold and twice as nasty, on Lacruz.

"Did you kill my daughter?"

Lacruz's eyes widened. Her pupils became big and round. Her mouth dropped open though no words came out. She met my glare. I could see sadness in her brown eyes. Her reply was soft, fierce and so protective. "Ken, my god no! I don't know who. I'd tell you if I did. I wouldn't keep that from you."

The silence stretched between us. The tension around my heart eased. Hearing the words coming from Lacruz instead of Dhyana made me believe. I closed the wound thoughts of my daughter always opened and thanked God. I didn't know what I would've done had she said yes. I took a deep breath.

"One more thing," I said. "Hijo de Dirige, what does it mean?"

She studied me. "The translation is closer to meaning, son of the dead. In Latin the word is just *Dirige*. The closest English approximation is dirge. A Dirge is a servant of La Parca or the servant of death. Beyond that I cannot say other that you are a key to stopping a mouros. How? I do not know."

I nodded. Hijo de Dirige, Dirge, or servant of death. Sounded fancy though I had no clue what I was supposed to do with that information. I wonder if my Mom knew. I never spoke to her about my Lengua-bruja or that I decided to take up monster killing as a career. Maybe we needed to have a heart to heart so I could find out what she knew. *Hey Mom, do you know your son is a servant of death?* On second thought, maybe I didn't want to know. My upbringing was pretty normal except for Dad getting possessed by an evil spirit. Yeah, maybe a chat with Octavia Ashe would clear things up… When I had the time, that is.

Lacruz rose from the chair and stood off to the right. I stared at the sharp protrusions reaching out from the vacated seat. Cursing, I climbed the dais. What I was about to do reeked of insanity and now that I was on the precipice I couldn't find a good reason to move forward. This could be a doorway to an addictive abyss I would never escape. For all I knew, I could be a Nescient and this could be my indoctrination.

I glanced at Lacruz. She frowned as if annoyed. The kind of grimace I had grown to trust. I found myself smiling in return. I returned my attention to the evil chair. Touching this abomination with bare skin was out of the question so I turned around and squatted to make sure I had a hefty set of cloth between it and me.

The Sangreino's cold hard planes invaded my flesh. A wintry evil radiated through my clothes to irritate the flesh beneath. I squirmed, which made the spines dig deeper. It was like riding an ice sculpted porcupine without a saddle. If I hadn't been clothed, the protrusions would've definitely pierced my skin. Sitting comfortably was impossible. As soon as I shifted my weight, a different set of pricks forced me to squirm again. Squirming created more discomfort. I settled with most of my weight on my heels. My ass hovered over the seat like I would do if I had to use a public toilet without the protective paper butt sheet.

Lacruz gripped my shoulder, pressed me against the chair, took my other hand, and raised my index finger to her mouth. I yelped in pain as the spines dug in. She ignored my discomfort as she nicked my finger with her fang. The pain was sharp, quick, and highly forgettable. A single dollop of blood pooled on my fingertip. She admired it as if it was the most magnificent jewel in the world before licking the gash clean. I retrieved my finger, rubbed it with my thumb, and the skin felt smooth, blemish free, as if it hadn't been nicked.

She released my shoulder and bit her own index finger. An indigo colored bead swirling with black pooled along the tip. I hadn't a clue as to what she meant to do with it until her finger edged closer to my lips.

My eyebrows shot up. I grimaced, scrunched my nose, and inched against the chair. "Have you been tested for STD's?"

"Kensington." Her voice was patient but firm. She repositioned her finger so that it was centimeters from my face like a mother offering spooned veggies to an infant. At least she didn't start cooing airplanes noises to coax my mouth open.

I sneered at the drop. There was no telling what that crap does. I could end up on the floor writhing in agony, transformed into a wight or some other monster entirely or, even worse, bonded as a Servant. One lick and whammy. Next thing I knew, I would be balancing a purse, shopping bags, and following her gleeful and drooling. Was this supposed to be corruption or seduction? I couldn't tell. I could still stop. I could walk away. She couldn't force me. Well, she could, but she hadn't. Her finger hovered. The spines pricking my shoulder blades twitched. Lacruz waited.

There had to be an upside. What if this drop of monster blood contained answers? Maybe. Yet I knew it was going to end in screams. Each passing second made her blood less appetizing. Rain and floods. I came too far to balk and besides when the dirty needed doing it was best to jump in the mud without hesitation. So that was what I did. I strangled my doubts and stuck out my tongue for a tiny taste. If I had to ingest evil, it was going to be as little as possible. There was no telling what evil might do to your bowels.

The guajona blood flooded my tongue with the pungent taste of burnt offal and started a countdown. When the clock hit zero, rich liquid heat exploded down my throat like a good whiskey. I heaved and jerked as every muscle in my body contracted simultaneously.

Lacruz gripped my arms so I wouldn't clock myself in the head with my uncontrollable flailing. Her blood's liquid heat seeped into my cells. I imagined it attempting to alter my DNA like in the sci-fi movies where the unlucky science guinea pig grew seven tentacles and started lusting after Japanese school girls.

Nothing so dramatic happened to my body. My Lengua-bruja reacted... oddly.

To my left, a fuzzed image began to form, an ultrasound shape of a hawkish man wearing a top hat. It opened its beak. The world faded to black except for a million scampering rats across hardwood. Which was odd because my death rattle never reacted to the living before, and guajona, despite what they could do, were very much alive.

It felt like I was slipping. I cried out (I knew there would be screams) and everything happened at once. My limbs turned to slush. My insides danced the jig. My nostrils clogged with sulfur and death. I was reduced to a raw lump of weeping meat surrounded by laughing darkness. Sound flared crisply and condensed into a three dimensional ultrasound silhouette. La Parca the grim reaper reached out a thin scything talon, pat me on the shoulder, and spoke:

Under the cover of moonlight, a raven haired maiden had huddled behind an outcrop of rocks, a mile from her home. She could scarcely believe he had chosen her, an only child amidst the more beauteous ladies of her town, to meet him this evening. A gentle chill blew through the surrounding forest causing browned leaves to scatter along the road. The mud splattered hem of her favorite red summer dress meant nothing to her wildly beating heart. She knew it was wrong without God and her parents' blessing. But as she imagined his child, a heavenly beauty like him, growing inside her she knew any sin would be forgiven.

The road she watched lay empty until a sudden sweep of dust scattered the dead leaves. It was if an angel descended. He appeared alone without mount or care shining in a crimson tunic, cream breeches, and golden rapier hanging purposefully at his waist. His chest was emblazoned with a crest she could not identify, for a king she could not name. She climbed from the rocks, lifted her skirts heedless of the mud, and ran to him knowing she would indulge anything he asked. He waited. Her hair tumbled loose from its long braid as her steps gathered speed. She heard his call and then frowned because his mouth had not moved. It was as if she had heard it within her blood. Any confusion she might have felt was quickly discarded as she drew in the comfort of his presence.

'Don Vega Nuberu,' she gasped while reaching for him. His smile burned like a thousand candles and she shivered at the cold touch of his pale slender hand sliding along

her cheek. She collapsed into his embrace, huddled against his bosom with closed eyes, and almost fainted with ecstasy at the scent and feel of him. He is my new home, she thought.

His fingers toyed with her most sacred places. She encouraged his sweet violation. Desire came unbidden. Her heart bounded into her expectant throat.

She pressed forward for a kiss and as her lips met flesh there was a meaty crunch. Her eyelids fluttered like hummingbird wings. She tasted thick red juice spilling with so much rapture she almost swooned. When her vision focused, she found herself, panting, on her knees in front of many fires whose charcoal burn no longer incited fear. She cradled someone in her lap. She looked into the face, expecting to see Don Vega's baby and yet she knew it was much too soon. Her thoughts whirled and jumbled upon another. She shook her head to clear the muskiness.

Neither Don Vega nor his child filled her arms. It was her mother, gentle Emile, whose neck hung crookedly in fleshy shreds with blood pouring out of the lifeless wound. The maiden's dress was soaked with a loved one's blood. The shock caused the maiden to drop her mother's head against the wooden floor. The maiden reeled; her hammering heart sucked the hot sticky from her mouth, down her throat, and into her veins where it filled her entire body.

She felt a connection cement into a ravenous song that provided strength bordering on bliss. She felt her hand go unbidden to the burning spot between her thighs. She wheedled frantic as something bestial awakened from her deeps, and hungered for more of the precious red juice. She rocked back and forth until, with a hiss of release, she shuddered.

Her home burned around her. Her mother slew by her appetite. A lone figure stood amidst the revelry; his coal black gaze devoured her every move. This time she was positive his mouth moved, for he spoke with a voice of thunder, a voice she would never find the strength to disobey.

'I am your Sire,' Don Vega Nuberu had said. 'You are now ready to come into your inheritance. Awaken Dhyana Nuberu, you are guajona, you are death, and your future stretches long ahead.'

The maiden screamed.

Normally after my Lengua-bruja kicked in, I was transported to a gray decibel wasteland where La Parca spoke. What was happening now was much different than anything else I had experienced. Somehow my Lengua-bruja wasn't translating the last moments of the recently deceased. It had somehow tapped in Lacruz's life. I saw Lacruz's indoctrination. Vega Nuberu made Lacruz murder her family. That had to be harsh. The pain, the guilt. I understood Lacruz a little better now. I wanted to honor her pain with my tears. The picture show wasn't over.

I sensed a gathering malevolent storm of more to come. My Lengua-bruja plunged into the storm's mouth of a second voice—close, dormant, evil. Old dusted words, a papyrus whisper reeking of century's bygone detailed blood, fury, and at the end, human fear. La Parca spoke:

Vasco sniffed contemptuously as his coal black eyes roved the tiny storage room caked with cobwebs and dust. Rotted barrels and other useless relics were hastily shoved aside to make room for hiding. Waiting in a half circle was Sergeant Colon Drac, leader of what remained of Vasco's household guard, and twenty-nine haggard-faced gargola warriors in soiled silver armor. The warriors gripped their gore crusted spears tightly.

The smell of packed flesh teased his appetite and almost overwhelmed his self-control. The Dirge had turned most of the traitorous gargola and guajona against him. Eventually, the Dirge and the traitors breached his defenses. Vasco was rushed into hiding. He wanted to make sure he was at his maximum strength before he faced the Dirge. He needed to feed. His keen hearing alerted him to the enemies converging on his position. He surveyed the gargola around him.

They could not protect him. He would have to save himself. That made his choice for a meal obvious. A guard who had one arm sheared off at the elbow.

Vasco Compelled, 'Come.'

The guard stiffened as if hit by a stone, dropped his spear, and limped to Vasco. Sergeant Colon, Vasco's page Tulin Drac, and the other surviving guards glared in uncomfortable silence.

The guard kneeled in front of Vasco and said, 'Master, would you do me the honor.'

Vasco snatched the guard by his shoulders and heard the bones break. The guard whimpered. Vasco squeezed his meal, crushed armor to his chest, and bit deep into the guard's throat.

Blood poured into the Vasco's mouth, but not as much as it should've been, still, he would savor each drop. What began as pleasure ended with a sting as a cold blaze pierced his back. He was dimly aware that it was a spear and growled at its annoyance until he felt several more pricks in rapid succession.

He collapsed backward as the muscles in his leg were severed. Spears sliced the muscles in his arms. He lost his grip on the one armed guard. His teeth, still firmly rooted in the dying guard's throat, pulled the gargola atop him as he collapsed backward. Vasco continued to drink until he heard a meaty tearing of his meal being ripped away. Sergeant Colon tore the guard from Vasco's jaws and threw the corpse against a wall. A bloody chunk of flesh remained in Vasco's mouth and he sucked the fleshy chunk clean of its juices and spat aside the remains.

More spears scything through organs and flesh pinned his body to the floor. The guards hacked shallow gashes in his limbs, the material of his clothes parted as easily as the flesh beneath. Blood leaked. Vasco realized too late. He attempted to shapeshift, but without enough blood the Cleave remained dormant. Vasco was more starved for power than before.

Colon kneeled at his side. Vasco met the Sergeant's hard and sad gaze, but could summon no words.

Colon's voice echoed with defeat as he spoke. 'I am sorry Milord. As of this moment, you are the last mouros in the world. We are surrounded and cannot escape. The tunnel...' Colon shook his head. 'The Dirge offers our lives in exchange for yours and in truth some of your household has joined him. We remain loyal.' Colon nodded to each man circling Vasco. 'Brothers come. Let us do our Lord this final service.' Tulin moved from his space near the rear. Colon saw him and held up a hand. 'Not you Tulin, it will be your duty to release Lord Vasco.'

Tulin nodded gravely, crossed his arms, and resumed leaning against the wall. Colon beckoned and the guards circled, bowed, and thirty hands held Vasco's body. Colon palmed Vasco's forehead and the mouros had the brief sensation of Colon's warmth before the familiar cold of the Cleave flared. Vasco gasped as his body shuddered in response.

'What are... you...?' Vasco finally managed to say. Had he been capable of sweat, huge droplets would have peppered his forehead. His heart hammered. He felt the increased pull of his hunger.

Colon's barked a mirthless laugh. 'Milord... Father, we are your children. We are Drac. We cannot shapeshift as you can, but we can focus our ability outward. We can reshape flesh. We will hide you. Young Tulin will pretend to betray you and join the Dirge. He tell him you escaped. The rest of us will give our lives to protect you. But in truth. You will go nowhere. You will remain here. Safe."

Their combined power overtook Vasco. He could feel his body losing solidity. He tried to fight the change, but the guards' combined strength had become a typhoon to his tiny flood. His skin rippled, then expanded, and finally hardened. They threw their complete power at him, including their lives, and one by one each guard fell dead to the floor.

Only Colon remained; the last fountainhead of an awesome power. Vasco could sense the Sergeant's strain and growing weakness. With a final defiant cry Colon shoved the last of the gathered power into his former Lord. Colon clutched his chest and collapsed. Dead.

Vasco shuddered. Power infused his body and began to reshape him. His bones warped and his stretched skin took on a blockish shape. He tried to move his limbs, but had none. He tried to scream. His mouth and vocal chords had fused. His vision gone, his connection to the Cleave neutered, he was trapped in a prison of his own flesh and tortured by never-ending hunger.

Vasco felt the admiring touch of a hand, he could still feel at least, and heard the soft voice he recognized as Tulin Drac.

'A blood throne,' Tulin mouthed in awe. 'Sangreino.'

Vasco, the last mouros would have wept, if he had eyes.

The vault's shadows appeared more foreboding. Pressure stretched my temples to their painful limits. A fuse in my brain exploded. My Lengua-bruja shut down. The ultrasound image of La Parca faded into the recesses of my imagination. The translation stopped. My head pounded to the tune of one hundred loathing hammers. I tried to scrub out the grime in my brain with my fingers except pesky things like hair, scalp, and skull barred the way.

My eyes snapped open. I sprang from the quivering seat so fast that I almost faceplanted. I came down hard on my hands and knees, pain shot through my thighs. I embraced the ache because physical pain was a familiar discomfort that would pass or be medicated into passing. My stomach heaved and thank god I was already on all fours.

The five color breakfast I kind of wanted to keep splashed onto the floor and exorcized the guajona and mouros blood I had ingested. My abdomen pushed against my ribcage forcing an icky liquid chorus through my lips. First came the chunks. Next, the brown bile lining the pit of my intestines. A few barking dry heaves later, it was over. Luckily, I managed to avoid spewing on my coat.

Lacruz kept a silent vigil until I was finished puking. When the last drips of saliva hung listless from my lower lip, she kneeled at my side, wiped my face with a hanky she produced from a pocket, and helped me stand. Once the wobbliness faded, I actually felt better. The vertical was back to vertical and the horizontal was back to horizontal. My stomach settled. I felt invigorated even though my breath tasted of ass and rot.

What the hell just happened?

I knew the basics about how my Lengua-bruja functioned, but knew very little about its origins. My ability translated La Parcas' grim reaper speech as they announced the arrival of someone passing into the afterlife. Blood, skin, hair, and clothing were the common catalysts that jumpstarted my Lengua-bruja, though sometimes, someone dying in close proximity or someone whose death was tied to specific place were enough to trigger it.

The consistent thing was, whoever's death rattle I tapped into was always, you know, dead. This was the first time my Lengua-bruja had translated for the living. It was a grand mystery, a new loose thread in an old suit, one I wouldn't be unraveling today. I had too much on my plate already. I decided to ignore my hiccupping Lengua-bruja to concentrate on the results it brought.

Tasting Lacruz's Sangreino tinged blood had sent me on a memory trip down hell lane. I felt sad about her indoctrination. I wanted to hug her, tell her I understood, and assure her I would never let anyone hurt her like that again.

"So the guy in the painting, Vega Nuberu, he pimped you?" I watched her face for changes—anger, embarrassment, shame.

Lacruz regarded me thoughtfully. She touched my face, traced a single digit along my cheek, down my jaw, to a spot on my neck over my pulse, and then her finger turned horizontal making a slow line. "Can it, Ashe."

There was no anger or malice in her tone and certainly no roughness in her touch. Vega was a sensitive subject, as love always was, and if there was one thing I knew, she had loved him as much as she hated him.

I glanced at the Sangreino. I had no love for this tainted thing. If it were up to me I would strap a nuke to it.

The last mouros was trapped as a stone chair. Vasco was the Sangreino. Say that ten times fast, I thought. I had experienced the moment before Vasco's imprisonment. Thirty silver clad loyal gargola had sacrificed their lives to hide Vasco from a big balls monster ass-kicker. Tulin Drac was supposed to free Vasco later. Tulin didn't and I thought I knew why. Tulin must've fed from the chair. He probably got addicted to the mouros-juice. Instead of freeing his former Lord, he tried to make himself a king. Mick mentioned Tulin Drac battled Vega Nuberu for the Sangreino. Vega won. Though I couldn't be sure of the chronological order of events, I did know the same Vega indoctrinated Lacruz. It wasn't a coincidence that she was the Sangreino's current caretaker. Did that mean Lacruz killed Vega? Probably.

Fast forward to the present. Lacruz found Roxana's father, realized he was a Drac bloodline, and killed him. Only, there was a small wrinkle. Gabriela was pregnant with another Drac bloodline. Instead of killing a pregnant woman, Lacruz takes Gabriela in and protects Roxana after she is born. Everything would've turned out perfect if Sera hadn't decided to steal the kid. With Roxana in hand, Sera had the means to free Vasco. I didn't know what she hoped to get for her trouble. From what I experienced in the death rattle flashback, Vasco was a nasty son of a bitch best left buried.

Lacruz saw my expression. She squeezed my shoulder and ushered me toward the door. "You are shaken. Perhaps some fresh air will replenish your resolve."

"We should kill it," I said, knowing it was the obvious being stated and also knowing it meant nothing. The Sangreino laughed at me.

"No blade can breach it. Fang can pierce its hide and yet there is no vital spot. Draining it dry is impossible; its foul power is eternal. However, periodic ingestions increases my lifespan and grants amazing regenerative abilities." She gestured around the vault. "This room was built to ensure it could never be removed without leveling this entire cave and the mall above it."

"I think you underestimate the power of C4," I said. I believed her. If there had been a way to destroy Vasco, the Dirge who had been hunting him would've found it. "Do you know how to release him?"

"*Si*", she replied without further explanation.

11 HAIL MARY

The mall's walkways were filled with roamers ignorant of the last mouros in the world sleeping beneath them. I followed the in and out traffic of the open storefronts, the stroller pushing mothers, their children, and hand holding couples lured by the smell of fresh baked chocolate chip cookies and Mongolian barbecue.

There were sellers and buyers, lookers and schemers. Mostly, it was a jovial place where citizens congregated in the illusion of community. Except this one creepy guy wearing a face obscuring hooded yellow parka, who had the misfortune of being stopped by a cell phone sales guy trying to hawk a new phone plan. The parka guy nodded while the sales guy spoke. I could tell the parka guy wasn't going to buy, hell, parka guy seemed ecstatic that anyone was talking to him. I chuckled, wondering how long it would take for sales guy to figure it out.

The mirth faded, killed by the realization that mouros weren't as dead and gone as I had been led to believe. After a traumatizing experience, it's always a good idea to treat yourself to icing topped sunshine as a reminder of why life is worth living. My destination was the Gigan-Ton Cinnamon Roll Cart on the second floor of the mall, which under normal circumstances I could locate blindfolded. Unfortunately, my head was too scrambled. I would have trouble finding shit in an outhouse right now.

Lacruz opted to stay below. She must've sensed my need to be alone or maybe she wanted more one on one with her crack chair. My heart was beating a rock band drum solo. I was in pretty good shape so I doubted my rapid heartbeat was from exertion. Besides, the onset felt like...

Panic, spiky and thick. I was seized by the urge to throw my hands in the air and scream for everyone to run for their lives. Somehow, I found the sanity to avoid lunacy and kept my mouth screwed shut.

My head snapped back and forth at the happy faces going on about their business. Didn't they have a clue about what was buried beneath their feet? I couldn't really blame them for their lack of survival instincts as much as I would've liked to. I had made many trips to the mall without suspecting anything other than the usual consumer price gouging. I mean, my Lengua-bruja kept silent about the evil below. How could I expect more from regular people with senses as dull as plastic?

My arms hung useless under my slumped shoulders. I began giggling at nothing in particular, my legs were starting to wobble, and I was nauseous again. There was no way I would keep down a cinnamon roll in this state. Oh crap, going nuts must feel like this. I was starting to feel lightheaded so locating a place to sit became my utmost priority.

Walking with no direction in mind, my thoughts were a fugue state. My brain needed a reboot. I was quite positive I wouldn't receive either. My feet took me past store after store until something green, white, and frilly in a display window caught my eye. I stopped in the middle of the walkway. People snorted rudely as they were forced to detour around me. I was staring at a dress a seven year old would wear, with puffy short white sleeves, ruffled frills at the hem, and a red happy faced dragon on the chest. I blinked, shook my head, and continued down the walkway.

I found an empty bench near a granite fountain with seven multi-leveled circular petals extending from a single base like a four leaf clover. Each petal held petite granite animal carvings—seahorses, clams, and starfish were on the lowest petals; salamanders, frogs, and caecilians took up the second level pads; the single topmost pad had a solitary turtle.

The sea animals had an uplifting grace as water arced out of their mouths (or in some cases other body parts) into a pool. Kids splashed their filthy little hands in the water while their parents threatened, coaxed, cajoled, and dragged them bawling and kicking from the fountain. At least, the water was shallow so drowning wasn't a hazard.

A teen with a blue polo shirt, pink highlights in her blonde hair, and an onyx lip stud supervised the pool. Mostly she looked too bored and frightened to confront the parents. Her effort was spent sighing at the children and then looking at their parents until the hint was successfully delivered.

I sat on the empty bench, leaned forward, and put my head in my hands. I needed a vacation. Like right now. Mick told me I should take breaks between jobs. I ignored his advice because I was too busy trying to drum up income.

Now I needed a vacation so that I could flush the Sangreino's images out of my head. I was soiled, lost, and dirtied in so many layers. I thought I knew darkness. I thought I knew pain. I learned a whole new definition. I took the canvas out of my pocket, unfolded it, and stared at the image. I recognized the face. It was Vasco, the guy stuck as a chair. The canvas' taint didn't affect me anymore after experiencing the real thing. I rewrapped the canvas and put in back in my pocket.

The Sangreino's chill had felt like ice sculpted ants were crawling over my body. If I had to do it over again I was not sure I would've sat on it. Too bad I couldn't rewind time to undo that choice.

Damn choice.

Sera's plan to free the mouros made no sense. I didn't see how releasing a competing grudge holding predator into the Crimson Consortium would benefit her. Unless… unless Sera found a way to leash Vasco. Mouros are rumored to possess tremendous power. They were said to be able destroy cities. Having a mouros under her thumb would be like owning the biggest baddest attack dog on the block. Sic 'em boy. Maul. Rule the neighborhood.

The bench lost its comfort and was starting to hurt my behind. I shifted in my seat so my weight would settle differently. People chuckled because it must've looked like I was bench scratching my butt. To hell with it. Sitting here wasn't going to unravel this mystery.

Since early this morning my phone had been vibrating nonstop with about a gazillion messages from Mick and Melody. Now that I had some privacy, it was a good time to let Mick know I was still alive and that whatever happened wasn't my fault. I put my cell to my ear.

"Ken," Mick said on the other end. "About time, Son. I knew you wouldn't be stupid enough to be involved in that Cattle Branch business, especially since we already had a plan in place."

Mick was trying too hard to sound like he was on a beach in Maui, which meant he had been fretting all night. "It was a Nuberu hit," I said. Well, it was true. Sort of. I had absolutely nothing to do with the lightning or explosives. That was Lacruz. "Sorry about the scare, but I've been diving for answers and just resurfaced for air. You check out the damage?"

"Ground zero's still crawling with the local authorities," Mick said. "I gave Jason a call in case he'd started the party early. He's still in transit."

"Seems like his handiwork," I added to be snippy.

Mick grunted. "So what did you find?"

I basically gave Mick the highlights about Roxana being a Drac whose bloodline is integral to cracking the Sangreino, which happens to be the last mouros trapped in stone. I even went through the whole reluctant admission of Mick being right about the Sangreino being real. I left out the weirdness of Lacruz being Dhyana Nuberu, me tasting her guajona/mouros blood cocktail, and the Lengua-bruja flashback acid trip.

"Are you sure?" Mick said, perking up at the mention of the *Sangreino*. "Do you know where the Sangreino is?."

"No clue."

The last thing I needed was Mick tearing the mall apart to find it. "I'm guessing Sera hasn't found the Sangreino yet or the sky would be raining fire. I'm on the trail though. I'll probably have to go silent again."

In the earlier days, a mouros' strength made them kings, lords, and nobles. It was easy for them to scare, seduce, seize power, and rule empires from the shadows. Mouros conspired in Egypt, Greece, Rome, Spain, and countless other empires. They molded human civilization. The idea of Zeus or Thor or all those other mythological folks probably came from seeing a mouros in action.

"You keep on it." Mick's voice thundered with excitement. "Call me as soon as you find anything new. If the Sangreino is what you say it is, then we have to destroy it. I hope you're wrong. If there's one mouros around, who's to say there isn't another."

I nodded. "Only making sure we're on the same page, Chief."

"You need anything from here?"

I needed to replace my lost weapons and ammo. Meeting Mick face to face would lead to questions that I might not want to answer. And I wouldn't have the protection of a phone call to hide my body language. I had to stay away from Sanctuary.

"No. I'm good. Just know that I'm on her ass." I heard Mick's growl of displeasure through the phone. "Hey, asses are biblical, Mary rode one." Silence. "Sorry," I corrected, "I meant butt."

"Don't do anything without backup," Mick said.

The call ended. I glanced up. Lacruz walked toward me. My throat tightened in a way I hadn't felt since walking by the girls' locker room in junior high. She made my heart beat hummingbird style. It was reminiscent of how Yanira used to make me feel: like I could fly. It was best to avoid women who inspired airborne fantasies because it hurts like hell when you fall.

Lacruz sauntered; the crowd parted as if she were royalty. The onlookers' expressions touched on many emotions: awe, lust, jealousy, desire. Lacruz focused on me while ignoring the men and pubescent boys definitely wanting to know her and the smattering of dry looks from women who were struck with an uncontrollable need to check their hair, clothes, and make up. Lacruz joined me on the bench, back stiff, and hands folded in her lap. My blood heated.

We both looked straight ahead like we were in the theatre and the mall shoppers were the movie. I checked the time on my phone to give myself something to do. We had a stalemate with Sera. Each side had a piece the other wanted. This standoff could last for weeks, decades, even centuries. Time was on Sera's side. I had to somehow come up with a plan to tip this situation in me and Lacruz's favor. I needed to put pressure on Sera. Enough to make her desperate. And then I needed to present her with a way out. If I could do that, Sera would come to me.

An out of breath pigtailed first grader full of excitement ran up to Lacruz and asked, "Are you a princess?"

Lacruz's smile made it clear she didn't want to be touched. She showed the kid her badge and laced a hint of cop in her response. "No Precious, I'm a police officer."

The girl's eyes lit up with glee. "Is it real? Can I have it?"

"It's real. You can't have it. It has to be earned. Listen to your mother, work hard in school, apply to the police academy, and you'll earn one." Lacruz shooed, "Go back to your parents and don't talk to strangers or next time I'll take you to jail."

With a smile from ear to ear, the young girl skipped back to her mother who dragged her away by the arm while scowling at Lacruz. Now that Her High-heel-ness was finished greeting the natives, she turned to me.

"I can bring Sera to us," I said before she could speak. Lacruz inclined her head and somehow I knew she wouldn't like my plan, but that was the beauty of it. I continued, "I need you to call the covens and tell them Sera has a Drac guajona. I want the whole Consortium hunting Sera. I want Sera to realize there's nowhere she can hide and no one she can hide with. I want her to realize that sooner or later someone will find her and take her to task. I want her to feel like she has the devil on her heels."

Lacruz considered my words carefully before she spoke. "If I were to inform the Consortium," she began. "Roxana's life is forfeit. Secrecy is her shield."

"You don't have to give them the kid's description or location. They won't know what she looks like or where she is. If we do this right, we can hide the kid before they find her."

Lacruz shook her head. "As to Roxana's description, it matters little; it's about scent, Cariño. All any Crimson would need is sufficient proximity to catch her scent. That would be enough to identify her as guajona. I brought Roxana to Tierra Santa because of the minimal Crimson presence. You do an excellent job of keeping us out of your territory. With you here, I worried little about her accidentally being scented."

Interesting, I hadn't realized scent played such a vital part in how gargola and guajona identified one another. It also explained why Lacruz had humans looking after Roxana and why she worked alone. "Then how was the kid discovered in the first place?"

Lacruz gazed into the distance. "It was Evan. I believe coincidence and ill luck was part and parcel to our current dilemma. I have thought about it and I believe Evan was a regular at the Jungle Gem. Parents have a lot of contact with their children, scents intermingle due to proximity and shared diet. He must have carried Roxana's scent, a hug or handshake, him to the club."

I understood what Lacruz meant. I remembered my daughter's fingers smelling of syrup and how I ended up smelling of syrup after a hug. Sera had claimed to be out smoking when she saw Roxana and me climbing the stairs. I don't remember anyone being around. Now that I knew about scent, I realized Sera had discovered the kid's proximity by a different means. Roxana must've plastered me with her scent when she hugged me as I left Winnie's. Sera picked up on it. With the kid so close, it would've been easy to track her.

So much hunting. So many kills. Yet, I knew next to nothing about them. Lacruz was right. My current crash course in guajona culture was proving invaluable. I would've never thought to take scent into account; in fact, my original plan didn't account for guajona noses though knowing about them still wasn't enough to warrant a change of plans. Exposing Roxana to the Consortium came with benefit of getting her free.

"There's also one last part," I began. Lacruz froze at the tone of my voice. I put my hand over hers. "I need you to tell Sera the Sangreino is here. Apologize. Make up with her. Say you'll be BFF's again. I don't care. She needs to know it's here."

"She will know it is a trap," Lacruz responded.

"Yeah, but she won't be able to resist because it's the truth. She'll probably send a scout. Once Sera has a confirmation she won't have a choice, especially with the Consortium breathing down her neck. She'll have to take the bait." Lacruz clearly didn't like my plan. I shrugged. "It's the only way to force the conflict on our terms."

As I spoke, one of the forty-eight inch TV's in the window of an electronic store display flashed a news update. I couldn't hear anything from where I sat, but as we watched Roxana, Gabriela, and Evan's photos popped onscreen. They showed a second overhead image of a suburban home surrounded by squad cars. This wasn't a fresh newsfeed but rather a replay of yesterday's hot stories. I could tell because one of the squad cars in the overhead shot was Lacruz's. This story was followed by another concerning The Cattle Branch.

Lacruz saw the images and pursed her lips. She turned to me and said, "Sera has contacts within the Consortium who are unaware of her betrayal. Poisoning those contacts with the truth is a good plan." Lacruz nodded toward the television. "Public pressure will also force her to act."

Lacruz stared like she was measuring me for a pine box, then she stood, walked a bit away, flipped out her cell, and started dialing. Her body language gave nothing away nor could I hear a word she said. Either she was doing what I asked or calling for a pizza. Honestly, I was hoping for the pizza. I leaned back against the bench. My stomach growled. Despite my prior failures, the pieces were moving into place. With luck, Sera should be desperate by this time tomorrow. The waiting remained, always the waiting.

A couple of years ago, Yanira had left me waiting. After work, I had stopped off for a couple of drinks. I needed a minute to consider what I discovered that morning and a whole day of selling car insurance sure as hell hadn't helped my mood.

Yanira had been using again.

I had left the bar. My car had veered wide as it crested the corner of my street and almost ran up on the curb. My façade of a home came into view; it was an illusion I was tired of keeping. After the tears and promises, there wasn't anything left for her to say. I got out of the car and staggered inside the house.

The front door rattled against the wall and startled my daughter. The dolls she had been holding fell from her grasp and bounced on carpet. She jumped up, body rigid, eyes quivering on the verge of tears. She recognized me, started to soften, until something about my face kept her from rushing to my arms like she always did. I tried to smile but my expression skewed at an odd angle like a table with a leg too short.

It took three tries to set down my briefcase so it didn't tip over. My arms tangled in my jacket sleeves as I yanked it off. I freed myself, threw my coat to the floor, stumbled over to my daughter who hadn't moved or spoken, dropped to my knees in front her, and pulled her into a sloppy hug. I remember the room spinning and her small hands touching my face asking me why it was wet. I couldn't answer. Words were clogged. I couldn't give her one simple answer.

Yanira had witnessed my entrance, hell, she probably smelled the alcohol and the despair. When I finished hugging my little girl, I stood and wobbled toward the bedroom. Yanira asked our daughter to play in her room. Yanira followed me and asked me what was wrong. I remember turning and giving her a look death incarnate, three times cold, and twice as nasty. Yanira paled, started babbling that she would go to rehab. Again. That she would do anything I asked. Again. She asked to be forgiven. Again. I dropped onto the bed, removed my shoes, and turned my back to her. I screwed my eyes shut to dam the building moisture.

I told her to go to hell.

Yanira's side of the bed had been cold when I awakened the next morning still in my clothes from the day before. I felt emptier than a wine bottle after New Year's Eve. The room was deathly silent and one of first things I noticed was her missing possessions—clothes, jewelry, pictures, the clutter people share when they live together. I crawled out of bed; my head pounded. Light filtering through the blinds stabbed my eyes.

Panic took root. I stumbled toward my daughter's room. I pushed open the door and there in the dim crisp morning was her sleeping form curled in a small S with her fist pressed against her lips. I smiled and released a pent up breath. I looked down on my Pequiñita and a feeling ten times stronger than relief slowed my frazzled heartbeat. My daughter fidgeted in her sleep and unclenched her little fist. Something metallic spilled onto her pillow; it was Yanira's wedding band on a necklace string.

My daughter's eyes opened, she yawned, and began rubbing at her face and nose. I stared at the ring that should've been on Yanira's finger and knew for certain she wasn't coming back. My daughter turned to look up at me. She opened her mouth to speak. There would be questions. I did the thing any responsible Dad could—thought of lies to tell my waking daughter.

Mommy was visiting abuela Marisela or tia Cecelia. She was working a new travel job. She was on vacation. She was in Canada. She was on vacation in Canada. She was anywhere that would keep her away long enough for you to figure it out for yourself. Now stop asking Daddy questions and eat your damn Fruit Loops.

I didn't report Yanira missing. The most investigating I did was ask Yanira's mother about Yanira's whereabouts. Abuela Marisela answered dodgy enough to let me know she was harboring a fugitive. Mariela even had the nerve to offer to take custody of Evelyn.

In retrospect, I should've let her have Evelyn. If I had, my daughter would still be alive. I thought Yanira would return as long as I had our daughter. I waited two years. Even at Evelyn's funeral, I waited. Yanira never showed. After that, I stopped wasting emotion on her existence. Whether she was curled up in some crack house or stone dead meant less to me than roadkill.

Lacruz finished her call, walked over, and sat down. Her brows furrowed as she clenched her hands. "It is done. I believe Sera will have to locate the Sangreino within the next two days."

My eyes widened as my eyebrows shot up. I knew what I was planning would force Sera to move fast, but I wasn't expecting that fast. "You sure?"

Lacruz nodded. "The Consortium has a long standing kill on sight order for a Drac bloodline. Every able bodied warrior will be on their way. I hope you are ready for the abundance of Crimson you are about to receive, Cariño."

"You told them she's here," I said. My jaw dropped open and my voice rose to a squeak. "Are you high?"

"I do not do things half measure," she said. "Tierra Santa will be infested with Crimson in forty-eight hours' time. Sera's window of opportunity will be tonight or tomorrow evening. She must act after sunset because, once released from his prison, Vasco will be unable to travel under the open sun."

For once an idea of my mine was turning out to be a solid game plan. Sure, there would be a few extra gargola and guajona roaming the city in the next couple of days, but Jason and his crew were on their way and for once the extra help would prove useful. I had my Sig, pistol-gripped axe, and a whole lot of fury. Why did I have the sick feeling it wasn't going to be enough?

12 LOSER'S WEEPERS

If there was anything resembling heaven, licking icing off my fingers came the closest. I munched on my Gigan-Ton cinnamon roll in the relative quiet of to a private security station not even mall security knew about. It was a station Lacruz had built for the explicit reason to monitor the Sangreino and the entire mall. I leaned back against the seat, a hard backed chair with metal armrests, with the weight of my black boots atop the control panel's plastic multi-colored switches. As the last bite of my cinnamon roll filled my mouth, I licked the gooey white icing off my fingers with a series of loud lip smacks.

On the floor were two cardboard containers smeared with icing. I reached down, opened the container, plucked the pastry with a giggle, the warm crust sending temperate waves into my fingertips, and took that large first bite. My teeth plunged into moistness and sugar surged inside my mouth creating an oral orgasm of pure and simple pleasure. I sighed.

The single door security office was large enough to fit about four people if they were friendly. The air conditioning blew in a constant stream of frigid air. One of the four walls was covered in about fifteen different screens transmitting images of various parts of the mall. There were two additional chairs, besides the two at the control panel, pushed under a petite rectangular table touching the back wall. The office lacked creature comforts, decorations, or personal effects; it was four plain walls.

Beside me, Lacruz focused on the monitors. Every time my lips smacked together, her eyes narrowed and she muttered something in Spanish. She would have to suck it up and deal with my eating habits.

Especially, since it was her brilliant idea to hide a mouros under a mall.

She adjusted the camera feed to display the service tunnels. The vault's interior popped up on one of the monitors.

She twisted a knob and the camera swiveled to display the entire room, which was as creepy as before. The camera appeared to be positioned over the Sangreino. I didn't remember anything poking out of the ceiling so I surmised the camera must be hidden.

"What if someone tried to dig their way in?" I asked.

"Along with the security keypad and door, the room is rigged with tripwires and explosives designed to collapse the entire vault," she said.

I grunted. I had to give it to her. She considered the angles which left me to wonder what my role was. Why would a guajona go through the trouble of working with an Inquisitor? Somehow the 'enemy of my enemy' explanation didn't quite cut it. That reminded me of something Sera said at The Cattle Branch about how she wanted me to kill Dhyana AKA Detective Natalie Lacruz.

Lacruz turned her attention to another camera covering the mall. She hit a button and the camera focused on a guy in a yellow parka.

Lacruz spoke, "For quite some time now, I have scented a wight heavily perfumed to obscure the reek of its death."

Her words caused my brain to trip over a piece of the out of the ordinary I hadn't been paying attention too—a darkened corner of a strip club, an idiot standing in line, and an odd conversation with a phone salesman.

"The weird guy in the yellow parka," I breathed.

Lacruz faced me, reached across the console, and gently squeezed my forearm. "You observed him."

It took my brain a moment to catch up. I had seen that guy everywhere. Outside Red Cat Liquor, at the Jungle Gem, and even in line at the Cattle Branch. "Do you think he's Sera's?"

"I do."

Shit. Sera knew I was here. She knew everywhere I had been. Winnie, Lacruz, Mick, Melody, and Deacon. I put them all in danger. "Why'd we come here if you knew we were being tailed?"

"You insisted on the truth, Cariño. And truths have their fair share of consequences." Lacruz's attention returned to the monitors.

"Why didn't Yellow Parka recognize you then? I mean as Lacruz?"

She looked thoughtful. "To be honest, I do not know. Sera was surprised to find us working together. Perhaps, he did not know what I looked like."

Or maybe her Lacruz transformation was so different, appearance, body language, clothing, manner of speaking, etcetera that he didn't recognize her.

I crossed my arms and sat back determined to sulk only to remember I had one last container of sugary deliciousness. I popped the seal on the last cinnamon roll and four bites later I tossed the empty carton aside while sucking icing off my fingers. It was sad to see the gooey pastry disappear though the warmth it left in my stomach was wonderful and the sugar replenished my faith in the world, which led to fantasies involving Lacruz and copious amounts of nudity.

Fantasies were good to pass time. Eventually, their potency dwindled as the hours dragged on. My sugar rush ebbed. Boredom set in. The screens showed normal mall people doing normal mall things.

I was fast asleep with my head on the control panel when Mick's text woke me. I fumbled for my phone and checked the screen. Jason's crew ambushed an Ojáncanu contingent about an hour outside of town. Mick wanted me back at Sanctuary to provide back up if necessary. I texted back that I was on a stakeout and ignored the follow-up texts asking me who and where. Sometime around sunrise, Mick's messages dwindled and boredom returned.

Hours passed into evening. Gabriela arrived to take Lacruz's watch so Lacruz could slip away for a bite to eat. Gabriela had changed into the black fatigues and the tactical vest she had worn during the Cattle Branch siege. She also brought a large silver combination lock suitcase. When I asked her what was inside, she smiled and held a finger to her lips in the universal sign of shush. I replied with my own universal middle finger sign for the bird. Sera was a no show for Sunday night so we ended up pulling an all-nighter.

Lacruz returned with breakfast at around seven the next morning. Monday's lunch and dinner came and went. The day's dull disappointment began stinking up the room. After a few sniffs of my armpits, I decided to take a few minutes and a few leftover wet wipes to wash. The remaining evening passed in slow agony until the lights started going out and stores began shutting their gates.

At midnight, the stores were all locked up and employees went home. Lacruz left the security station to check the floors for any janitorial staff or retail workers on graveyard shifts. I had sneaking suspicion she was nibbling. She returned flushed and humming like someone who had the perfect steak dinner.

It was close to 2 a.m. when I heard a quickened *tickety-tap* and glanced at the monitors. Lacruz was perched on the edge of her seat. Her fingers danced among the keys. Her mood shifted to red alert. One of the feeds zoomed in on a couple of storefronts on the first floor near the movie theatres. She hit a second set of numbered keys and the picture began jumping to different parts of the mall.

Giovanna's Hideaway, a lingerie store popped onto the screen. The store's lights were on and there was movement inside. We traded speculative glances before I recognized the monster who had been talking to the cell phone retailer, Yellow Parka pulled up the security gate and scanned the empty walkway before turning and speaking to someone behind him. The bad camera angle combined with the shadows inside the store made it impossible to make out who and how many were coming to the surprise party.

"Is there another camera you can switch too?" I asked.

Dhyana shook her head. "Each store handles its own interior security. These are external feeds. I will attempt another angle."

The image sharpened. At least now we could see three additional figures moving between the Hideaway's clothing racks. They didn't linger. I could see them moving toward the front of the store. It wasn't until they stepped onto the walkway that the camera was able to capture their full detail.

A humorless grin split my face wide. The bait had been swallowed. Here on my doorstep, on my terms, was Sera fucking Nuberu. I released a dry chuckle. Now was time for vengeance, pain, and the hard knocks that go with them. Screw the stone chair, the world, humanity, good, and evil; in this moment I only cared how many bullets it would take to split the center of Sera's head.

I studied the rest of her party. With the beaucoup of wights she brought before, it was disappointing to see only two. Yellow Parka and a second wight stood on either side of Sera in guard dog mode.

The second wight had seen its share of fights and wore its scars on its thin emaciated form. Crisscross slashes were gored out of its sunken gray face. Its left eye, a portion of its cheek, and jaw were gone leaving a black hole where broken teeth and a dried shriveled tongue lolled out. Little of its security guard uniform remained. I followed the uniform's tatters to a missing sleeve and the arm that should've filled it.

I glanced at Lacruz. "It takes about three days to reanimate a wight, right?"

"Three nights for most guajona. Seravina can do it in two," Lacruz replied.

The only reason for Sera to bring along One Arm was if he was the last of her vaunted army. When I considered the carnage I caused and the time it took to reanimate a wight, it became clear Sera couldn't replenish her army in so few days. My forays into Delta Terrace and the Cattle Branch changed the odds.

Onscreen, a frowning Sera took the lead as they moved from Giovanna's. Her hair lacked its usual meticulous bounce and no amount of makeup could hide her exhaustion. She wore red leather pants stuffed into black boots, a white corset crisscrossed by a gold chain cinching her waist, and the Easter egg-sized ruby gleaming in a gold setting around her neck matched her lipstick.

Gabriela's voice caught in her throat. Her daughter appeared onscreen. Roxana skipped barefoot beside Sera, a cruel empty smile on her adolescent stilted lips. The pale foundation caking her face made her appear clownish. Crimson stained lips combined with the shadowed circles of mascara made her look like a raccoon in drag or one of those pageant toddlers. The outfit didn't help.

Draped over her thin frame was an oversized sack-like gray cocktail dress trimmed with tassels and sequins. She was unrecognizable as the daughter Gabriela left under my protective custody. Her bearing was… skewed; the curiosity, insecurity, timidity, awkwardness, and energy of a young girl learning how to move inside her skin were absent. Arrogance, hunger, and sadism were repackaged in their place. She stared straight ahead as if the walk nor the destination mattered.

The blood drained from my face, a knot lodged in my throat, and the thrill at kicking Sera's ass was dashed by the horror of what she did to my Peq—I mean Gabriela's daughter. I smashed my fist against the control panel and ignored the painful jolt howling up to my elbow. Any misguided belief I harbored that Roxana was still a Nescient was shattered.

My glare drifted to Sera. Time was always on her side. She only needed two days to turn an innocent into a monster.

Gabriela sobbed and wrung her hands. Silently, Lacruz rose from her seat, embraced Gabriela, and whispered into her ear. Gabriela's face became stone. Tears stopped. Lacruz released the embrace and used her thumbs to wipe the moisture from Gabriela cheeks.

Gabriela's expression became more businesslike and therefore alien due to the context. It was as if Lacruz's words had lobotomized Gabriela's maternal instincts. Like a robot, Gabriela turned away from the screens, grabbed her silver suitcase, and popped it open on the back table.

With clenched fists, Lacruz glanced at me as if to ask if I had a problem with what she did. I shrugged. For Lacruz, this was about saving the world. She understood we needed Gabriela cold, professional, and detached. Somebody had to cover our backs and make sure no other surprises were headed our way.

Despite the ache of my daughter's passing, I would kill anyone who tried to rip her resonance from my heart. Chasing her ghost was too precious a pain. That pain filled my lungs in the morning and gave me the bitterness I needed to survive the day. Without that pain, I wouldn't be... I didn't know. I wouldn't be me.

The cameras followed Sera's party down the escalator. It didn't take long to figure out they were headed toward the service tunnels.

"Lacruz and I will cover the service tunnels." I turned to Gabriela. "Check out Giovanna's. We don't need any other wights crawling up our backside."

Gabriela looked to Lacruz, who nodded. Gabriela reached into the suitcase and brought out a Steyr AUG A3, a sleek black mini submachine gun for the up close and personal. I saw the way the light hit the sleek delicious beast and suddenly my Sig and pistol-grip axe felt extremely inadequate.

"Why grandma what big guns you have there," I said.

"The better to wage war with," Gabriela replied.

Gabriela hoisted the AUG and slid its strap over her shoulder. She reached inside the suitcase, removed the top tray to reveal a second tray of packed explosives and ammunition. When I thought it would stop there, she removed the second tray, and underneath was one more.

My heart rate rocketed to eleven as she offered me the contents. Rain and floods, someone must've told her what boys like. I smiled and accepted her offering with genuine thanks. This would do well to replace the one I had lost.

The Remington 870 shotgun was cold, sleek, dirty-gray with perfect weight and balance. A warm and wet voice in my head laughed. The shotgun felt good in my hands like an old lover whose curves you caressed so regularly they become part of your muscle memory. I took a shooting stance and stared down its sights and mock pulled the trigger.

I didn't hunt monsters for the right or wrong of it. There was no cosmic balance sheet. What I did was beyond revenge or indulgence. I liked to kill and was damn good at it. Monsters excised my daughter from this world and I would do anything to revisit that same evil on them. Sera was mistaken if she thought she could take my kid... I mean Gabriela's kid away.

Lacruz ignored the case's contents. Since abandoning her Detective Lacruz persona she'd done away with her Chief's Special. She, like most guajona, preferred to fight empty handed.

Gabriela and I finished loading up on ammo. Gabriela left to scout Giovanna's Hideaway. Lacruz motioned for me to follow and we jogged to the entrance to the service tunnels where we found Sera and company waiting.

Sera paced in her finery while Roxana stared at a movie poster. The two wights, Yellow Parka and One Arm posted protective spots in front of their master. Yellow Parka sniffed the air and looked our direction.

"Mistress," Yellow Parka said and pointed at us.

She glanced at him and then over her shoulder. Her tsunami blue eyes met mine and a seductive smile ghosted her lips.

Roxana edged closer and reached for Sera's hand. As the kid stretched for contact, my chest ached as if someone put a bullet through it. Some misguided part of me expected Roxana to come running into my arms proclaiming me her grand savior. I wanted... no, needed the fantasy. I already lost a daughter and it burned to lose a second chance.

What made it worse was that I didn't even rate her attention. Roxana focused on Lacruz; her lower lip curled into a snarl. How could the kid act this way? Didn't she notice I was willing to swim the river Styx for her? Then again, she was a teenager and nowhere near old enough to understand the depths of devotion a parent has. From the Roxana's perspective, she'd been abandoned twice by adults who were supposed to care.

"Have no fear, child," Sera snapped as she slapped Roxana's hand away. "Dhyana Nuberu," Sera said eying Lacruz up and down. "I was somewhat surprised to receive your call."

Lacruz's expression remained unreadable except that her lips firmed into a thin line. She started forward. Sera's party backed up and circled away from the door. I circled opposite them, my shotgun at the ready. Lacruz unlocked the door, entered the service tunnels, and I came up behind her, keeping one eye on Sera's posse.

Suddenly wary, I began looking for trouble. As far as I could tell, the tunnels were empty. I strained my hearing for footfalls and sniffed the air, which revealed the same piss odor from before. When nothing came out of hiding to bite my face, I should've felt at ease. But I didn't ease well, never had. Easing made me want to kick someone in the junk.

"Ambush?" I whispered so only Lacruz could hear.

"Of sorts. Come." Lacruz scanned the hallway and flared her nostrils to scent the air. She started down the tunnels at an increased pace without saying more.

I used the same low tone I had before. "How far we taking this?"

Her silence made me grind my teeth. She had to realize being glib and secretive was really starting to grate on my nerves. I considered tripping her to the floor to knock some sense into her.

The smart thing to do was to open a calm and rational dialog, real civil like. I didn't do either of those well. I was more of a smart-ass. Hmm, maybe talking wasn't such a great idea. In fact, if I remembered correctly, silence was supposed to be golden. I decided to save my energy for the looming conflict rather than deal with the paradoxes of two glib and secretive people trying to have a meaningful conversation.

Sera and her group followed a few feet behind us and I couldn't help but to keep looking over my shoulder. We reached the door leading to the stairs and descended into the vault without incident. Lacruz punched the code disarming the tripwires and explosives and continued toward the vault door.

"What the hell are you doing?" My gaze ping ponged between Sera and Lacruz. Sera smirked. Lacruz's expression remained fixed. This had gone far enough. "Stop," I commanded. I pressed the shotgun to the back of Lacruz's head. Supernatural speed or not, at this range I was pretty sure I couldn't miss. Though once I pulled the trigger, I was pretty sure Sera and company would shred me before my second shot.

"Oh now, this is quite fun," Sera clapped.

Lacruz didn't pause. "Trust me."

I should've pulled the trigger and lord knows I wanted to. Hell, I should've pulled it yesterday when I found out she was a guajona. My instincts told me she was on my side and that I still had a part to play. For some reason, I kept trusting her though logic made me ask the obvious question. Did I trust me?

Lacruz finished with the tumbler, grabbed the ring, and began pulling. Now that the vault was open a hair, the two wights helped. Their combined strength created an opening wider than the crevice I had been forced to shimmy through.

My stomach lurched as the Sangreino's presence fouled up the air with its chill, hate, and hunger. Both Sera and Roxana were straining to glimpse the cursed seat. I glared at everyone refusing to believe this was a double double-cross because as the solitary human present, I would be the surprise dinner for Vasco's welcome back party.

Rain and floods.

It made no sense. Lacruz could've chosen anyone, Gabriela, a security guard, or a janitor for meat. In fact, she could've released Vasco any time she wanted—she had the kid for fifteen years. What changed? Why was Lacruz taking it this far when the plan was to get Sera here and yank her lungs through her nostrils? I was missing something.

"Somebody really needs to fucking tell me what the hell is going on," I growled. Though I admit it might have sounded more petulant than threatening.

"Freedom, Kensington," Lacruz explained. "This has always been about freedom."

Before I could ask her to use the English language in a way that implied coherence, Lacruz and Sera snapped their bodies toward the darkened stairway and dropped into crouches. The Cleave poured from their cores and flooded against their skin, muscles rippled beneath their clothes, inky blackness filled their eyes, claws sprouted from fingers, and a solitary fang lengthened.

Power battered to be set free. Neither beasted out yet, but they were on the hair trigger verge. Gargola and guajona didn't carry weapons because they were weapons. Calling on the Cleave was like cocking the hammer on a gun.

I pointed my shotgun at the staircase.

The Cleave from a different source blew into the vault carrying the cadence of marching soldiers. Beasted gargola, loads of them, stepped into the light of the vault.

One by—giant, meaty, muscled, reptilian—one, they formed a wall until they blocked the exit. I counted twelve but I could feel the presence of more lurking in shadow. The newcomers were dressed in black body armor, part ninja and part Camelot, studded with citrines. Well, except the one guy with the different cut of clothes that screamed, *Me be the leader!*

The lead gargola, the sole monster using the pretense of a human face, stood as careless as a lit match around dynamite. He smirked arrogance and murder. He radiated the smarmy confidence of someone who got laid way too easily. His long golden hair glistened as it brushed past his shoulders. He had a smooth forehead and perfect cobalt eyes that gave a masturbatory beauty to his hawkish nose.

He wore his expensive corporate starched shirt open at the neck to show off his pecs, a black leather belt with a big medieval gold buckle, and gray business slacks cut to accentuate well-toned legs that probably squat pressed engine blocks. Two citrine earrings and a larger gem on his pinky finger glittered. He curled a single beckoning finger at a lackey.

I heard a wet scrape as a lackey with short cropped sandy hair and an apple shaped face stepped forward dragging a black bundle dripping blood. Apple Face tossed the bundle toward Lacruz. It smacked with a fleshy *thump,* and streaked blood over the gray floor as it slid to a stop at her feet.

In my time on this planet I had seen many bodies in grisly states of death so trust me when I say it was bad. The head lolled at the neck like an old bobblehead with worn springs, limbs were turned back at odd angles so they appeared boneless, and the black covering turned out to be clothing rather than fur. Brown bloodied hair was plastered against a pummeled face.

I scanned the features; my mind did reconstructive surgery so that the eyes, nose, and mouth fit together like they were supposed to. Recognition flared. My evening had become more complicated than being the only human trapped in an enclosed space packed with a gaggle of blood drinkers.

The world's color bled into a wasteland of Armageddon gray as the sound of a million scampering rats across hardwood. La Parca spoke:

She had run to Giovanna's Hideaway like he had asked and stumbled into an ambush. She was struck several times before her mind registered the threat. She collapsed into a fetal position and was pummeled. She cried out for her daughter with her final breath as her bones turned to paste under the onslaught of numerous fists. Mistress Dhyana hadn't been able to erase everything.

The world regained color ending the temporal pause of the death rattle.

My head whipped to Roxana. The kid's face was caught somewhere between confusion and hunger. Her fang spilled over her adolescent lips. Her eyes had gone inky. She stared at the dripping blood with a fanaticism bordering idolatry.

I wanted to shield her eyes before she realized who it was. A quick glance around the room confirmed the newcomers' complete focus on Lacruz and Sera, which was both good and bad. If I made a move for Roxana, I ran the risk of that attention shifting. For now, the kid was flying under the radar and I had a feeling it was best to keep it that way. I planted my feet and ignored the kid in case someone noticed me noticing her. Who knows, maybe luck would hold and Roxana wouldn't recognize her mother. Yeah, maybe.

"*Lo veo*, Dueño Lauder of Coven Ojáncanu," Lacruz bowed her head.

Rain and fucking floods. So leader guy was the head honcho himself, the actual leader of coven Ojáncanu. My mouth went dry as I took a second solid look. The sheer bravado of his presence made sense. This guy was predator supreme. The Inquisition as a general rule avoids Dueños unless it's a group effort and by group I mean twenty to thirty gun toting sociopaths. I really should've told Mick where I was.

"*Lo veo*, Sovereign Dhyana," Lauder sneered. "And you Apprentice Seravina. Though I have to say I am somewhat surprised at this welcome." Lauder snorted at Sera. "That you require my assistance to clean up your failure is a sure sign the Consortium needs another to take up the role of Sovereign."

Sera chewed her bottom lip, caught herself, stopped, and straightened, breasts out with hips held in a show of relaxed casual sensuality. It was a stance most men would take as an invitation. The effect was somewhat marred, for me at least, by the bristling fang, claws, and inky eyes. "Do not speak to me of weakness," Sera answered. "You lack comprehension of the sacrifice needed to safeguard our most vile shame."

Lacruz wrinkled her nose in contempt as she cut her eyes at Sera. Lacruz had to be wondering how Lauder arrived so quickly.

Lauder dismissed Sera with a short bark of laughter. His eyes locked onto Roxana. "She offends the nose."

"The child is of Drac bloodline, Dueño Lauder," Sera said tentatively. "The Sovereign was going to free him. Now that you have arrived we can—"

"Why is she not dead?" Lauder asked. He put his hands behind his back and began pacing. "The Consortium is quite *clear* concerning Drac bloodlines. Surely you can handle one Crimson, one child, and cattle."

"Who's cattle?" I asked.

Sera flicked blonde highlights over her shoulder with practiced flair, batted eyelashes, and teased her lips into an irresistible pout. "Dueño, The Sangreino is beyond that door." Sera pointed at Lacruz. "She has allied with our enemy, an Inquisitor. Her scent covers him. They destroyed your Cattle Branch and laid waste to your bloodline. I contacted you—"

"You contacted me to do your job for you," Lauder sneered. "You wish the Sovereignty, but lack the resolve to take it." He smiled coldly. "I have resolve."

Now this was the double double-cross. Sera knew Lacruz's invitation was a trap so she formulated her own trap and brought Lauder as backup thinking he would be so pissy about the Cattle Branch, he would clear the way for her to take the Sangreino.

Sera didn't count on Lauder's greed and from what I gathered he had plans for the chair. He could eliminate us, grab the Sangreino, increase his personal power, and his covens standing within the Crimson Consortium in one move. It was all win for him. Sera's trap backfired and now she was stuck with us if she wanted to live through the next few minutes. With this much backbiting, it's no surprise guajona and gargola hadn't managed to rule the world like the mouros of old.

I started laughing.

I don't know where it came from, but it bubbled and exploded. We catch up with Sera and end up surrounded by Ojáncanu meatheads including the head cheese himself. I mean there was fucked, really fucked, and direly fucked. I continued laughing like a crazy bastard until I had everyone's attention. Me, lone big balls human, was going to set matters straight.

"You'd have to be the stupidest motherfucker on the planet to believe that," I said. I pointed at Sera. "If you're paying attention, it's a double-cross. Sera lied to you. Not that I really think you care about the truth, but here it is. The awakening thing is her idea. *We're* trying to stop *her*. Think about it. Could I, a measly human, blow up a whole freaking Crimoire?" The meatheads started frowning. Good, someone was paying attention. "Lauder, you're a pawn in someone else's game."

Lauder's soldiers traded stares. Anger and doubt clouded their faces. They hated being chumps and liked it even less that their leader hadn't seen it coming. Life was somewhat simple with predators. They despised weakness and had to pounce whenever they found it.

Lauder's loss of a Crimoire and a large chunk of men must've cost him tons of face for him to march from South America to personally hunt whoever was responsible. If I made him look weak enough, perhaps, one of his more ambitious lackeys might take the opportunity to stab him in the back.

"Are we to listen to the words of cattle who presumes to hunt Crimson? His mouth is full of twists only death will straighten." Lauder glared at his lackeys.

They remained unmoved.

"You must be able to taste shoe because it sure sounds like your bootlicking," I said.

Lauder made a major mistake by acknowledging my words instead of ripping out my throat. He put himself on the level of cattle. I grinned triumphant. I successfully neutered a Dueño leaving him no options except... uh oh, maybe I didn't quite think this through. I whipped my shotgun to shoot from the hip.

Lauder moved fast.

As fast as he was though, Lacruz was faster. She dashed in front of me. Guajona and gargola exchanged blows, quick and hard. Red spurted as they disengaged with bloodied claws. The Ojáncanu fighters looked on. They were content to let him do his own dirty work. Score one for the human. Things couldn't have possibly turned out better.

"Moooom!" Roxana wailed at the top of her lungs.

Her goring shriek echoed off the walls, battered my eardrums, and snapped the spell of indifference I had spun over the room. Everyone eyed Roxana. She bristled in gray. A black halo surrounded her. The Cleave vomited from her pores; the energy, a whole hell of a lot of it for someone so young, gathered above her head and shaped into a quivering three fingered claw.

Roxana thrust her hand forward. The Cleave-claw sailed across the room trailing a black tail, clutched Apple Face, the guajona who carried Gabriela's corpse into the room. The Cleave-claw squeezed like toothpaste. Apple Face arched. Her jaws stretched wide in an inhuman scream.

The other lackeys looking on in horror backed away to put space between them and Apple Face. Torn flesh, strangled screams, and snapped bones filled the air. Apple Face soiled her pants; her twisted skeleton erupted from of her flesh as if yanked by invisible strings.

Roxana retracted her hand. Apple Face's scream ceased. Her entire skeleton exploded free of flesh in shower of gore. Bone shrapnel demolished the two Ojáncanu closest to the blast zone. The others managed to avoid injury. Blood and lumpy bits of tissue covered the floor, walls, and ceiling. The gore covered lackeys, their expressions filled with fear and disbelief, stiffened.

Oblivious to their wariness, Roxana glared and snarled, "I'll kill you!"

I thought she was going to jump into the pile of Ojáncanu lackeys and start ripping out entrails so I moved to intercept. I was wrong. She spun on her heel and sprinted into the vault.

Oh hell. Everyone knew what that meant.

No longer content to sit on the sidelines, the Ojáncanu lackeys rushed to fight. Lacruz and Sera whipped up wind and ice. The two wights, Yellow Parka and One Arm, threw themselves at the lackeys. My shotgun blasted a lackey in the chest. He collapsed lifeless and gray.

Sera chucked ice stakes, deftly ducked a swipe from one Ojáncanu, buried her stake in the throat of a second, twisted her wrist and yanked to decapitate him, and spun to face the one she dodged. He lunged at Sera with a downward claw swipe. She caught his wrist and impaled him through the gut with the ice spike in her other hand. Blood splashed across her forearm. The gargola collapsed at her feet. Sera pivoted and met Lauder's eyes. She recognized his malice and prepared for his onrush.

About eight Ojáncanu corpses littered the floor in a haphazard mess making the footing perilous. More lackeys poured into the room from the stairs. This fight was warming up and I didn't have time to see it through. Someone had to stop the kid from ending the world.

"Lacruz!" I pointed frantically at the vault. She glanced at me and then the vault, nodded understanding, and returned her attention to the fight. I felt bad leaving her in the thick of it, but I had to have faith she could hold out. I pumped a few more apologetic shotgun shells at the incoming Ojáncanu and stole one last look. Lacruz had repositioned herself to keep the remaining Ojáncanu at bay while Sera and Lauder battled. Knowing she was buying me time, I plunged into the vault.

Roxana stood at the base of the Sangreino, her arms hung limp at her sides. She was still surrounded by the black power, which inched toward the chair. I screamed her name. She flinched and turned.

She carried death in her eyes, her mother's, Evan, and those she fed on.

Roxana's first taste was taken in self-defense. Sera probably forced a second, third—hell, a twentieth taste to get the kid's power up to this level. Roxana probably tried to resist, but starving, captured with no hope, she cracked, and sucked several poor saps dry. She probably believed that if she had been born normal, her mother, father, and stepfather would've lived.

She was wrong.

Blame rested on the questionable choices made by Lacruz's manipulations, Gabriela's Faustian deal, Evan's failure to resist Sera's charms, and my inability to protect her. And now fan and shit were having a windy brown orgy, and it was on me to mop the floor.

I ransacked my brain for the magic day-saving words. Roxana's gaze slid past my left shoulder. I snapped my head to where Roxana looked. Too late. Sera's fist slammed into my back and sent me dribbling well past the Sangreino where my head replicated a basketball bouncing against hardwood. My shotgun clattered out of my hand during the skid-dribble. I tumbled to stop by smacking against the far wall. I struggled to regain my breath.

Most people hated pain. We were hardwired to avoid it because doing so maximized our chances at survival. There was another side to pain most didn't consider and that was its ability to motivate. Pain improved us if we took its lessons to heart. His or her pain, there was no difference. Pain was gender equal. It was how you handled it and how it handled you.

Pain grabbed me by the collar and screamed at me to rise in Sergeant Calhoun's voice. Sergeant 'Never Call Me Sarge' Calhoun, the toughest drill instructor in basic, was a bronze skinned, five foot six, pug-nosed, fire hydrant full of chin and sadism. His bellowing voice was fused to my most painful experiences as a burgeoning soldier. He shoved, kicked, and pummeled me through the wall that made other men quit. He trained me to act despite suffering or injury. He taught me that pain existed to make me stand.

I ignored the aches and the cobwebs that made everything fuzzy. I scrambled to my feet to escape Sergeant Calhoun's incessant bellowing. I moved fast and regretted it. I clutched my back and almost collapsed. A cervical muscle must've torn. Despite the pain, a cold bubbling stirred beneath my navel and swelled into my mouth where it awakened my Lengua-bruja.

I blinked. I couldn't see anything.

I must've taken a pretty hard crack to the noggin because my vision had gone blind to the details. I saw Sera. Not saw, more like I could locate where she was. She buzzed on a frequency only I could pick up. It was like I had become a radio antenna. No, more like sonar antenna. This was some weird kind of echolocation.

My Lengua-bruja was pulsing signals that echoed off the Cleave inside Sera. That couldn't be right. Only it was. Sera fuzzed like an ultrasound image fleshed out in three dimensions. I could trace the crackle of energy filling her legs.

Sera sprinted toward me. That same power filled her arm. She cocked her fist to throw a punch. I could predict her actions by listening to the echo of her Cleave. It seemed simple. The pain in my back was forgotten; I sidestepped right so that Sera's fist kissed open air.

She stiffened with shock, spun, and faced me. I fought the urge to pump my fist skyward and whoop. The handiness of this new ability was boundless; it revealed Sera's intentions in a way that was kinetopathic, the ability to read the body rather than telepathic, the ability to read the mind.

I could also tell that despite her aggressive posture, she wasn't using enough force to kill. She was holding back when there was no reason to treat me with kid gloves. I still had no clue why I was so important. I should've asked Mick about the Hijo de Dirige crap when I had the chance.

My shotgun echoed a few feet away. This new echolocation ability worked on inanimate objects too. Awesome!

Sera had no idea the situation changed. I heard her impending attacks and dodged while edging closer to my shotgun. Doubt leached into each of her swings. She couldn't understand why she wasn't connecting. Her punches became more erratic. Her whiffing more spectacular.

I laughed, buffeted in my world of sound…wait, sound? As in the armageddon-gray of the death rattle? It couldn't be. As the realization hit me, *zap*, the plug was pulled and the world slammed back to normal. The ultrasound look faded and Sera was once more looking like she always had, sexy and sinister.

Oh shit. I was out of batteries.

I started stalling. I had to figure out how to restart the echolocation or… "Do you know what he is? What he'll do if you free him?"

"He will remake us in his image," Sera smirked as she stalked toward me.

Remake in his image? Wait, was that what this was about? Sera's plan suddenly made sense. Vasco's release wasn't about power it was about hate.

Self-hate to be exact. Sera despised guajona. She hated what she was. "You want Vasco to change you," I said.

"So there is a brain in that head of yours."

"What you want isn't even possible, Einstein." I circled away from her. To be honest I wasn't sure.

"Says who? The Consortium? It's a lie spun by the Dueños to keep the rest of us in line. They fear his power. They fear any power that surpasses their own. I don't. I tire of this half existence. We are rejected by humanity because we drink blood. We are sneered at by other monsters for being impure. We are neither cursed nor gifted. We are a tragedy of genetics. There is no place for us." Her voice took on an edge. "Vasco Drac will change me and Roxana into something greater because we are worthy and because I will give him no choice. You will see to that." She lunged.

I yelped and dove as her fist hurtled toward me. She struck my shoulder. The blow spun me. I came down hard on my ribs and wasn't able to keep the air from blasting out of my lungs. Gasping, I crawled.

Sera snatched my ankle and yanked. I growled, spun to my back, and kicked upward into her chest. The impact made a solid satisfying crunch that rocked her back a step and freed my ankle from her grip. I rolled into a crouch and reached for my axe.

Dolor slid out of its side draw smooth. I whipped it upward as she lunged forward. The blade kissed her left forearm and sheared it off at the elbow. Meat and bone parted without resistance. I roared in satisfaction as Sera's hand sailed over my head spraying blood. She screamed and stumbled waving her stump in surprised agony.

Bitch should've killed me when she had the chance.

I pivoted on my knee letting the momentum carry me around for another swing, this time slicing at her legs. The axe tasted flesh for a second time and opened a deep gash above her right knee severing important tendons. Her leg gave out, she screamed in pain and clutched at her leg as she crashed down on her hip.

I stood and readied the axe for a final strike. As I loomed, Sera tried to make ice with her free hand. Before she could form more than a snowflake I stomped her wrist to the floor and ground my heel. My adrenaline pumped. My blood raged. I glared into the terrified face of a would-be-ruler.

Sera shrieked, "Hijo de Dirige!"

Her power hit me like before and twisted my insides. Determination, grit, or maybe old fashioned stubbornness kept my head together. I swung with my full strength. *Dolor's* edge passed through Sera's throat with a meaty *thunk* and her head spun across the floor.

My momentum carried me forward causing my foot to tangle on her twitching leg. I tripped and fell sprawling atop her corpse with a *squelch* that sent blood shooting out of her neck like a busted tap on a beer keg. My face smacked against the floor, agony shot through my jaw. I tasted blood from inside my mouth.

From my angle on the floor, I could see the fighting continued outside the vault. Lauder and Lacruz faced off while the nine remaining Ojáncanu circled, looking for an opening. Lauder raked acid across Lacruz's cheek, scorching her to the bone. She grunted in pain and made a desperate lunge to regain the offensive. Lauder sidestepped as she overreached and kicked her legs out from under her. Horror filled her features as she fell leaving her back exposed. Already she twisted to minimize her vulnerability. It was clear she would be too slow.

My chest tightened as Lauder moved to finish it. The Dueño flattened his hand like a spearhead, thrust down, and impaled his acidic claws into Lacruz's back, barely missing her spine. Flesh sizzled and melted as the snap crackle of white smoke filled the air.

Wide eyed, Lacruz screamed saliva and blood. Any other guajona would've gone to their maker, not her. As her head snapped forward she twisted at the waist and drove the point of her elbow into the wrist impaling her. There was a loud crunch. Lauder hissed and quickly withdrew his broken wrist. Free, she pivoted on her knees to face him.

Her hand shot forward, clamped on his crotch, and twisted. Lauder yelped in shock and grabbed her forearm with his unbroken hand. Smoke rose as acid seared her arm. The acid burned for a few seconds before Lacruz compressed wind and ignited a mini tornado point blank into his junk. The force shredded Lauder's slacks and the flesh beneath and sent him spiraling into five of his lackeys.

One of the remaining four lackeys tried to exploit her weakened state, but Lacruz summoned the Cleave. A black halo of power flared transforming her into the beasted killing beauty. She bounced to her feet. Her skin shone reptilian white. Muscles rippled sleek and deadly beneath her clothes as she caught the lackey by the throat, crushed his windpipe, and threw him into the lackeys skirting the fight.

Her acid scorched forearm stopped sizzling as fresh pink scar tissue formed. The hole in her back sealed leaving a dark black stain of blood. She dove at Lauder who was extricating himself from a pile of injured lackeys.

I was torn. I wanted to help, but Roxana demanded my attention. My face, back, and shoulder throbbed. My ribs caught fire when I inhaled. It took a few moments to gather my wits. I sat upright, spat, wiped my lips on my sleeve, and pushed away from Sera's twitching corpse. Testing my strength, I wobbled to my full height. *Dolor* felt so heavy; I was barely able to return it to its side harness.

Roxana knelt in front of the Sangreino. The expression she carried was miles beyond horror, disgust, or repulsion. Bloodied vomit stained the front of her dress and from what I could tell, there wasn't much of actual food in it, which confirmed her diet over the last few days. At first, I thought her eyes were unfocused only to realize something in them had died. Gone was the child. Gone was the beast. In its place was a victim longing for eternal rest.

Aww hell. "Kid, you okay?"

Her head swiveled woodenly to pinpoint the sound of my voice. Her dead eyes touched me uncomprehending. I was ashamed of my appearance. My shirt was covered in Sera's blood. I was a walking red smear. My coat was unsullied. Whatever mojo Lacruz wove into the material caused blood to bead and roll off, which left it clean and crisp as the first time I laid eyes on it. Cool. I cinched my coat tight to cover my shirt and pants, which didn't have the mojo and thus were blood soaked.

My grisly appearance and the decapitation were traumatic enough to send an adult into years of therapy. No teenager could remain sane after everything Roxana had experienced this weekend. The poor kid had been kidnapped, forced fed blood, saw her mother's corpse treated like refuse, and witnessed Sera hacked to pieces. Any teenager would probably come to the conclusion the world was a cruel, unforgivable, and screwed up place.

A lopsided grin formed on her spittle covered lips. She tilted her head drunkenly and listened as if the Sangreino had spoken.

"Don't do it," I pleaded even knowing she was too far gone to hear me.

She reached to pet the Sangreino like a dog.

And like that, I was reliving the night Evelyn died.

I had a decent job, but the pay didn't always cover the bills so when I needed extra money I punched the overtime card and hired the neighbor's kid to babysit my Pequiñita. I had believed as long as my daughter was supervised she would be okay. It took a guajona looking for an easy meal to end everything that mattered to me. I came home to two broken young lives expired on a kitchen floor covered in blood and milk. The overturned dairy carton on the dinner table dripped its dregs next to a sodden box of *Fruit Loops* and two broken bowls. The neighbor's kid was dead. My daughter was dead. My stint as a single dad wasn't supposed to end like that.

My gaze snapped to my shotgun lying where I dropped it.

I wasn't helpless if I had the resolve to do what was necessary. I ran, scooped up my shotgun, and took aim. One trigger pull would finish it. *She wanted to die. I would be doing her a favor. I wouldn't have to worry about mouros.* These were the lies I repeated to gain the courage. Signals surged from my brain to my finger. Somewhere along the way my heart intercepted my brains earnest commands. Paralyzed, I watched the world end.

Roxana touched the chair. The Cleave inside her reached for the Cleave inside the Sangreino. The two energies connected and fused building an intricate latticework that filled the air like dark nasty spider web of thousands upon thousands of intricate woven strands. It hung in the air in wicked splendor before the first tendril snapped followed by another. As the web's decay gained momentum and speed, the Sangreino cracked and sections of stone crumbled. A deep black seepage of ooze like crude oil gushed from the new crevasses, flooded the dais, and washed over Roxana's ankles.

The smell of old death took center stage as the main body of ooze bubbled upward into a humanoid shape. Appendages sprouted and stretched into arms, hands, legs, and feet. A large bubble atop the center mass sloughed away until it became a recognizable head and neck. The facial features were hidden behind the steady slide of still moving liquid, but that changed when the ooze lightened from obsidian to gray, to white, and finally a pale more fleshy tone. Eyes, nose, and mouth gained prominence and shaggy dark hair grew rapidly out of a bald head.

The entire transformation from ooze to monster had taken five maybe ten seconds and when the process reached completion a seven-foot, nude, lizard scaled, pearl Adonis with moon colored rakish hair sweeping to his waist stood on the dais. The mouros yawned. Flaring nostrils scented the air. His slit obsidian eyes snapped open and peered down on the child in front of him. His visage, a face identical to the one on the canvas in my pocket, split into a gruesome grin.

The remaining ooze dried, flaked, and disintegrated into dust. The last of the web exploded into a shower of dark motes that descended like spent fireworks before disappearing.

Under the ebbing shower of sparks, Vasco snatched Roxana by the hair, crushed her to his bosom, and tore into her throat. I heard the crunch, the slurp, and the release of her bowels. This was terror at its most pure. Walking death.

The last mouros was awake.

13 ALL'S WELL THAT ENDS HELL

Aww-fucking-hell.

Sometimes when the night was cold and your underwear was wedged in the wrong spots, you were treated to a moment of absolute clarity.

The devil always got his due and he never took what you were willing to lose.

Vasco flexed his muscles for the first time in over a thousand years and the results were pure butchery. His teeth sunk neck deep causing blood to soak the neckline of Roxana's dress. Her body shuddered, limbs flailed, and eyelids twitched. The kid hadn't uttered a sound; in fact, it was impossible to tell if she was even conscious.

Suddenly, the image of my daughter, her brown hair, dimples, and pert nose, transposed over Roxana. A false memory. I hadn't been there to see my daughter being fed upon in the middle of my old kitchen.

And yet… And yet, my Pequiñita was dying right in front of me.

And me?

My heart stopped beating or I couldn't hear it over the anvil pounding my skull. A clammy calm laced the pit of my stomach. I waded beyond the shores of pissed off and out into the wild well-worn storm-ridden seas of vengeance. I felt anguish like the tearing of fleshy nibs of fingernails. That anguish, liquid heat and foaming acid, seared away my crippling indecision.

My paralysis evaporated. I might've balked at killing a teenager. I had no problem decking the walls with Vasco's brains *Fa la la la la, La la la la*. However, I was seriously lacking the seasonal jolly of a clear shot. Mouros crushed Roxana to his chest. Roxana's lithe neck obscured the sideways tilt

179

of the mouros' nose and mouth while the rest of his face remained partially concealed under the tender fall of her disheveled hair.

I didn't know how long it took for a mouros to completely drain a victim though I would guess a minute, maybe two, which didn't leave me a lot of time. Each second brought the kid closer to a pine box and a eulogy. I wanted to avoid being that guy standing over her grave trying to think of nice things to say. I had very few options with her body shielding him. Moving within arm's length was suicide. I needed to drive a wedge between them and draw Vasco's attention. I had a good idea how.

Vasco knew next to nothing of twenty-first century advances. He missed a millennium's worth of technological innovations—microchips, potato chips, shortwave radio, microwavable food, baby powder, gun powder. I glanced at my shotgun. The answer, but not in the way I originally intended.

I pointed the barrel skyward and pulled the trigger. *Boom!* The bark startled the mouros out of his socks, that is, if he had been wearing any. Vasco dropped Roxana and somersaulted backward, his hands and feet shapeshifted into claws mid-leap. He stuck to the wall. His claws dug into the stone. He hung like a spider. Roxana crumpled in a tangle of limbs and remained motionless except for the rise and fall of her chest.

Vasco hung onto the wall and snarled as his ears oriented on the origin of the noise. He sniffed the air, sneezed, fixed his eyes on me, and licked his lips clean of blood while muscles undulated. I waved the shotgun like a signal torch. He scrambled up the wall until he touched the ceiling.

His eyes swiveled from me to the shotgun like he was trying to puzzle out what I was holding. His animal instincts subsided and a human-like intelligence filled his eyes. His shoulders straightened, his nose curled in suspicion, he released his hold on the wall, dropped down, and landed lightly on his feet.

He spoke.

I paused for a second to understand what he said. The language possessed an archaic, severe, silky, Spanish rhythm and tone I never heard before. I could feel the beginning pull unlike any I ever encountered, an encompassing vortex that tried to devour my entire identity.

His power, the pulsing infinite maw, pushed at the edges of my consciousness in its attempt to defile my mind. I let the attack wash over me as if it were nothing more than steam. His mind control probably would've worked if I could understand what he was saying. All his deliberate gibberish was doing was giving me a headache.

The mouros edged to within ten yards with growing confidence. He was unaware of my immunity. Good, at least I had his undivided attention for the sneaky I had in mind. I relaxed my posture as if his mental pull had taken effect and leaned forward with my bestest buddy smile.

"I'm about to give you a crash course in the twentieth century," I said still grinning like a loon. "There are things you need to know like Internet, nukes, fast food, cable TV, and this." I held the shotgun sideways so that he could see the full length of its sleek design. "You see this? This is like... hmmm. Let's see, how can I explain it so you would understand?"

His brow furrowed. He was perplexed by my speech. Apparently, they didn't have American English in his century. He adapted. Rather than decipher my words I could tell he had begun paying more attention to my tone, which had become patronizing like how you'd talk to an idiot who was smart enough to know you were talking to him like he was an idiot.

I placed a hand on my chin in mock thought. "I could say it's a boomstick, but that's trademarked. Let's say it's a coffin maker. You see I point and squeeze and then somebody needs to make a coffin."

I think Vasco started to understand because his lips pulled back into snarl. He lifted his chin, tossed back his head, and stared down his nose at me like an aristocratic slave owner would.

"Watch close," I said, tapping the shotgun's barrel. I angled the weapon's nozzle so he could see down the barrel.

He flinched at first. When nothing happened, he actually stepped forward to look into the hole. I mean that was basic brain wiring. You see a strange dark hole and you look in it. Vasco tensed, his eyes narrowed, and he leaned.

"See this finger." I wiggled my trigger finger then pointed it at the gun's nozzle again. He cocked his head in confusion. That was when I slid my finger back onto the trigger and squeezed.

The gun sparked and to my surprise Vasco didn't move. He held a brief oh-the-pretty-lights expression before the shot sailed the distance between us and struck his noggin above his left eye and exited out the back of his head taking a chunk of skull with it. The force sent him hurtling against the wall leaving dark red smear sliding down its surface.

Screaming, Vasco smacked the ground on his side. His arms and legs curled fetal protective around a body that had begun shapeshifting. Hair bristled hedgehog spiky, black bones sprouted from his back, chest, and shoulders to interlock into an exoskeleton while muscles hardened to elephantine density.

I pumped more shots to take his head off knowing that if I failed he would heal. Buckshot ripped chunks of flesh free when they hit. Most of them ricocheted off his new exoskeleton. I fired with a fanatic's sense of urgency until I heard the stomach churning *click* of an empty weapon.

Vasco heard it too because he lowered his right arm enough to take a peek, saw me reloading, and must've figured out that I couldn't shoot forever. He roared, dropped to all fours, and as he dashed at me something odd happened.

His exoskeleton melted away, shoulders spread, and neck thickened with overlapping bestial muscle. As he gained speed his fingers and toes were absorbed, feet fused with ankles, hands fused with wrists, and four appendages became cat paws. White fur covered his entire body. The ruins of his face twisted into a feline countenance bearing the two large tusks of a saber tooth tiger. Without missing a stride Vasco hacked up and spat out the buckshot still lodged in his body with no more difficulty than furballs.

I had seen guajona and gargola shapeshift. This was my first experience with a mouros shapeshifting into five hundred pounds of black fanged, white-furred saber-toothed tiger in a handful of heartbeats. The differences between their transformations were stark. Guajona and gargola transformations are brutal swelling of the body. Vasco's transformation was the silent sleek liquid of modeling clay.

The saber-toothed tiger roared with promised pain as he sprang. I sidestepped and swung the shotgun like a baseball bat because I knew I wouldn't have enough time for another shot. The barrel hammered against the side of the tiger's skull and snapped in two from the impact. The jarring rattle numbed my hands, the gun's remnants clattered to the floor. I shook off the tingles biting my palms, drew my Sig with a shaky hand, and backpedaled.

Vasco shrugged off my swing with a headshake. He spun to face me. I took aim with an unsteady hand. When Vasco saw the Sig, he bolted out of my line of sight leaving my missed shot to tear a chunk out of the floor. I cursed, took another bead on the saber-toothed tiger, and steadied my hand.

Vasco baited me by waiting until I committed to a shot before dodging at last possible moment. Even though I was using a different weapon, the mouros had figured out how to handle it. He made the connection between the shotgun and my Sig.

I aimed. He would zig. I pulled the trigger. He would zag. I stole a quick glance Roxana's way. Air moved in and out of her lungs though she laid unmoving. I needed another tactic quick or we were both done. Vasco noticed my brief shift in attention and jetted toward me. When I drew a bead on him, he altered his course and darted straight for Roxana.

Aww hell.

I sprinted to interpose myself between them. Emptied my clip way too quickly. Gouts of blood splashed as a couple of my shots scored across his neck and shoulders; however, neither the caliber nor the new pain were enough to divert him.

Vasco proved he could be a sneaky bastard, too. He swerved his tiger bulk with a quickness that should've defied the laws of physics concerning mass and speed. He dove at me. Claws scratched air. Dual maxillary canines gleamed in a maw of wide serrated teeth. His untamed breath, fetid enough to straighten hair, bellowed right into my face.

Unable to stop my momentum, I fell backward and slid on my rear. Vasco's jaws and claws snapped empty air. I thought he would sail right over me while I glided underneath until I saw the darkened contour of hairy tiger jewels coming toward my face.

Imagine the horror of five hundred pounds of cat butt smacking against your chest and ribs. Vasco's flanks slapped down with enough thunderous impact to compress my diaphragm and knock the wind out of me. My ribcage snapped and jammed into my lungs.

I tried to yelp but between the smothering cat musk, fur, and his crushing weight I couldn't breathe. Trapped with the mass of the world on my face, I thought how humiliating it would be to die suffocated by cat ass. My pondering was thankfully cut short as his weight lifted as his forward momentum carried his flanks, swishing tail and all, off me.

Not that it mattered.

Vasco made a sharp left turn and slid sideways. When his paws found traction, he darted forward and clamped down on my right arm. I felt the points of his teeth dig in and expected them to rip the limb in half. My coat's knife and bullet proof durability saved me from the piercing portion of his assault though it did next to nothing for the crushing force of his jaw. I screamed and flailed as the bones in my forearm snapped under the onslaught of twelve hundred pounds per square inch of bite.

I tried to yank my arm out of his mouth. Vasco held on, dug his forepaws into the floor, leaned back to gain leverage, whipped his head sideways, and yanked my entire bulk into the air. He let go when I was at the apex of my arc. I looked cool for a moment, arms and legs billowing out like a skydiver, and my long coat stretched behind me like a cape. But like eighties cool, it came to a tragic end.

I hit the floor with a devastating *smack*, pinballed, missed the flippers, and fell into the game over pit. I came to rest face down on tilt feeling like I broke everything. I was too hurt to move and yet, I had to because a referee had started counting the knockout.

Where the hell did the referee come from?

Before attempting to stand, I tried to take stock of my injuries. My legs tingled so I knew they were still attached. I wasn't feeling any sensation in my right arm. Not good. My left hand twitched. I felt wet prickles along the palm. The dampness soaking my face told me my nose had been shattered, not to mention that I was having a hell of a hard time breathing because of my chest pain. I gulped shallow breaths through my mouth.

At least, I still had my teeth. Miracles do happen.

Agony blazed furious as my brain's pain centers registered the full brunt of my injuries. My broken ribs pierced my lungs. I was hemorrhaging internally. I was dying. I whimpered in helpless agony. Alone. Human. Dead. The disembodied voice of the referee counted ten, though I think he skipped a few numbers. The knockout was official.

I would've closed my eyes except they were already shut. Abandoned to the dark, I lost. Death wanted its due. My Lengua-bruja activated. Instead of hearing someone else's death rattle, I tuned into mine. La Parca spoke:

A soiled glow wreathed with gray pulsed at the edge of his awareness and Hijo de Dirige knew it wasn't heaven because he was definitely headed in the other direction. The glow bathed him in a pool he recognized not as light but as entity.

La Parca stood over Hijo de Dirige. This La Parca differed from the one he had encountered before, its stooped bearing was that of a leader carrying a millennium old burden. La Parca's top hat complemented the large feather tufts on either side of a face decorated with glowing white vertical lines bisected by half-moons.

La Parca kneeled and tilted its face down. 'We can restore your life in exchange for a boon.'

Its voice was aged, more like three million rats scampering across hardwood than one million. It was the first time La Parca addressed him directly. Hijo de Dirige did not like it. Its voice needled his nerves and caused the back of his teeth to itch.

He wanted to tell La Parca to shut the hell up and let him die in peace except his mouth refused to budge. For once, he was glad for the censorship it probably was not a good idea to cuss out a grim reaper.

La Parca chuckled as if reading his mind. 'We are La Parca. We are the path beyond life. All living must submit to our judgment as it should be. All do except the immortal spawn of Cuélebre's cursed blood,' La Parca spat. 'Their attempt to sidestep La Parca unbalances the natural order. Serve us. Be our scythe in the living path. Reap the eternal ones.'

Mouros? Hijo de Dirige thought.

'And others, many others…' La Parca trailed off.

Hijo de Dirige did not understand what other immortals La Parca spoke of, but any boon would be worth the price if he had the opportunity to payback Vasco and save Roxana. He could always fudge the fine print later. What was the worse they could do? Kill him twice?

Hijo de Dirige was sucked into the abyss of La Parca's face. Fear curdled in that special dark place that leeched bravado and the strongest of confidences. Hijo de Dirige trembled. La Parca was not to be fucked with.

La Parca nodded satisfied, pulled Hijo de Dirige to a sitting position, placed long, thick, curved, talons on either side of the his skull, and pressed deeply. La Parca spoke, 'Grieve for her.'

La Parca scrapped against Hijo de Dirige's skull and severed Hijo de Dirige's ears in one smooth motion. The contact jolted Hijo de Dirige's body. Pain bored into his skull with growing pressure. Hijo de Dirige flinched and gasped overcome by too much heat. La Parca admired the curve of Hijo de Dirige's ears before tilting back its head and dropping them down its endless beak.

Hijo de Dirige fought for control of his flailing limbs. He burned. Apparently, he was going to hell anyway. He searched for solace and found a single bead of ice so old and familiar; he recognized it as the seed of his Lengua-bruja.

He reached for it with his thoughts and frost erupted from his core in a volatile hiss of opposing temperatures clashing for dominance. The war waged across the soul. No matter how feverish, the conflagration couldn't match death incarnate, three times cold, and twice as nasty.

His smiling Pequiñita appeared hovering against his chest, her diminutive arms encircled his neck, and little fingers caressed the pits of his missing ears. He embraced her. She melted into smoke leaving the echo of laughter; the one thing he missed so very very much.

The burn was quenched by a flood of love. His internal war ended. He lowered his head to weep a redemptive joy.

A bright orb blinked open on his forehead and out poured a large crystalline teardrop shining like a lighthouse in dense fog. The tear ran down his forehead onto the bridge of his nose where it multiplied and trailed against gravity toward his hurts. When the tears touched arms, legs, ribs, and ears, he gasped.

La Parca watched. Its face full of intensity. Then with a wry turn of his beak he announced, 'The Dirge awakes.'

My death rattle ended. The experience sparked the memory of a mother and son playing in the evening shade as a father's beat-up green truck swerved drunkenly into the driveway. *Can we go inside?* I had asked. Somehow at seven, I knew when evil was on the horizon. The truck door swung open and my father's cowboy boots plodded into the dirt. Red faced, he stumbled toward us. His were eyes the color of kerosene. My mother pulled me against her thigh so my head rested on her hip and replied with words I didn't understand at the time. *What's coming is coming no use runnin' ya hear.*

She was right. I had been running for most of my life. From family. From my daughter's death. From my heritage. Not anymore.

My Lengua-bruja translates grim reaper speech. It never occurred to me I could use it to negotiate with the afterlife. La Parca granted me a second chance if I agreed to kill the immortal children of Cuélebre.

La Parca's power thundered through me. Over a hundred hurts dueled for the right to be vented. Grief crashed against my closed eyelids until the pressure battered for release. A sob reverberated from the far reaches of my toenails traveling up into my thighs, chest, and throat until the strain built to explosive levels.

My eyelids snapped open and two tears burned a white-blue fire trail down my cheeks to the tip of my chin where they suspended for a second before dropping to the floor with a gentle splash that ignited the old blood whose legacy expanded centuries.

Energy burned as accelerant to heighten my body's ability to rebuild bones, re-inflate lungs, and reunite flesh. I shuddered with grit teeth while enduring the greasy gut clench of being pieced back together with spit, cobwebs, and bile. Bones snapped into place at an alarming rate, my radius and ulna mended, leaving my forearm throbbing. My ribcage's healing reduced the pressure in my chest. My lungs stuttered back to pumping and forced up chunky red vomit encrusted with shards of bone.

I doubled over and hugged my heaving stomach. With each wracking cough, other internal organs kick-started, more or less, back to working. It was a hard reboot, the body's version of rebirth. The shuddering stopped. I was left like a wet sheet hanging on a clothesline. In terms of endurance, I felt waterless like a desert; the healing dried everything.

Let's be clear, I was a career ass kicker who had been in dust ups since daycare when I crawled over to Nolan McKenzie and knocked the pacifier out of his mouth by courtesy of a Lincoln Log upside his noggin. True story. The first round wasn't indicative of the last because fighting was about having the guts to go longer and dirtier than the other guy. Vasco hit me with his best and I was still standing, well, more like crawling to an upright position.

Muscles burned with weakness. I wanted to rest except I had murder work that needed doing. I grabbed weakness by the throat, strangled it, and robbed its pockets. I abandoned agony and despair one limb at a time, my elbows, then my knees, until finally I straightened my shoulders, jutted out my chin, and smirked. I fixed Vasco with my Dirge's stare, death incarnate, three times cold, and twice as nasty.

The entirety of my conversation with La Parca and the quick healing took seconds; Vasco was still a few feet from where he threw me. His red gaze narrowed into twin sets of suspicion. He probably wondered why the scent of my death disappeared and how the hell I was standing.

Smoothing my coat, I walked toward him with a cold dead grin fixed on my face. How confused and uncertain he must feel right now to guess at what kind of bad ass could shake off death. I drew *Dolor* and shook its glistening edge. "Come get some."

My Lengua-bruja began pulsing and the world altered. Visual color and detail melted and coalesced into auditory black, white, and gray shapes like when I fought Sera. This time the effect was stronger—resonances, especially those connected to the Cleave, were more precise.

Though my eyes were open I was blind. My experience of the world was through three dimensional sound. My Lengua-bruja pulsed echolocation that revealed the proportions of the room, the raised dais, and the open vault door. As an added bonus, my echolocation was three hundred and sixty degrees allowing me to sense Roxana and her fading Cleave signature without turning my head.

Thanks to the walls, I couldn't pick up any other signatures outside of the room so I had to take it on faith that Lacruz was still holding off Lauder.

The echolocation made the mouros appear like an ultrasound image, a strong white silhouette chased by darker shadows. I sensed the Cleave anchored to his brain and heart like a nervous systems composed of snakes. I could discern the direction of his momentum by the way the energy oriented.

I knew Vasco would attack when the Cleave bundled in his haunches. Within a few feet, he rose up on his hind legs and extended large brutish forepaws capped with razor claws. I used the flat of the axe blade to shield. His claws raked against the metal causing a shower of sparks. I shoved the flat of the axe against his shoulder with all my strength to reorient his momentum away from me. He recovered quickly by digging four legs into the floor and driving his weight into my hips.

His echo provided ample forewarning. By the time he rammed his shoulders, I was already moving toward his exposed haunches. I swung *Dolor*. The satisfactory reverberation of contact travelled from my hands and into my shoulders as the blade entering and exiting his flesh left a gash a foot and a half long in his right rear leg.

Vasco roared and leapt away limping.

I pressed him. If I gave him a moment, he would shapeshift to erase the damage. I hacked at him repeatedly and scored each time. Each frenzied cut sent bloodied chunks flying and reduced him from fearsome saber-toothed to an oversized kitten. My arms were beginning to tire. My heaving lungs burned. There wasn't any way I would let weakness derail me. The fury of my assault backed him against the wall. His flanks and forelegs were bleeding heavily. Pretty soon, he wouldn't be able to move.

Vasco launched at my wrist. Had I been relying on my eyesight, he would've moved too fast for me to follow and I would've lost a hand. Fortunately, his echo let me hear him coming. I dodged his teeth, lifted the axe over my head, and swung down. I heard the whistle of the descending metal, felt the *thunk* of contact, and the sensation of separation right before mouth and nose parted from his face in an end over end trajectory spraying red across the room.

I followed up his facelift with a knee to his muscled neck, it felt like I hit a tree. The strike disrupted Vasco's footing. He toppled to his side, legs twitching. He began to shapeshift as he hit the ground. His head shrank as flesh poured over the open facial wound, his body narrowed, arms and legs began to fuse with his torso, and his tail lengthened.

Panic blasted away fatigue. Before Vasco finished shapeshifting, I brought down *Dolor* headman's style and separated head from neck. The partially morphed tiger head bounced across the floor. The body shuddered, but continued to shapeshift. Already Vasco's rear legs had fused with the tiger tail to become a snake's tail. I sensed the Cleave struggling to hold on to its anchor point in Vasco's heart.

I focused my echolocation on that anchor and hacked open his chest to expose the dead organ pulsing with the last remnants of his dark power. I severed his heart and as the organ tumbled to the floor, I stamped it into mush for good measure. Vasco stilled. My Lengua-bruja ceased echoing. My normal vision returned. The last mouros' skin grayed into a sandy texture before it collapsed into a pile of ash.

The easy part was over.

I dropped *Dolor* and sprinted to Roxana's side. I fell to my knees. My arms hovered over her, unsure what to do because I wasn't a doctor nor did I play one on TV. Her neck looked so mangled that I didn't dare risk moving her. Two finger thick holes in her neck dripped red. She lay on her side; her back curled like limp string with one arm twisted at the elbow. Her closed eyes were sunken pits against a purple bruised cheek resting on a pile of tussled hair.

"Kid, you okay? Come on, be okay," I took the risk and embraced her gingerly. Her blood smeared across my shirt. She felt like a bag of broken ice cradled against my chest. I smoothed hair away from her face. She barely breathed. Damn, she was weakening fast. Her body was cooling to corpse temperature. She needed to heal.

Guajona low on gas didn't refuse fresh blood. Bloodlust combined with the body's need to heal made them tear at anything for it. I rolled up my sleeve, took out my knife, and cut a diagonal slash in my wrist. I let the blood drip along her cheek before I pressed it against her lips.

"Eat," I chided gently while stroking her matted crown.

Roxana's eyes flickered open, bleary, and distant. She gulped some of my offering. The ragged neck tissue stopped bleeding and a gentle wisp of sound came from a dry throat. "Shhwwaffles?"

I forced a smile and coughed to jumpstart my voice. "Sorry kid, I don't have any on me."

I offered my wrist a second time. She wrinkled her nose, inched away from the blood, and tightened her lips into a barricade of denial.

Thinking like a teenage girl was about as difficult and disturbing as life gets. Other than ponies and *Lady Gaga*, I was clueless as to what she wanted. When we first met, she reminded me of Little Red Riding Hood.

Maybe that was what she wanted? Happily ever after.

"Your mom fought for you," I said. "She was a Queen. You know what that makes you? A Princess, a long lost Princess. You'll have a palace, ponies, laptops, and... that other stuff. The whole works. All you have to do is heal."

I pushed my wrist against her lips to force the blood in. Her eyes locked on mine. I froze. It was if she reached into my chest and grabbed my heart. Her silence begged me not to do this. I looked away. A slow creep of shame came over me. She had to feed. Her life depended on it. I felt that same lack of resolve like when I had her in my crosshairs. I couldn't pull the trigger then, I couldn't pull it now. Not to her. She accidentally killed her stepdad. She extinguished lives. She never been given a choice and that was what she wanted most.

I sucked in a sob as I used my sleeve to wipe the blood off her lips, making sure none remained.

"Shhssorry," she slurred. No... Hurtsshh... friendsshh. I... want... nnnever... want... to bbbreak," she choked. "I... want to... be... Evvvelynn..."

A baseball-sized lump lodged into my throat as understanding came. She suffered from the lack of family and the desire to be normal. She knew about her inner monster and hoped someone would accept her and make her feel regular. I trembled. DNA, supernatural or otherwise, didn't make monsters; choices did. She tasted blood and knew she couldn't turn away from it. She killed and enjoyed it. She realized cherishing life was what made you human. Her humanity mattered more than her life. She understood. Even with the hunger gnawing at her, she made a choice. She would be a girl, a daughter, my daughter even if it killed her.

"Close your eyes," I said. She obeyed and relaxed. I kissed her cheek, rocked her gently, and pretended this was a stormy night and she was my Pequiñita. I cooed tender encouragement, more sounds than syllables, and gave one last tight hug. "My darling daughter, Roxana. I love you."

Her smile claimed me. I closed my eyes. The shockwave of her last convulsive breath traveled up my arm, into my shoulders, and down into my chest where it hung with a dull stinging ache.

Her bruised cheeks smoothed into a thin smile. No gurgling or shuddering, a complete relaxation of muscle as she turned ashen gray and became papery light in my arms. I touched my nose to her hair etching the dirty, musky, and metallic scent of her last moments into memory so she would never be gone. I waited for a wellspring of tears to open up inside me or for some reserve of sadness I kept in case of emergencies. The crying didn't come. My forearm tattoos were my only tears.

I listened for her death rattle. She didn't have one. She was at peace.

14 CRY FOR ME

With enough friends in low places, it's pretty easy to find funerals done off the books. It cost me twenty-five hundred dollars—the last of the cash I received from Gabriela. On a sunny Friday afternoon, a week from when Gabriela and Roxana stumbled onto my doorstep, I found myself at a quiet service for one in the bowels of Skyline Cemetery.

I had an empty casket buried in Roxana's honor in the plot (formerly reserved for my ex-wife) next to my daughter Evelyn. I had been standing over it for hours, staring at Roxana's headstone wreathed with angels unable to read the inscription without my throat seizing.

ROXANA RODRIGUEZ ASHE

BELOVED DAUGHTER

A GOOD HEART

A BETTER SOUL

LOVED WAFFLES

The events of last weekend droned like elevator music. I was tired of sifting through the pieces to find answers where there were none. Roxana died. Gone. The only good that came out of it was Vasco's death and Coven Ojáncanu's major bitch slap to the face. Mouros were finally extinct this time. Dueño Lauder escaped, though I guess that was to be expected, he was too crafty to become an easy casualty. My dealings with him were far from over.

I blamed Lacruz.

After Roxana, I had been too distraught to decapitate Lacruz for letting Lauder run, which in the end turned out to be a positive because she cleaned up the mess, disappeared the bodies, and walled up the stairway to the vault so the public wouldn't find out what went down under their favorite mall.

Somehow after the fight, I managed to lay Roxana's body aside and climb up from the mall's depths to make my way over to Sanctuary. Exhausted, half crazed, and bitter I had broken down after sunrise and told Mick everything. I omitted becoming a Dirge. I didn't know how Mick would react to La Parca when his belief was founded on God and angels. Hell, I didn't know how I felt about it or how it was going to affect the rest my life. I might not be human anymore.

Mick downplayed my failures and argued that I struck a major blow against evil and nastiness while chiding me for partnering with a guajona instead of calling for Inquisition help. By the time his lecturing ended, I was falling off the stool with fatigue so he pointed me to a cot and some rest.

I didn't stir for twenty-four hours though I do have some hazy memories of Melody periodically bringing food and drink. By the time I fully roused and gathered the courage to see Winnie, I had already received her voicemail saying she had been released from the hospital and was staying with family—she had also included the date for Brody's funeral. Though Mick let me leave Sanctuary without fuss he had stooped to having one of Jason's stooges follow me. Not that I worried. This was my city. I could lose a tail any time I wanted. Still, it hurt.

So much for trust.

The word of Sangreino's demise spread like wildfire and now gargola and guajona all over the world were kicking up a ruckus. Some of the covens frowned on having a cultural relic destroyed while others celebrated in the streets. Fights ensued; bystanders caught in the crossfire were being slaughtered across the globe leaving the Inquisition more unrest to quell.

Tierra Santa was only a few bullets shy of a war zone; the gargola and guajona who had shown up when Lacruz had leaked Roxana's whereabouts continued searching the city. I wasn't sure whether they wanted to confirm Vasco's death or solidify a foothold for their covens. Not that I had to worry. Jason's Crew was having a field day tagging and bagging the stragglers though they had a bad habit of failing to keep any alive for questioning.

The Cattle Branch remained a smoldering pit.

Daz got paid.

As I continued to stare at Roxana's tombstone, I smelled apples and gun oil, a scent I knew like the cool metal grip of my Sig. Lacruz took brisk steps in her approach, a bouquet of white roses in one hand. She smiled a hello, laid flowers on Roxana's grave, and stepped back so we were shoulder to shoulder facing the headstone.

"She would have loved it," Lacruz said, reading the script.

My hand slid to *Dolor*, an easy draw since I sported the custom coat she designed for me. Hey, don't judge. It was a damn fine coat. I took my eyes off the headstone and studied her profile.

"Why'd you open the vault?" I asked. For the life of me, I couldn't figure out her last minute change in allegiance. "I thought the whole plan was to kill Sera."

Lacruz stared straight ahead, eyes shining with the weight of thoughts that must've kept her up nights. "I told the truth, Kensington. This entire cruel twist has been about freedom," she responded. "For me. For Roxana Drac. Even for Vasco." She pawed the grass with the toe of her shoe. "The duty of a Sovereign is to safeguard the Sangreino and I have been diligent in that respect for over four centuries. A Sovereign must exist outside of the Consortium. She cannot have friends, lovers, or allies because her loyalty to the Sangreino must remain absolute. In short, it is to have no life. The only way to escape my service was with my destruction or Vasco's."

"So you freed him to kill him." I started to ask why she didn't bury the chair in and walk away. I realized that in a way she had and it still didn't stop Sera from looking for it. As long as the Sangreino existed, there would always be gargola or guajona scheming to use it. Walking away wasn't an option.

My problem with her plan came down to execution. Everything would've backfired if not for the dumb luck of my Lengua-bruja manifesting a new ability. Maybe that was the real reason she called the Consortium, maybe a guajona on mouros gangbang was her plan B? I asked as much.

Lacruz studied me out the corner of her eyes. "The thought occurred to me when you proposed your idea, but no Kensington. The reason I let the Consortium know Roxana's location are for the reasons you specified, to pressure Seravina into action. Giving Coven Ojáncanu our exact location was, as you say, Seravina's plan B." Lacruz licked her lips. "Had my original plan gone as I desired, you and Roxana would have had years to come into your full powers before you faced Vasco."

I remained silent.

Lacruz exhaled between pursed lips. "Vasco's destruction always required a key element, the one kind of man immortals truly fear, the Hijo de Dirige also called a Dirge." She paused to let me absorb the meaning. "It is why Seravina jockeyed for your favor. She harbored no illusions that the newly awakened mouros would rather kill her than do her bidding. Your presence was supposed to be an ever present threat to keep him tractable. When I called, I told her I had made you my Servant. My 'control' over you left her no other option except agreeing to my terms. She knew it was a trap but could not achieve her goals without you. She took the risk and showed up."

It hurt to hear that neither of them were truly interested in me. It hurt more to hear Lacruz had always intended for Roxana to be a pawn. That was why she kept the kid's existence a secret from the Consortium. The whole time I thought Roxana was Vasco's leash and it turned out to be me. It was why Lacruz and Sera kept me alive when I had been fighting outside of my weight class all weekend long. It was why they tried to seduce me.

"You stoked the coals of hell and hoped I could stamp out the flames," I said. "You put the world at risk on a whim." Lacruz knew more about my heritage than she originally led on. I could ask her about it, but wouldn't. Some truths needed to be discovered on their own.

She frowned, took a careful breath, and started moving her hands in conversation before any sound left her throat. "I know you better than you realize. I know you don't quit." Our eyes met. "Given time you're pigheaded self will realize there is an *us* even if you're too stubborn to admit it. I'll be around."

Her attention shifted to the sky. "The choices you'll have to make. The beings you'll have to stomp." Her voice picked up steam. "I'm with you because you've given me freedom. I choose to have your back because I believe you'll shake this world. And also—" She stared at the headstone. "To honor her sacrifice."

I gripped the axe handle so tight I had to admit I wanted to cut her down right there except Dhyana's verbal ticks faded as the Lacruz I loved took center stage. I avoided relationships because I was unwilling to risk my damaged heart. She was as damaged as I was. I guess that was the point. We couldn't hurt one another anymore than others had already hurt us.

She glanced at the headstone one last time. Wetness appeared among her lashes and she used her thumbs to clear it away. She leaned toward me and planted a chaste kiss on my cheek. "That is a blessed thing you did,

Ken."

"I couldn't save her," I whispered.

Lacruz's genuine grin outshone the sun even as it said I was an idiot. "You saved the best part of her." Lacruz turned to leave the way she came. "Learn your heritage. Master your birthright. Be the Dirge this world needs."

"You still suspended?"

"Three months of desk duty."

Maybe Detective Natalie Lacruz of the TSPD wasn't gone. Maybe with a little urging from me, Dhyana Nuberu would never return. I rubbed the tingle where her lips touched and called out, "How'd you find me anyway?"

She stopped and glanced over her shoulder looking perplexed as if the question was obvious as light against dark. "Cemeteries are for grieving."

I nodded.

I turned back to Roxana's headstone. This was the first time since Evelyn's death that I felt changed. I had more resolve and understood killing wasn't about getting my jollies.

I was a fighter. I was a protector. I could swing a pretty mean axe. It was those qualities that made me suited for a life in the dark. It was my duty to ensure that night didn't spill into the day because that was when innocents suffered. That was the lesson I was supposed to learn when my daughter died. It took a double feature of harsh events for me to realize my purpose.

I read her inscription aloud, closed my eyes, titled my face toward the sun, and let its heat dry my cheeks. My hand dropped away from *Dolor*. I still hadn't given up on killing Lacruz. I would when the moment called for it. Now wasn't the time. The cemetery wasn't the place. In fact, it was best to forget about death altogether and instead celebrate the importance of a waffle breakfast. Grieving was about honoring how those you loved lived.

GLOSSARY OF TERMS

Bruja: A human using witchcraft based on incantations, wards, and talismans.

Brujeria: Witchcraft.

Cariño: Term of endearment meaning Love.

Cleave: Blood magic primarily used by mouros, gargola, and guajona.

Coven: Refers to a specific bloodline of gargola and guajona.

Crimson: Inclusive term referring to both gargola and guajona.

Crimson Consortium: The collection of all covens.

Cuélebre: The first monster from which all monsters spawn.

Dirge: A servant of death possessing several supernatural abilities including the power to kill immortals.

Dolor: It means pain. The name of Kensington's pistol-grip axe.

Drac: Coven bloodline with the ability to shapeshift others.

Dueño: Coven leader.

Gargola: A male blood-witch.

Guajona: A female blood-witch.

Hijo de Dirige: Son of the dead. See Dirge.

La Parca: Death gods who announce the death rattles of those who die tragically. They transport the souls of the dead into afterlife and keep the oral histories of every monster in existence.

Lengua-bruja: Witch tongue. Allows Kensington to speak and understand the language of La Parca.

Nescient: A potential gargola or guajona who retains their humanity by not drinking blood.

Nuberu: Coven bloodline with the ability to manipulate the weather.

Ojáncanu: Coven bloodline with the ability to secrete toxins.

Pequiñita: Term of endearment meaning Little One.

Ramidreju: Coven bloodline of unknown ability.

Sangreino: Blood throne. Stone prison for the mouros Vasco.

Sovereign: Royal protector of the Crimson Consortium whose primary responsibility is to ensure the mouros Vasco stays imprisoned.

Mouros: A blood drinking demon scion of Cuélebre.

Wight: A corpse reanimated by a gargola or guajona's poisonous bite.

ABOUT THE AUTHOR

D.W. White has a Bachelor's in Psychology from UCLA and a Master's in English from California State University, Northridge. He is currently working for an educational consulting company. His short fiction has appeared in the Northridge Review. He is currently working on his next novel, Anansi the Butcher.

Darryl.White.96@mycsun.edu